MW00623869

ANTON
CHEKHOV

RUSSIAN CLASSICS

RADUGA PUBLISHERS MOSCOW 2001

ANTON
CHEKHOV

STORIES

RADUGA PUBLISHERS MOSCOW 2001

ББК 84. Р 1-4
    Ч 56

Translated from the Russian by *Ivy Litvinov*
Designed by *E. Kouznetsova*

А. П. Чехов

ПОВЕСТИ И РАССКАЗЫ

На английском языке

First printing 1973

On the cover:
Drawing by D. A. Dubinsky
and portrait of A. P. Chekhov by I. Braz. 1898, Nice

ISBN 5-05-004815-X   © Raduga Publishers, 1999, 2001

CONTENTS

ANTON CHEKHOV
by Maxim Gorky

He once invited me to visit him in the village of
Kuchuk-Koi, where he had a tiny plot of ground and
a white two-storey house. He showed me over his
"estate", talking animatedly all the time:

"If I had lots of money I would build a sanatorium
here for sick village teachers. A building full of light,
you know, very light, with big windows and high
ceilings. I'd have a splendid library, all sorts of musical
instruments, an apiary, a vegetable garden, an orchard.
I'd have lectures on agronomy, meteorology, and so on
—teachers ought to know everything, old man, everything."

He broke off suddenly, coughed, cast an oblique
glance at me, and smiled his sweet, gentle smile, a
smile which had an irresistible charm, forcing one to
follow his words with the keenest attention.

"Does it bore you to listen to my dreams? I love
talking about this. If you only knew the absolute
necessity for the Russian countryside of good, clever,
educated teachers! In Russia we have simply got to
create exceptional conditions for teachers, and that as
soon as possible, since we realise that unless the people get an all-round education the state will collapse
like a house built from insufficiently baked bricks. The
teacher must be an actor, an artist, passionately in love
with his work, and our teachers are navvies, half-
educated individuals, who go to the village to teach
children about as willingly as they would go to exile.
They are famished, down-trodden, they live in perpetual fear of losing their livelihood. And the teacher
ought to be the first man in the village, able to answer

all the questions put to him by the peasants, to instil in the peasants a respect for his power worthy of attention and respect, whom no one will dare to shout at ... to lower his dignity, as in our country everybody does—the village policeman, the rich shopkeeper, the priest, the school patron, the elder and that official who, though he is called a school inspector, busies himself, not over the improvement of conditions for education, but simply and solely over the carrying out district circulars to the letter. It's absurd to pay a niggardly pittance to one who is called upon to educate the people —to educate the people, mind! It is intolerable that such a one should go about in rags, shiver in a damp, dilapidated school, be poisoned by fumes from badly ventilated stoves, be always catching cold, and by the age of thirty be a mass of disease—laryngitis, rheumatism, tuberculosis. It's a disgrace to us! For nine or ten months in the year our teachers live the lives of hermits, without a soul to speak to, they grow stupid from loneliness, without books or amusements. And if they venture to invite friends to come and see them, people think they are disaffected—that idiotic word with which cunning folk terrify fools.... All this is disgusting ... a kind of mockery of human beings doing a great and terribly important work. I tell you, when I meet a teacher I feel quite awkward in front of him—for his timidity, and for his shabbiness. I feel as if I myself were somehow to blame for the teacher's wretched state—I do, really!"

Pausing for a moment, he threw out his arm and said softly:

"What an absurd, clumsy country our Russia is!"

A shadow of profound sorrow darkened his fine eyes, and a fine network of wrinkles showed at the corners, deepening his glance. He looked around him and began making fun of himself.

"There you are—I've treated you to a full-length leading article from a liberal newspaper. Come on, I'll give you some tea as a reward for your patience...."

This was often the way with him. One moment he would be talking with warmth, gravity and sincerity, and the next, he would be laughing at himself and his own words. And beneath this gentle, sorrowful laughter could be felt the subtle scepticism of a man who knew the value of words, the value of dreams. There was a shade of his attractive modesty, his intuitive delicacy in this laughter, too.

We walked back to the house in silence. It was a warm, bright day; the sound of waves sparkling in the vivid rays of the sun could be heard. In the valley, a dog was squealing its delight about something. Chekhov took me by the arm and said slowly, his speech interrupted by coughs:

"It's disgraceful and very sad, but it is true—there are many people who envy dogs...."

And then he added, laughing:

"Everything I say today sounds senile—I must be getting old."

Again and again I would hear from him:

"Listen—a teacher has just arrived ... he's ill, he has a wife— you couldn't do anything for him, could you? I've fixed him up for the moment...."

Or:

"Listen, Gorky! A teacher wants to meet you. He is bedridden, sick. Won't you go to see him?"

Or:

"There's a schoolmistress asking for books to be sent...."

Sometimes I would find this "teacher" in his house—usually a teacher, flushed with the consciousness of his own awkwardness, sitting on the edge of a chair, sweating and picking his words, trying to speak as smoothly and "educatedly" as he could, or, with the over-familiarity of a morbidly shy individual, entirely absorbed in the desire not to appear stupid in the eyes of the writer, showering Anton Pavlovich with questions that had probably only just come into his head.

Anton Pavlovich would listen attentively to the clumsy speech; and a smile would light up his mournful eyes, setting the wrinkles on his temples in play, and in his deep, gentle, hushed voice, he would begin speaking, using simple, clear words, words close to life, which immediately put his visitor at ease, so that he stopped trying to be clever and consequently became both cleverer and more interesting....

I remember one of these teachers—tall, lean, with a sallow, emaciated face and a long, hooked nose drooping mournfully towards his chin—he sat opposite Anton Pavlovich, gazing steadily into his face with his dark eyes, and droning on in a morose bass:

"Impressions of this sort gathered from living conditions throughout the period of the pedagogical season accumulate in a psychic conglomerate which entirely eliminates the slightest possibility of an objective attitude to the world around. The world is, of course, nothing but our own conception of it...."

Here he embarked upon philosophical ground, slipping about like a drunk man on ice.

"Tell me," asked Chekhov, quietly and kindly, "who is it that beats the children in your district?"

The teacher leaped from his chair and began waving his arms indignantly.

"What? Me? Never! *Beat* them?"

And he snorted offendedly.

"Don't get upset," continued Anton Pavlovich, smiling to pacify him. "Did I say it was you? But I remember reading in the paper that there was someone who beat the school-children in your district...."

The teacher sat down again, mopped his perspiring countenance, and sighed in relief, saying in his deep bass:

"Quite right. There was a case. It was Makarov. And no wonder! It's fantastic, but it is understandable. He's married, has four children, his wife is ill, he is, too, consumptive, his salary is twenty rubles ... and the school's like a cellar, with only one room for the teacher. In such circumstances one would cuff an angel from heaven for the slightest misdemeanour, and the pupils are far from angels, beleive me!"

And this man, who had the moment before been trying to impress Chekhov by his stock of grand words, suddenly, wagging his hooked nose ominously, came out with words like stones, simple and heavy, words which threw a bright light on the accursed, sinister truth of the life going on in the Russian village....

When taking leave of his host the teacher pressed Chekhov's small, dry-skinned hand with its slender fingers in both of his.

"I went to see you as if I were going to see a superior," he said, "shaking in my shoes. I swelled like a turkey-cock, determined to show you that I was worth something too, and I go away as if I were leaving a good, close friend, who understands everything. What a great thing it is—to understand everything! Thank you! I'm going. I take away with me a good, precious thought: great people are simpler, they understand more, they are closer to us poor mortals than the small fry we live amidst. Good-bye, I shall never forget you."

His nose quivered, his lips relaxed in a nice smile, and he added unexpectedly:

"Bad people are unfortunate, too—damn them!"

When he had gone Anton Pavlovich, following him with his

eyes, smiled, and said: "Nice chap. He won't be teaching long, though."

"Why not?"

"They'll hound him out ... get rid of him."

After a pause he added, in low, gentle tones:

"In Russia an honest man is something like a chimney-sweep for nurses to frighten little children with. . . ."

It seems to me that in the presence of Anton Pavlovich everyone felt an unconscious desire to be simple, more truthful, more himself, and I had many opportunities of observing how people threw off their attire of grand bookish phrases, fashionable expressions, and all the rest of the cheap trifles with which Russians, in their anxiety to appear Europeans, adorn themselves, as savages deck themselves with shells and fishes' teeth. Anton Pavlovich was not fond of fishes' teeth and cocks' feathers; all that is tawdry, tinkling, alien, donned by human beings for the sake of an "imposing appearance", embarrassed him, and I noticed that whenever he met with one of these dressed-up individuals he felt an overmastering impulse to free him from his ponderous and superfluous trappings, distorting the true face and living soul of his interlocutor. All his life Anton Pavlovich lived the life of the soul, was always himself, inwardly free, and took no notice of what some expected, and others—less delicate—demanded of Anton Chekhov. He did not like conversations on "lofty" subjects—conversations which Russians, in the simplicity of their hearts, find so amusing, forgetting that it is absurd, and not in the least witty, to talk about the velvet apparel of the future, while not even possessing in the present a decent pair of trousers.

Of a beautiful simplicity himself, he loved all that was simple, real, sincere, and he had a way of his own of making others simple.

He was once visited by three extremely dressy ladies. Filling his room with the rustle of silk petticoats and the fragrance of heady perfumes, they seated themselves pompously opposite their host and, feigning an intense interest in politics, began "putting questions" to him.

"How do you think the war will end, Anton Pavlovich?"

Anton Pavlovich coughed, paused for thought and replied in his soft, grave, kindly voice:

"No doubt in peace."

"That, of course. But who will win? The Greeks or the Turks?"

"It seems to me that the stronger side will win."

"And which do you consider the stronger side?" the ladies asked in one voice.

"The side which is better fed and better educated."

"Isn't he witty?" cried one of the ladies.

"And which do you prefer—the Greeks or the Turks?" asked another.

Anton Pavlovich looked at her kindly and replied with his meek, courteous smile:

"I like fruit pastilles—do you?"

"Oh, yes!" cried the lady eagerly.

"They have such a delicious taste," corroborated the other gravely.

And all three began an animated conversation about fruit pastilles, displaying marvellous erudition and intricate knowledge of the subject. They were obviously delighted not to have to tax their brains and pretend a serious interest in Turks and Greeks, to whom till the present moment they had never given a thought.

On leaving, they promised Anton Pavlovich gaily:

"We're going to send you a box of fruit pastilles."

"You had a nice talk," I remarked, when they had gone.

Anton Pavlovich laughed softly.

"Everyone ought to speak in his own language," he said.

Another time I found a good-looking young assistant procurator in his room. Standing in front of Chekhov, tossing back his curly head, he was saying in confident tones:

"In your *Miscreant* you confront me with an extremely complex problem, Anton Pavlovich. If I recognise in Denis Grigoryev the existence of a deliberate will to evil, it is my duty to commit Denis to gaol unhesitatingly, since the interests of society demand it. But he is a savage, he is unconscious of the criminality of his act, I am sorry for him. If I regard him as a subject acting irrationally and yield to feelings of pity, how am I to guarantee society that Denis will not again unscrew the bolts and derail the train? That is the question. What is to be done?"

He paused, throwing himself back in his chair and fixing a searching glance on the face of Anton Pavlovich. His uniform was brand new, and the buttons down the front of it gleamed as confidently and stupidly as the eyes in the freshly-washed countenance of the youthful zealot.

"If I were the judge," said Anton Pavlovich gravely, "I would have acquitted Denis."

"On what grounds?"

"I would have said to him: 'You haven't grown into a type of the conscious criminal yet, Denis, go and do so.' "

The lawyer laughed, but immediately recovered his portentous gravity and continued:

"No, esteemed Anton Pavlovich, the problem you have raised can only be solved in the interests of society, the life and property of which I am called upon to protect. Denis is a savage, it is true, but he is a criminal, and therein lies the truth."

"Do you like listening to the gramophone?" asked Anton Pavlovich suddenly.

"Oh, yes! Very much. It's a marvellous invention," the youth hastened to reply.

"And I can't bear the gramophone," admitted Anton Pavlovich sorrowfully.

"Why not?"

"Oh well, it talks and sings, without feeling anything. All the sounds coming from it are so empty and lifeless. And do you go in for photography?"

The lawyer turned out to be a passionate admirer of photography. He began immediately to speak about it with enthusiasm, no longer taking the slightest interest in the gramophone, despite his own likeness to that "marvellous invention", which Chekhov had noticed with such subtlety and precision. Once again I saw beneath the uniform a lively and not uninteresting human being, one who was still as young in the ways of life as a puppy taken hunting.

After seeing the young man out, Anton Pavlovich said morosely:

"And it's pimples like that on the backside of justice who dispose of the destinies of men."

After a pause he added: "Prosecutors are always fond of fishing. Especially for perch."

He had the art of exposing vulgarity everywhere, an art which can only be mastered by one whose own demands on life are very high, and which springs from the ardent desire to see simplicity, beauty and harmony in man. He was a severe and merciless judge of vulgarity.

Someone said in his presence that the editor of a popular magazine, a man perpetually talking about the necessity for love and sympathy for others, had insulted a railway guard without the slightest provocation, and was in the habit of treating his subordinates roughly.

"Naturally," said Anton Pavlovich, with a grim chuckle. "He's an aristocrat, a cultivated man ... he went to a seminary. His father went about in bast shoes, but *he* wears patent-leather boots."

And the tone in which these words were spoken at once dismissed the "aristocrat" as a mediocre and ridiculous individual.

"A very gifted person," he said of a certain journalist. "His writing is always so lofty, so humane ... saccharine. He calls his wife a fool in front of people. His servants sleep in a damp room, and they all develop rheumatism...."

"Do you like So-and-So, Anton Pavlovich?"

"Oh, yes. A nice man," replies Anton Pavlovich, coughing. "He knows everything. He reads a lot. He took three books of mine and never returned them. A bit absent-minded, tells you one day that you're a fine fellow, and the next tells someone else that you stole the black silk socks with blue stripes of your mistress's husband."

Someone was heard to complain in his presence that the "serious" sections of the "heavy" magazines were dull and difficult.

"Just don't read those articles," Anton Pavlovich advised with the utmost conviction. "They're co-operative literature ... the literature written by Messrs. Krasnov, Chernov and Belov.* One writes an article, the other criticises it, and the third reconciles the illogicalities of the first two. It's like playing vint with a dummy. But why the reader needs all this none of them ask themselves."

He was once visited by a stout lady, healthy, good-looking, well-dressed, who immediately began to talk "the Chekhov way".

"Life is so dull, Anton Pavlovich. Everything is so dingy—people, the sky, the sea, even flowers seem dingy to me. And there's nothing to wish for—my heart aches. It's like a kind of disease...."

"It is a disease," said Anton Pavlovich energetically. "That's just what it is. The Latin name for it is morbus sham-itis."

Fortunately for herself the lady did not understand Latin, or perhaps she pretended not to.

---

* Red, Black and White.—*Tr.*

"Critics are like horse-flies which hinder the horses in their ploughing of the soil," he said with his wise chuckle. "The muscles of the horse are as taut as fiddle-strings, and suddenly a horse-fly alights on its croup, buzzing and stinging. The horse's skin quivers, it waves its tail. What is the fly buzzing about? It probably doesn't know itself. It simply has a restless nature and wants to make itself felt—'I'm alive, too, you know!' it seems to say. 'Look, I know how to buzz, there's nothing I can't buzz about!' I've been reading reviews of my stories for twenty-five years, and can't remember a single useful point in any of them, or the slightest good advice. The only reviewer who ever made an impression on me was Skabichevsky, who prophesied that I would die drunk in the bottom of a ditch. . . ."

A subtle mockery almost always twinkled gently in his grey mournful eyes, but occasionally these eyes would become cold, keen, harsh, and at such moments a hard note would creep into the smooth, cordial tones of his voice, and then I felt that this modest, kindly man could stand up against any hostile force, stand up firmly, without knuckling under to it.

It sometimes seemed to me that there was a shade of hopelessness in his attitude to others, something akin to a cold, still despair.

"The Russian is a strange being," he said once. "He is like a sieve, he can hold nothing for long. In his youth he crams himself eagerly with everything that comes his way, and by the time he is thirty nothing is left of it all but a heap of colourless rubbish. If one wants to lead a good life, a human life, one must work. Work with love and with faith. And we don't know how to do that in our country. An architect, having built two or three decent houses, sits down to play cards for the rest of his life or hangs about the backstage of a theatre. As soon as a doctor acquires a practice he stops keeping up with science, never reads anything but *Novosti Terapii* (Therapeutical News) and by the age of forty is firmly convinced that all diseases come from colds. I have never met a single official who had even the slightest idea of the significance of his work—they usually dig themselves in in the capital, or some provincial town, and invent papers which they dispatch to Zmiyev and Smorgon for fulfilment. And whose freedom of movement is impeded in Zmiyev or Smorgon by these documents, the official no more cares than an atheist does about the torments of hell. Having made a name by a successful defence the barrister ceases to bother about the defence of truth and does nothing but defend the rights of property, put money on horses, eat oysters, and pass himself off as a connoisseur of all the arts. An actor, having performed two or three parts with fair success, no longer learns his parts, but puts on a top hat and considers himself a genius. Russia is a land of greedy idlers. People eat and drink enormously, love to sleep in the daytime, and snore in their sleep. They marry for the sake of order in their homes, and take a mistress for the sake of social prestige. Their psychology is a dog's psychology. Beat them and they squeal meekly and sneak off to their kennels. Caress them, and they lie on their backs with their paws up, wagging their tails."

A cold, sorrowful contempt underlay these words. But while despising, he could pity, and when anyone was abused in his presence, Anton Pavlovich was sure to stick up for him.

"Come now! He's an old man, he's seventy...."

Or:

"He's still young, it's just his stupidity...."

And when he spoke like this I could see no signs of disgust in his face....

When one is young, vulgarity seems to be simply amusing and insignificant, but it gradually surrounds the individual, its grey mist creeping into his brains and blood, like poison or charcoal fumes, till he becomes like an old tavern-sign, eaten up with rust—there seems to be something depicted on it, but what, it is impossible to make out.

From the very first Anton Pavlovich managed to reveal, in the grey ocean of vulgarity, its tragically sombre jokes. One only has to read his "humorous" stories carefully, to realise how much that was cruel was seen and shame-facedly concealed by the author in comic narrative and situations.

He had an almost virginal modesty, he could never bring himself to challenge people loudly and openly: "Be more decent—can't you!" vainly trusting that they would themselves realise the urgent necessity for being more decent. Detesting all that was vulgar and unclean, he described the seamy side of life in the lofty language of the poet, with the gentle smile of the humorist, and the bitter inner reproach beneath the polished surface of his stories is scarcely noticeable.

The esteemed public, reading *A Daughter of Albion*, laughs, and is probably unable to see in this story the detestable sneers of the well-nourished squire at a forlorn individual, a stranger to everything and everyone. And throughout all Chekhov's humorous stories I hear the gentle, profound sigh of a pure, truly human heart, a despairing sigh of pity for human beings unable to maintain their self-respect, and yielding without a struggle to brute force, living like slaves, believing in nothing but the necessity for the cabbage soup they daily swallow to be as succulent as possible, feeling nothing but the fear of being beaten by the powerful and the insolent.

No one ever understood the tragic nature of life's trifles so clearly and intuitively as Chekhov did, never before has a writer been able to hold up to human beings such a ruthlessly truthful picture of all that was shameful and pitiable in the dingy chaos of middle-class life.

His enemy was vulgarity. All his life he fought against it, held it up to scorn, depicted it with a keen impartial pen, discovering the fungus of vulgarity even where, at first glance, everything seemed to be ordered for the best, the most convenient, and even brilliant. And vulgarity got back on him with an ugly trick when his dead body—the body of a poet—was sent to Moscow in an oyster wagon.

This dingy green wagon strikes me as the broad triumphant grin of vulgarity at its weary foe, and the innumerable "reminiscences" of the yellow press—mere hypocritical grief, behind which I seem to feel the cold, stinking breath of that very vulgarity which secretly rejoiced in the death of its enemy.

Reading the works of Chekhov makes one feel as if it were a sad day in late autumn, when the air is transparent, the bare trees stand out in bold relief against the sky, the houses are huddled together, and people are dim and dreary. Everything is so strange, so lonely, motionless, powerless. The remote distances are blue and void, merging with the pale sky, breathing a dreary cold on the half-frozen mud. But the mind of the author, like the autumn sunshine, lights up the well-trodden roads, the crooked streets, the dirty, cramped houses in which pitiful "little" people gasp out their lives in boredom and idleness, filling their dwellings with a meaningless, drowsy bustle. There goes "the darling", as nervous as a little grey mouse, a sweet, humble woman, who loves so indiscriminately and so slavishly. Strike her a blow on the cheek and she will not even dare, meek slave, to cry out. Beside her stands the melancholy Olga from *The Three Sisters*; she, too, is capable of loving and submits patiently to the whims of the depraved, vulgar wife of her fainéant brother; the lives of her sisters fall in ruins around her and she only cries, incapable of doing anything about it, while not a single living, strong word of protest against vulgarity is formed within her.

And there go the tearful Ranevskaya and the rest of the former owners of *The Cherry Orchard*—selfish as children, and flabby as old people. They, who should have been dead long ago, whine and snivel, blind to what is going on around them, comprehending nothing, parasites unable to fasten their suckers into life again. The worthless student Trofimov holds forth eloquently on the need for working, and fritters away his time, amusing himself by dull-witted taunts at Varya, who works unceasingly for the welfare of the idlers.

Vershinin* dreams of the good life to come in three hundred years, and in the meantime does not notice that everything around him is falling to pieces, that before his very eyes Solyony is ready, out of boredom and stupidity, to kill the pitiable Baron Tusenbach.

A long procession of slaves to love, to their own stupidity and laziness, to their greed for earthly blessings passes before the reader's eyes. Here are the slaves to the obscure fear of life, moving in vague anxiety and filling the air with inarticulate ravings about the future, feeling that there is no place for them in the present....

Sometimes the report of a gun is heard from the grey mass— this is Ivanov or Treplev, who, having suddenly discovered the only thing to do, has given up the ghost.

Many of them indulge in beautiful dreams of the glorious life to come in two hundred years, and nobody thinks of asking the simple question: who is to make it glorious, if we do nothing but dream?

And now a great, wise man passes by this dull, dreary crowd of impotent creatures, casting an attentive glance on them all, these dreary inhabitants of his native land, and says, with his sad smile, in tones of gentle but profound reproach, with despairing grief on his face and in his heart, in a voice of exquisite sincerity:

"What a dull life you lead, gentlemen!"

---

* The hero of *The Three Sisters.—Tr.*

Five days of fever, but no desire to rest. The grey Finnish rain sprinkles the earth with a moist dust. The guns of Fort Ino thunder continuously. At night the long tongue of a searchlight licks up the clouds, a loathsome sight, for it is a constant reminder of the fiendish disease—war.

I read Chekhov. If he had not died ten years ago the war would probably have killed him, first poisoning him by hatred of men. I remembered his funeral.

The coffin of the writer, so "tenderly loved" by Moscow, was brought in a green wagon bearing the inscription "Oysters" in big letters on the door. A section of the small crowd which had gathered at the station to meet the writer followed the coffin of General Keller just arrived from Manchuria, and wondered why Chekhov was being carried to his grave to the music of a military band. When the mistake was discovered certain genial persons began laughing and sniggering. Chekhov's coffin was followed by about a hundred people, not more. Two lawyers stand out in my memory, both in new boots and gaily patterned ties, like bridegrooms. Walking behind them I heard one of them, V. A. Maklakov, talking about the cleverness of dogs, and the other, whom I did not know, boasting of the convenience of his summer cottage and the beauty of its environments. And some lady in a purple dress, holding up a lace sunshade, was assuring an old gentleman in horn-rimmed spectacles:

"Oh, he was such a darling, and so witty...."

The old gentleman coughed incredulously. It was a hot, dusty day. The procession was headed by a stout police officer on a stout white horse. All this and much more was disgustingly vulgar and highly inappropriate to the memory of the great and subtle artist.

In a letter to old A. S. Suvorin, Chekhov wrote:

"There is nothing drearier and more unpoetical than the prosaic struggle for existence, destroying the joy of life, and creating apathy."

These words are the expression of an extremely Russian mood which in my opinion is not at all like A. P. In Russia, where there is so much of everything, but where people have no love of work, most people think like this. Russians admire energy, but do not really believe in it. A writer who is the exponent of the active mood, Jack London, for instance, would be impossible in Russia. Jack London's books are very popular in Russia, but I have not observed that they stimulate the will of Russians to action, they merely stir their imaginations. But Chekhov was not very Russian in that sense of the word. From his earliest youth the "struggle for existence" had to be waged in the joyless, colourless form of daily petty cares for a crust of bread—and a big crust was needed, for others as well as himself. To these cares, devoid of joy, he gave all his youthful energies, and the wonder is how he managed to preserve his sense of humour. He saw life as nothing but the weary striving for food and repose. Its great dramas and tragedies were concealed from him by a thick layer of the commonplace. And it was only when he no longer had to worry so much about earning bread for others that he could cast a keen glance at the truth about these dramas.

I have never met anyone who felt the importance of work as the basis of culture so profoundly and diversely as A. P. This feeling showed itself in all the trifles of his home life, in the selection of things for the home, in that love for things in themselves, and while quite untainted by the desire to collect, he never wearied of admiring them as the product of man's creative spirit. He loved building, planting gardens, adorning the earth, he felt the poetry of work. With what touching care he watched the growth of the fruit-trees and shrubs he had himself planted. In the midst of the innumerable cares connected with the building of his house at Autka, he said:

"If everyone in the world did all he was capable of on his own plot of land, what a beautiful world it would be!"

I was just then in the throes of writing my play *Vasily Buslayev* and I read Vasily's boastful monologue to him:

> *If I only had more strength in me!*
> *With hot breath I'd melt the snows around,*
> *Go about the world and plough its lands;*
> *Stately towns and cities I would found,*
> *Churches would I build, and orchards plant,*
> *Like a lovely girl the world would look!*
> *In my arms I'd take it, like a bride,*
> *To my bosom I would hold the earth,*
> *Take it up and bear it to the Lord.*
> *Look, Lord God, look down upon the world,*
> *See how pretty I have made it now!*
> *You had tossed it like a stone to heaven,*

> *I have made it like a precious jewel!*
> *Look at it, and let your heart rejoice!*
> *See how green it shines beneath the sun!*
> *Gladly would I give it up to you,*
> *But I cannot—it's too dear to me.*

Chekhov liked this monologue, and, coughing nervously, said to me and Dr. A. N. Aleksin:

"Good.... Very good.... Real, human. That's precisely where the 'meaning of all philosophy' lies. Man inhabited the world, he will make it a good place for him to live in." Nodding his head resolutely, he repeated: "He will!"

He asked me to read Vasily's monologue again, and listened, looking out of the window.

"The last two lines won't do. They're defiant. Superfluous."

He spoke little and reluctantly about his literary work. I might almost say, with the same virginal reserve with which he spoke about Lev Tolstoy. Very occasionally, when in high spirits, he would relate the plot of a story, chuckling—it was always a humorous story.

"I say, I'm going to write a story about a schoolmistress, an atheist—she adores Darwin, is convinced of the necessity for fighting the prejudices and superstitions of the people, and herself goes to the bath-house at midnight to scald a black cat to get a wishbone for attracting a man and arousing his love—there is such a bone, you know...."

He always spoke of his plays as "amusing", and really seemed to be sincerely convinced that he wrote "amusing plays". No doubt Savva Morozov was repeating Chekhov's own words when he stubbornly maintained: "Chekhov's plays must be produced as lyrical comedies."

But to literature in general he always gave the keenest attention, especially touching in the case of "beginners". He read the lengthy manuscripts of B. Lazarevsky, N. Oliger and many others with admirable patience.

"We need more writers," he said. "Literature is still a new thing in our daily life, even for the 'elect'. There is a writer for every two hundred and twenty-six people in Norway, and here only one for every million."

His disease sometimes called into being a hypochondriac, or even a misanthropical, mood. At such times he would be extremely critical, and very hard to get on with.

One day, lying on the sofa, giving dry coughs, and playing with the thermometer, he said:

"To live simply to die is by no means amusing, but to live with the knowledge that you will die before your time, that really is idiotic...."

Another time, seated at the open window and gazing out into the distance, at the sea, he suddenly said peevishly:

"We are accustomed to live in hopes of good weather, a good harvest, a nice love-affair, hopes of becoming rich or getting the office of chief of police, but I've never noticed anyone hoping to get wiser. We say to ourselves: it'll be better under a new tsar, and in two hundred years it'll be still better, and nobody tries to make this good time come tomorrow. On the whole, life gets more and more complex every day and moves on at its own sweet will, and people get more and more stupid, and get isolated from life in ever-increasing numbers."

After a pause he added, wrinkling up his forehead:

"Like crippled beggars in a religious procession."

He was a doctor, and the illness of a doctor is always worse than the illness of his patients. The patients only feel, but the doctor, as well as feeling, has a pretty good idea of the destructive effect of the disease on his constitution. This is a case in which knowledge brings death nearer.

His eyes were very fine when he laughed—there was a feminine gentleness in them then, something soft and tender. And his laughter, almost noiseless, had something particularly attractive about it. When he laughed he really enjoyed himself. I have never known anybody who could laugh so "spiritually".

Indecent stories never made him laugh.

He once said to me, with his charming, sympathetic laugh:

"Do you know why Tolstoy is so fickle in his treatment of you? He's jealous, he's afraid Sulerzhitsky likes you more than him. He is, really! He said to me yesterday: 'I don't know why, but somehow I can never be myself with Gorky. I don't like Suler living with him. It's bad for Suler. Gorky's wicked. He's like a divinity student who has been forced to take monastic vows and has a grievance against the whole world. He has the soul of an emissary, he has

come from somewhere to the land of Canaan, an alien land for
him, and he keeps looking round, noting everything, so as to report
about it all to some god of his own. And his god is a monster, a
wood-sprite or a water-sprite, like the ones countrywomen fear.' "

Chekhov laughed till he cried as he told me this, and continued,
wiping away his tears:

"I said: 'Gorky's a good sort.' But he said: 'No, no, don't tell
me! He has a nose like a duck's bill, only unfortunate and bad-
tempered people have such noses. And women don't like him, and
women are like dogs, they always know a good man. Suler, now,
he has the priceless gift of disinterested love. In that respect he's
a genius. To be capable of loving is to be capable of anything. . . .' "

After a pause Chekhov went on:

"Yes, the old boy's jealous . . . isn't he marvellous? . . ."

When he spoke about Tolstoy, there was always an almost im-
perceptible smile, at once tender and shy, in his eyes, and he lowered
his voice, as if speaking of something fragile and mysterious,
something that must be handled with care and affection.

He constantly deplored the fact that there was no Eckermann by
Tolstoy's side, to jot down the keen, unexpected, and frequently
contradictory utterances of the old sage.

"*You* ought to do it," he assured Sulerzhitsky. "Tolstoi's so fond
of you, he talks such a lot to you, and says such wonderful things."

Of Suler himself, Chekhov said to me:

"He is a wise child."

Very well said.

I once heard Tolstoy praise a story of Chekhov's—*The Darling*
I think it was.

"It's like lace woven by a virtuous maiden," he said. "There
used to be girl lace-makers in the old days, who, their whole lives
long, wove their dreams of happiness into the pattern. They wove
their fondest dreams, their lace was saturated with vague, pure aspi-
rations of love." Tolstoy spoke with true emotion, with tears in
his eyes.

But that day Chekhov had a temperature, and sat with his head
bent, vivid spots of colour on his cheeks, carefully wiping his pince-
nez. He said nothing for some time, and at last, sighing, said softly
and awkwardly: "There are misprints in it."

Much could be written of Chekhov, but this would require close, precise narration, and that is what I'm no good at. He should be written about as he himself wrote *The Steppe*, a fragrant, open-air, very Russian story, pensive and wistful. A story for one's self.

It does one good to remember a man like that, it is like a sudden visitation of cheerfulness, it gives a clear meaning to life again.

Man is the axis of the Universe.

And his vices, you ask, his shortcomings?

We all hunger for the love of our fellow creatures, and when one is hungry, even a half-baked loaf tastes sweet.

STORIES

DEATH OF A CLERK

It was an excellent night when the excellent clerk, Ivan Dmitrich Chervyakov,* sat in the second row of the stalls, enjoying *Les Cloches de Corneville* with the aid of opera-glasses. He watched the stage and thought himself the happiest of mortals, when all of a sudden. . . . "All of a sudden" has become a hackneyed expression, but how can authors help using it, since life is full of surprises? All of a sudden, then, his face puckered up, his eyes rolled heavenwards, his breath was suspended . . . turning his face away from the opera-glasses, he doubled up in his seat and—a-shoo! That is to say he sneezed. Now everyone has a right to sneeze wherever he likes. Peasants, police inspectors, even privy councillors sneeze. Everyone sneezes—everyone. Chervyakov felt no embarrassment, dabbed at his nose with his pocket handkerchief, and, like a well-bred man, looked round to see whether his sneezing had incommoded anyone. And then he did feel embarrassed. For he saw a little old man sitting in the first row, just in front of him, carefully wiping his bald cranium and neck with his glove, muttering something the while. Chervyakov recognised in the old man Civil General Brizhalov of the Ministry for Communications.

"I sneezed over him!" thought Chervyakov. "He's not my chief, it's true, but still it's very awkward. I must apologise."

* From the Russian *chervyak*, worm.—*Tr.*

Chervyakov leaned forward with a little cough, and whispered in the General's ear:

"I beg your pardon, Your Excellency, I sneezed.... I didn't mean to...."

"Don't mention it."

"Do forgive me. I ... it wasn't premeditated!"

"Can't you keep quiet, for goodness' sake! Let me listen!"

Chervyakov, somewhat disconcerted, smiled sheepishly and tried to turn his attention to the stage. He watched the actors, but no longer felt the happiest of mortals. He was devoured by remorse. Walking up to Brizhalov in the interval, he hung about for a while and at last, conquering his timidity, mumbled:

"I sneezed at you, Your Excellency.... Pardon me.... You know ... I didn't mean...."

"Oh, really ... I have forgotten it, must you go on?" the General said, his underlip twitching impatiently.

"He says he's forgotten, but I don't like the look in his eyes," thought Chervyakov, glancing distrustfully in the General's direction. "Doesn't want to talk to me. I must explain to him that I didn't mean to ... that it's a law of nature, otherwise he might think I meant to spit on him. Even if he doesn't think so now, he might afterwards!..."

When he got home, Chervyakov told his wife of his ungentlemanly conduct. It seemed to him that his wife received his story with undue levity. True, she was alarmed for a moment, but finding Brizhalov was not "our" chief, she was reassured.

"I think you ought to go and apologise, though," she said. "Or he'll think you don't know how to behave in company."

"That's it! I tried to apologise, but he was so strange. Didn't say a word of sense. Besides, there was no time for talking."

Next day Chervyakov put on his new official frock-coat, had his hair cut, and went to explain his conduct to Brizhalov. The General's reception-room was full of petitioners, and the General himself was there, receiving petitions. After interviewing a few of them, the General raised his eyes to Chervyakov's face.

"Last night, in The Arcadia, if you remember, Your Excellency," began the clerk, "I—er-sneezed, and—er-happened to ... I beg...."

"Pshaw, what nonsense!" said the General. "What can I do for you?" he asked, addressing the next man.

"Won't listen to me!" thought Chervyakov, turning pale. "It means he's angry.... I can't leave it at that.... I must explain to him...."

When the General, having received the last petitioner, turned to go back to his private apartment, Chervyakov pursued him, muttering:

"Excuse me, Your Excellency! Nothing but my heart-felt repentance emboldens me to trouble Your Excellency...."

The General looked as if he were going to cry, and waved him away.

"You are laughing at me, Sir!" he said and shut the door in his face.

"Laughing!" thought Chervyakov. "I don't see anything funny in it. Doesn't he understand, and he a General? Very well, I won't bother the fine gentleman with my apologies any more. Devil take him! I'll write him a letter, I won't go to him any more! I won't, and that's all!"

Such were Chervyakov's thoughts as he walked home. But he did not write the letter. He thought and thought but could not think how to word it. So he had to go to the General the next day, to get things straight.

"I ventured to trouble you yesterday, Your Excellency," he began when the General turned a questioning glance upon him, "not to laugh at you, as Your Excellency suggested. I came to bring my apologies for having inconvenienced you by sneezing.... As for laughing at you, I would never think of such a thing. How would I dare to! If we took it into our heads to laugh at people, there would be no respect left ... no respect for superiors...."

"Get out of here!" barked the General, livid and shaking with rage.

"I beg your pardon?" whispered Chervyakov, numb with terror.

"Get out!" repeated the General, stamping his foot.

Chervyakov felt as if something had snapped inside him. He neither heard nor saw anything as he backed towards the door, walked out into the street and wandered on. He stumbled mechanically home, lay down on the sofa, just as he was, in his official frock-coat, and died.

1883

CHAMELEON

Police Inspector Ochumelov* crossed the market-place in a new great-coat holding a bundle in his hand. After him strode a red-haired constable carrying a sieve filled to the brim with confiscated gooseberries. All around was silence.... There was not a soul in the market-place.... The open doors of small shops and taverns gaped drearily out at God's world, like so many hungry jaws. There were not even any beggars standing near them.

All of a sudden the sound of a voice came to Ochumelov's ears. "So you'd bite, would you, you cur! Don't let it go, lads! Biting is not allowed nowadays. Hold it! Ow!"

A dog's whine was heard. Ochumelov glanced in the direction of the sound and this is what he saw: a dog came running out of the timber-yard of the merchant Pichugin on three legs, pursued by a man in a starched print shirt and an unbuttoned waistcoat, his whole body bent forward; the man stumbled and caught hold of the dog by one of its hind legs. There was another whine, and again a shout of: "Don't let it go!" Drowsy faces were thrust out of shops, and in no time a crowd which seemed to have sprung out of the earth had gathered around the timber-yard.

"Looks like a public disturbance, Your Honour!" said the constable.

Ochumelov turned and marched up to the crowd. Right in front of the gate of the yard he saw the above-mentioned individual in the unbuttoned waistcoat, who stood there with his right hand raised, displaying a bleeding

---

* From the Russian *ochumely*, crazed.—*Tr.*

finger to the crowd. The words: "I'll give it to you, you
devil!" seemed to be written on his tipsy countenance,
and the finger itself looked like a banner of victory.
Ochumelov recognised in this individual Khryukin,* the
goldsmith. In the very middle of the crowd, its forelegs
well apart, sat the culprit, its whole body a-tremble—a
white *borzoi* pup, with a pointed nose and a yellow spot
on its back. In its tearful eyes was an expression of
misery and horror.

"What's all this about?" asked Ochumelov, shoulder-
ing his way through the crowd. "What are you doing
here? Why are you holding up your finger? Who shouted?"

"I was walking along, Your Honour, as quiet as a
lamb," began Khryukin, coughing into his fist. "I had
business about some wood with Mitri Mitrich here, and
suddenly, for no reason whatever, that nuisance bit my
finger. Excuse me, but I'm a working man.... Mine is a
very intricate trade. Make them pay me compensation—
perhaps I won't be able to move this finger for a week. It
doesn't say in the law, Your Honour, that we have to put
up with ferocious animals. If everyone's to start biting,
life won't be worth living...."

"H'm... well, well," said Ochumelov severely, coughing and twitching his eyebrows. "Well, well ... whose
dog is it? I shan't leave it at this. I'll teach people to let
dogs run about! It's time something was done about gentlemen who are not willing to obey the regulations! He'll
get such a fine, the scoundrel—I'll teach him what it
means to let dogs and cattle of all sorts rove about! I'll
show him what's what! Eldirin," he continued, turning
to the constable, "find out whose dog it is, and draw
up a statement. And the dog must be exterminated
without delay. It's probably mad ... whose dog is it,
I ask?"

"I think it belongs to General Zhigalov," said a voice
from the crowd.

"General Zhigalov! H'm. Help me off with my coat,
Eldirin.... Phew, how hot it is! It must be going to rain."

---

* From the Russian *khryu-khryu*—pig's grunt.—*Tr.*

He turned to Khryukin: "One thing I don't understand—
how did it happen to bite you? How could it have got at
your finger? Such a little dog, and you such a strapping
fellow! You must have scratched your finger with a nail,
and then taken it into your head to get paid for it. I know
you fellows! A set of devils!"

"He burned the end of its nose with a lighted cigarette
for a joke, Your Honour, and it snapped at him, it's nobody's fool! That Khryukin's always up to some mischief,
Your Honour!"

"None of your lies, Squinty! You didn't see me do it,
so why lie? His Honour is a wise gentleman, he knows
who's lying and who's telling a God's truth. May the justice of the peace try me if I'm lying! It says in the law ...
all men are equal now. I have a brother in the police
myself, if you want to know...."

"Don't argue!"

"No, that isn't the General's dog," remarked the constable profoundly. "The General hasn't got a dog like that.
All his dogs are pointers."

"Are you sure?"

"Quite sure, Your Honour."

"And you're right! The General's dogs are expensive,
breed-dogs, and this one—just look at it! Ugly, mangy
cur! Why should anyone keep a dog like that? Are you
crazy? If a dog like that were to find itself in Moscow or
Petersburg, d'you know what would happen to it? Nobody would worry about the law, it would be got rid of
in a minute. You're a victim, Khryukin, and mind you
don't leave it at that. He must be taught a lesson! It's
high time...."

"Perhaps it is the General's after all," said the constable, thinking aloud. "You can't tell by looking at it. I
saw one just like it in his yard the other day."

"Of course it's the General's!" came the voice from the
crowd.

"H'm! Help me on with my coat, Eldirin.... I felt a
gust of wind. I'm shivery. Take it to the General's and
ask them. Say I found it, and sent it. And tell them not
to let it into the street. Perhaps it's an expensive dog, and
it'll soon get spoilt if every brute thinks he can stick ciga-

rettes into its nose. A dog's a delicate creature. And you put down your hand, blockhead! Stop showing everyone your silly finger. It's your own fault. . . ."

"Here comes the General's chef, we'll ask him. . . . Hi, there, Prokhor! Come here, old man! Have a look at this dog . . . is it yours?"

"What next! We've never had one like that in our lives!"

"No need to make any more enquiries," said Ochumelov. "It's a stray. What's the good of standing here talking. You've been told it's a stray, so a stray it is. Destroy it and have done with the matter."

"It isn't ours," continued Prokhor. "It belongs to the General's brother, who came a short time ago. Our General takes no interest in *borzois*. His brother now, he likes. . . ."

"What, has the General's brother come? Vladimir Ivanich?" exclaimed Ochumelov, an ecstatic smile spreading over his features. "Fancy that! And I didn't know. Come to stay?"

"That's right."

"Just fancy! Wanted to see his brother! And I didn't know. So it's *his* dog? Very glad! Take it . . . it's a nice little doggie! Snap at his finger? Ha-ha-ha! Come now, don't tremble! Gr-gr . . . the little rascal's angry. . . . What a pup!"

Prokhor called the dog and walked out of the timber-yard with it. The crowd laughed at Khryukin.

"I'll have you yet!" Ochumelov threatened him, and, wrapping his great-coat round him, he continued his way across the market-place.

1884

VANKA

Nine-year-old Vanka Zhukov, who had been apprenticed three months ago to Alyakhin the shoemaker, did not go to bed on Christmas Eve. He waited till his master and mistress and the senior apprentices had gone to church, and then took from the cupboard a bottle of ink and a pen with a rusty nib, spread out a crumpled sheet of paper, and was all ready to write. Before tracing the first letter he glanced several times anxiously at the door and window, peered at the dark icon, with shelves holding cobbler's lasts stretching on either side of it, and gave a quivering sigh. The paper lay on the bench, and Vanka knelt on the floor at the bench.

"Dear Grandad Konstantin Makarich," he wrote. "I am writing a letter to you. I send you Christmas greetings and hope God will send you his blessings. I have no father and no Mummie and you are all I have left."

Vanka raised his eyes to the dark window-pane, in which the reflection of the candle flickered, and in his imagination distinctly saw his grandfather, Konstantin Makarich, who was night watchman on the estate of some gentlefolk called Zhivarev. He was a small, lean old man about sixty-five, but remarkably lively and agile, with a smiling face and eyes bleary with drink. In the day-time he either slept in the back kitchen, or sat joking with the cook and the kitchen-maids, and in the night, wrapped in a great sheepskin coat, he walked round and round the estate, sounding his rattle. After him, with drooping heads, went old Kashtanka and another dog, called Eel, on account of his black coat and long, weasel-like body. Eel was wonderfully respectful and insinuating, and turned the same appealing glance on friends and strangers alike, but he inspired confidence in no one. His deferential manner and docility were a cloak for the most Jesuitical spite and malice. He was an adept at stealing up, to snap at a foot, creeping into the ice-house, or snatching a peasant's chicken. His hind legs had been slashed again and again, twice he had been strung up, he was beaten within an inch of his life every week, but he survived it all.

Grandad was probably standing at the gate at this moment, screwing up his eyes to look at the bright red light coming from the church windows, or stumping about in his felt boots, fooling with the servants. His rattle would be fastened to his belt. He would be throwing out his arms and hugging himself against the cold, or, with his old man's titter, pinching a maid, or one of the cooks.

"Have a nip," he would say, holding out his snuffbox to the women.

The women would take a pinch and sneeze. Grandfather would be overcome with delight, breaking out into jolly laughter, and shouting:

"Good for frozen noses!"

Even the dogs would be given a snuff. Kashtanka would sneeze, shake her head and walk away, offended. But Eel, too polite to sneeze, would wag his tail. And the weather was glorious. The air still, transparent, fresh. It was a dark night, but the whole village with its white roofs, the smoke rising from the chimneys, the trees, silver with rime, the snow-drifts, could be seen distinctly. The sky was sprinkled with gaily twinkling stars, and the Milky Way stood out as clearly as if newly scrubbed for the holiday and polished with snow. . . .

Vanka sighed, dipped his pen in the ink, and went on writing:

"And yesterday I had such a hiding. The master took me by the hair and dragged me out into the yard and beat me with the stirrup-strap because by mistake I went to sleep rocking their baby. And one day last week the mistress told me to gut a herring and I began from the tail and she picked up the herring and rubbed my face with the head. The other apprentices make fun of me they send me to the tavern for vodka and make me steal the masters cucumbers and the master beats me with the first thing he finds. And there is nothing to eat. They give me bread in the morning and gruel for dinner and in the evening bread again but I never get tea or cabbage soup they gobble it all up themselves. And they make me sleep in the passage and when their baby cries I don't get any sleep at all I have to rock it. Dear Grandad for the dear Lords sake take me away from here take me home to the village I cant bear it any longer. Oh Grandad I beg and implore you and I will always pray for you do take me away from here or I'll die...."

Vanka's lips twitched, he rubbed his eyes with a black fist and gave a sob.

"I will grind your snuff for you," he went on. "I will pray for you and you can flog me as hard as you like if I am naughty. And if you think there is nothing for me to do I will ask the steward to take pity on me and let me clean the boots or I will go as a shepherd-boy instead of Fedya. Dear Grandad I cant stand it it is killing me. I thought I would run away on foot to the village but I have no boots and I was afraid of the frost. And when I grow up to be a man I will look after you and I will not let anyone hurt you and when you die I will pray for your soul like I do for my Mummie.

"Moscow is such a big town there are so many gentlemens houses and such a lot of horses and no sheep and the dogs are not a bit fierce. The boys dont go about with the star at Christmas and they dont let you sing in church and once I saw them selling fish-hooks in the shop all together with the lines and for any fish you like very good ones and there was one would hold a sheat-fish weighing a pood and I have seen shops where there are all sorts of guns just like the master has at home they must cost a hundred rubles each. And in the butchers shops there are grouse and wood-cock and hares but the people in the shop dont say where they were shot.

"Dear Grandad when they have a Christmas tree at the big house take a gilded nut for me and put it away in the green chest. Ask Miss Olga Ignatyevna tell her its for Vanka."

Vanka gave a sharp sigh and once more gazed at the

window-pane. He remembered his grandfather going to get a Christmas tree for the gentry, and taking his grandson with him. Oh, what happy times those had been! Grandfather would give a chuckle, and the frost-bound wood chuckled, and Vanka, following their example, chuckled, too. Before chopping down the fir-tree, Grandfather would smoke a pipe, take a long pinch of snuff, and laugh at the shivering Vanka.... The young fir-trees, coated with rime, stood motionless, waiting to see which one of them was to die. And suddenly a hare would come leaping over a snow-drift, swift as an arrow.... Grandfather could never help shouting:

"Stop it, stop it ... stop it! Oh, you stub-tailed devil!"

Grandfather would drag the tree to the big house, and they would start decorating it.... Miss Olga Ignatyevna, Vanka's favourite, was the busiest of all. While Pelageya, Vanka's mother, was alive and in service at the big house, Olga Ignatyevna used to give Vanka sweets, and amuse herself by teaching him to read, write and count to a hundred, and even to dance the quadrille. But when Pelageya died, the orphaned Vanka was sent down to the back kitchen to his grandfather, and from there to Moscow, to Alyakhin the shoemaker....

"Come to me dear Grandad," continued Vanka. "I beg you for Christs sake take me away from here. Pity me unhappy orphan they beat me all the time and I am always hungry and I am so miserable here I can't tell you I cry all the time. And one day the master hit me over the head with a last and I fell down and thought I would never get up again. I have such a miserable life worse than a dogs. And I send my love to Alyona one-eyed Yegor and the coachman and dont give my concertina to anyone. I remain your grandson Ivan Zhukov dear Grandad come."

Vanka folded the sheet of paper in four and put it into an envelope which he had bought the day before for a kopek.... Then he paused to think, dipped his pen into the ink-pot, wrote: *"GRANDAD"*, scratched his head, thought again, and added:

"KONSTANTIN MAKARICH THE VILLAGE"

Pleased that no one had prevented him from writing, he put on his cap and ran out into the street without putting his coat on over his shirt.

The men at the butcher's told him, when he asked them the day before, that letters are put into letter-boxes, and from these boxes sent all over the world on mail coaches with three horses and drunken drivers and jingling bells. Vanka ran as far as the nearest letter-box and dropped his precious letter into the slit....

An hour later, lulled by rosy hopes, he was fast asleep.... He dreamed of a stove. On the stove-ledge sat his grandfather, his bare feet dangling, reading the letter to the cooks.... Eel was walking backwards and forwards in front of the stove, wagging his tail....

1886

THE GRASSHOPPER

I

All Olga Ivanovna's friends and acquaintances went to her wedding.

"Look at him—there *is* something about him, isn't there?" she said to her friends, nodding towards her husband—apparently anxious to explain how it was that she had agreed to marry a commonplace, in no way remarkable man.

Ossip Stepanovich Dimov, her husband, was a doctor with the rank of titular counsellor. He worked in two hospitals, in one as non-resident physician, and in the other as prosector. From nine till noon he received out-patients and visited his ward, and in the afternoon took the horse-tram to another hospital, where he performed post-mortems on patients who had died there. His private practice amounted to very little, about 500 rubles a year. And that is all. There is nothing more to say about him. Whereas Olga Ivanovna and her friends and acquaintances were by no means ordinary people. Each of them was distinguished in some way or other, and not altogether unknown, having already made a name and gained a certain celebrity, or, if not exactly celebrated yet, all gave promise of a brilliant future. One was an actor, whose genuine dramatic talents had already found recognition; he was elegant, clever and discreet, recited beautifully, and gave Olga Ivanovna lessons in elocution; another was an opera singer, fat and good-humoured, who assured Olga Ivanovna with a sigh that she was ruining herself—if she were not so lazy, if she would only take herself in hand, she would make a fine singer; as well as these there were several artists, chief among them Ryabovsky, who went in for painting problem pictures, animals and landscapes, and was an extremely handsome fair young man of about twenty-five, whose pictures made a hit at exhibitions—his latest had fetched five hundred rubles. He used to finish off Olga Ivanovna's sketches for her, and always said that something might come of her painting. Then there was a 'cellist who could make his 'cello "weep", and who declared openly that of all the women whom he knew, the only one capable of accompanying him was Olga Ivanovna. And a writer, young, but already well known, who had produced short novels, plays and stories. Who else? Oh, yes, there was Vasili Vasilievich, a genteel landowner, amateur book-illustrator and creator of vignettes; he had a true feeling for the old Russian style, and for the legendary epic. He could produce veritable miracles on paper, on china, and on smoked plates. Amidst this artistic, liberal society, these favourites of fortune, who, while perfectly urbane and well-bred, only remembered the existence of doctors when they were ill, and in whose ears the name of Dimov was equivalent to such common names as Sidorov or Tarasov, Dimov seemed like a stranger, superfluous, small, though he was actually very tall and broad-shouldered. His frock-coat seemed to have been made for someone else, and he had a beard like a tradesman's. Of course, if he had been a writer or an artist everyone would have said that his beard made him look like Zola.

The actor told Olga Ivanovna that with her flaxen hair and in her wedding attire she was exactly like a slender cherry-tree, when covered in the spring with delicate white blossom.

"No, but listen!" Olga Ivanovna said, seizing him by the hand. "How could it have happened? Listen to me, listen.... My father and Dimov worked in the same hospital, you know. When poor father fell ill Dimov watched by his bed-side day and night. Such a self-sacrifice! Listen, Ryabovsky! And you listen, writer, you'll find it very interesting. Come nearer. Such self-sacrifice, such sincere sympathy. I didn't sleep at night, either, I sat by my father, and all of a sudden—I won the heart of the lusty youth—just like that! My Dimov was head-over-ears in love. How queer fate can be! Well, after my father died Dimov came to see me sómetimes, and we sometimes met out-of-doors, and one fine day—lo and behold—a proposal, like a bolt from the blue! I cried all night, I fell madly in love, too. And here I am a married woman. There *is* something strong, something powerful, bearish, about him, isn't there, now? He's three-quarter face to us now, the light's all wrong, but when he turns full face just have a look at his forehead. What have you to say to such a forehead, Ryabovsky? Dimov, we're talking about you!" she shouted to her husband. "Come here! Give Ryabovsky your honest hand.... That's right. You must be friends."

Dimov held his hand out to Ryabovsky with a naive, good-humoured smile.

"Delighted," he said. "There was a Ryabovsky with me at college. He's no relation of yours, I suppose?"

II

Olga Ivanovna was twenty-two, Dimov, thirty-one. They had a wonderful life after their marriage. Olga Ivanovna covered the walls of her drawing-room with sketches, framed and unframed, by herself and her friends, and surrounded the grand piano and the furniture with an artistic jumble of Chinese parasols, easels, many-coloured drapes, daggers, small busts, photographs.... In the dining-room she hung cheap coloured prints, bast shoes, and scythes on the wall, and grouped a scythe and a rake in the corner, thus achieving a dining-room *à la russe*. She draped the ceiling and walls of the bedroom with dark cloth, to make it look like a cave, hung a Venetian lantern over the beds, and placed a figure holding an halberd at the door. And everyone said that the young couple had made themselves a very cosy nest.

Olga Ivanovna got up at eleven every day, played the piano, or, if there was sunshine, painted in oils. A little after twelve she went to her dressmaker. She and Dimov had very little money, only just enough for their needs, and if she was to appear constantly in new dresses, and look effective, the dressmaker and she had to resort to all sorts of cunning. Again and again sheer miracles were achieved, and a thing of utter enchantment, not a dress, but a dream, was created from an old, dyed frock and some odd bits of tulle and lace. From the dressmaker Olga Ivanovna usually went on to an actress friend, and while she was about it, tried to wangle tickets for some first-night, or somebody's benefit. From the actress she had to visit an artist's studio, or go to a picture-show, and then on to some celebrity to invite him to her house, to return a call, or simply to chatter. And everywhere she was greeted with gaiety and cordiality and assured that she was good, sweet, unusual.... Those whom she called celebrated and great received her as one of themselves, on an equal footing, and declared unanimously that with her gifts, taste and mind she would come to something big, if only she would stop wasting her talents in so many directions. She sang, played the piano, painted in oils, modelled in clay, acted in amateur theatricals, and all this not just anyhow, but displaying real talent. Whatever she did, whether it was making lanterns for illuminations, dressing up, or simply tying somebody's tie, turned out artistic, graceful, charming. But in nothing did her talents display themselves so vividly as in her ability to strike up lightning friendships and get on intimate terms with celebrated folk. The moment anyone distinguished himself in the very slightest degree, or got himself talked about, she scraped up an acquaintance with him, made friends instantly, and invited him to her house. Every time she made a new acquaintance was a veritable red-letter day for her. She worshipped the famous, she was proud of them, she dreamed of them every night. She thirsted for celebrities and could never slake this thirst. Old friends disappeared and were forgotten, new ones came to take their place, but she soon grew tired of these, too, or they disappointed her, and she began eagerly seeking new friends, new celebrities, and, when she had found them, looking for others. And why?

Between four and five she had dinner at home with her husband. His simplicity, common sense and good humour reduced her to a state of admiration and ecstasy. She was continually jumping up, flinging her arms round his neck, and showering kisses on him.

"You are a wise, high-minded man, Dimov," she told him. "But you have one very grave defect. You take no interest whatever in art. You quite ignore music and painting."

"I don't understand them," he said humbly. "I have worked at natural science and medicine my whole life, and I never had any time to go in for art."

"But that's awful, Dimov!"

"Why? Your friends know nothing about natural science or medicine, and you don't hold it against them. Everyone to his own. I don't understand landscapes or operas, but I look at it this way: since some clever people devote their whole lives to them, and other clever people pay enormous sums for them, they must be necessary. I don't understand, but that doesn't mean that I ignore them."

"Let me press your honest hand!"

After dinner Olga Ivanovna paid calls, then she went to the theatre or a concert, and did not get home till after midnight. And this went on every day.

On Wednesday evenings she was at home to visitors. There was no card-playing or dancing on these Wednesday evenings, and the company entertained themselves with the arts. The well-known actor recited, the singer sang, the artists made drawings in Olga's innumerable albums, the 'cellist played, and the hostess herself drew, modelled, sang and played accompaniments. In the intervals between reciting, playing and singing, they talked and argued about literature, the theatre, art. There were no ladies present, for Olga Ivanovna considered all women, except actresses and her dressmaker, trivial and boring. There was not a single Wednesday evening when the hostess did not start at every ring at the door-bell, saying with a triumphant countenance: "It's him!" by which pronoun she indicated some newly invited celebrity. Dimov was never in the drawing-room, and nobody so much as remembered his existence. But precisely at half past eleven, the door into the dining-room opened and Dimov appeared in the doorway, with his good-natured, gentle smile, rubbing the palms of his hands together, and saying:

"Come to supper, gentlemen!"

Everyone filed into the dining-room, and every time their eyes were greeted by the same objects: a dish of oysters, a round of ham or veal, sardines, cheese, caviare, pickled mushrooms, vodka and two decanters of wine.

"My darling *maître d'hôtel*," Olga Ivanovna would say, clasping her hands in ecstasy. "You're simply charming! Do look at his forehead, everyone! Dimov, turn your profile to us! Look, everyone—the face of a Bengal tiger, and an expression as sweet and kind as a doe's! You pet!"

The guests ate, glancing at Dimov and thinking: "He really is a nice chap"; but they soon forgot about him and went on talking about the theatre, music, art.

The young couple were happy, and their life went smoothly on. True, the third week of their honeymoon did not pass quite happily, indeed it was sad. Dimov caught erysipelas at the hospital, and had to stay in bed six days and have his beautiful black hair cropped to the roots. Olga Ivanovna sat at his bedside weeping bitterly, but when he got a little better she tied a white kerchief over his cropped head and began painting him as a Bedouin. And they both thought it great fun. Three days after he had quite recovered and begun going to the hospital again, a fresh misfortune overtook him.

"I have no luck, Mums," he said to her one day at dinner. "I had four post-mortems today, and I got two of my fingers cut at once. And I only noticed after I got home."

Olga Ivanovna was alarmed. He smiled and said it was a trifle and that he often cut his hands during post-mortems.

"I get carried away, Mums, and then I'm absent-minded."

Olga Ivanovna nervously awaited the onset of blood poisoning, and prayed every night that it might be averted; it all passed off harmlessly. And the old happy, tranquil life, untouched by grief or anxiety, was resumed. The present was splendid, and soon spring would be coming, smiling at them from afar, and promising a hundred joys. Happiness would go on for ever. For April, May and June there would be the country cottage a long way from Moscow, walks, sketches, fishing, nightingales, and then, from July right up to the autumn, the artists' excursion on the Volga, an excursion in which Olga Ivanovna, as a permanent member of their circle, would take part. She had already had herself made two travelling costumes of crash, and had bought paints, brushes, canvas and a new palette for the journey. Ryabovsky visited her almost every day to see how her painting was getting on. When she showed him her work he would thrust his hands deep into his pockets, compress his lips firmly, sniff and say:

"Well, well.... That cloud screams: that's not an evening light. The foreground is a bit messy, and there's something, you know what I mean—lacking.... Your hut looks as if it had been squashed and was whining piteously.... Make that corner darker. But on the whole it's not so dusty.... I'm pleased."

And the more obscure his way of speaking, the more easily Olga Ivanovna understood what he meant.

III

On Whitmonday Dimov went out in the afternoon and bought some snacks and sweets to take to his wife in the country. He had not seen her for a fortnight, and missed her sorely. In the railway carriage and afterwards, while trying to find his cottage in a thick copse, he felt the pangs of hunger, and indulged in dreams of sitting down to a leisurely supper with his wife, and afterwards tumbling into bed. It cheered him up to look at his parcel, which contained caviare, cheese, and smoked fish.

By the time he had found and recognised the cottage the sun had gone down. The elderly servant told him that the mistress was not at home, but that she would probably soon be back. The cottage, a highly unattractive structure, with low ceilings, note-paper on the walls, and uneven floors, full of gaps, contained only three rooms. In one was a bed, in the next canvases, paint-brushes, a piece of dirty paper, men's coats and hats on chairs and window-sills; and in the third Dimov came upon three strange men. Two were dark and bearded, and the third was clean-shaven and stout, an actor apparently. A samovar was steaming on the table.

"What do you want?" asked the actor in a bass voice, casting an unfriendly glance at Dimov. "To see Olga Ivanovna? Wait a minute. She'll be here soon."

Dimov sat down and waited. One of the dark men, looking at him with drowsy languor, poured out some tea, and asked:

"Have some tea?"

Dimov was both hungry and thirsty, but he refused the tea so as not to take the edge off his appetite. Soon steps were heard and a familiar laugh. A door banged and Olga Ivanovna burst into the room, in a broad-brimmed hat, carrying a box; after her, holding a big parasol and a folding stool, came Ryabovsky, red-cheeked and in high spirits.

"Dimov!" screamed Olga Ivanovna, flushing up with delight. "Dimov!" she repeated, laying her head and both her hands on his chest. "It's you! Why haven't you been for such a long time? Why? Why?"

"When could I, Mums? I'm always busy, and when I have any free time it always happens there's no suitable train."

"Oh, how glad I am to see you! I dreamed of you all night, all night, I was afraid you were ill or something. Oh, if only you knew what a darling you are, and how lucky it is you came! You are my deliverer! You're the only one who can save me! There's going to be the most original wedding here tomorrow," she went on, laughing and re-tying her husband's tie. "The telegraph-operator at the station is going to be married, Chikeldeyev his name is. Good-looking boy, and no fool, there's something strong, bearish about his face, you know.... He could sit for the portrait of a youthful Varangian. All we summer visitors take an interest in him and have given our word of honour to be at his wedding.... He's hard up, lonely, shy, it would be a sin to refuse him our sympathy. Fancy, the wedding will be just after the service, and everyone is going straight from the church to the home of the bride.... The grove, the singing of birds, spots of sun on the grass, you know, and all of us coloured spots against a bright green background—ever so original, just like the French expressionists. But, Dimov, what am I to wear at church?" said Olga Ivanovna, making a dolorous face. "I have nothing here, literally nothing. No dress, no flowers, no gloves.... You simply must save me! Your coming just now means fate intended you to save me. Take my keys, darling, go home, and get me my pink dress out of the wardrobe. You know it, it's hanging right in front.... And on the floor of the box-room you'll see two cardboard boxes. When you open the top one you'll see nothing but tulle, tulle, tulle and all sorts of scraps, and underneath them, flowers. Take out all the flowers very carefully, try not to crumple them, my pet. I'll choose something from them afterwards. And buy me a pair of gloves."

"Very well," said Dimov. "I'll go back tomorrow and send them."

"Tomorrow?" repeated Olga Ivanovna, gazing at him in consternation. "You couldn't possibly be in time tomorrow! The first train leaves at nine tomorrow, and the wedding's at eleven. No, ducky, you'll have to go today, you'll simply have to! If you can't come tomorrow yourself, send everything with a messenger. Go on, now.... The train will be here soon. Don't be late, my pet."

"All right."

"How I hate to let you go!" said Olga Ivanovna, and tears welled up in her eyes. "What a fool I was to promise the telegraph-operator!"

Dimov, gulping down a glass of tea and picking up a cracknel, smiled meekly and went to the station. The caviare, cheese and smoked fish were eaten by the two dark men and the fat actor.

IV

On a still moonlit night in July, Olga Ivanovna stood on the deck of a Volga steamer, looking in turns at the water and the exquisite river bank. Beside her stood Ryabovsky, telling her that the black shadows on the surface of the water were not shadows but a dream, that it would be good to forget everything, to die, to become a memory, surrounded by this magical, gleaming water, this infinite sky, these mournful, pensive banks, all speaking to us of the vanity of our lives, and of the existence of something higher, something eternal, blissful. The past was trivial and devoid of interest, the future was blank, and even this divine, never-to-be-repeated night would soon end, would become part of eternity—why, then, live?

And Olga Ivanovna listened in turn to Ryabovsky's voice and to the silence of the night, and told herself that she was immortal, that she would never die. The opalescent water, which was like nothing she had ever before seen, the sky, the banks, the black shadows, and the unaccountable joy filling her soul, all told her that she would one day be a great artist, and that somewhere, beyond the distance, beyond the moonlit night, in infinite space, there awaited her success, glory, the love of the people.... When she gazed long and unblinkingly into the distance she seemed to see crowds, lights, the sounds of solemn music, cries of enthusiasm, herself in a white dress, and flowers raining upon her from all sides. She told herself, too, that beside her, leaning on the rail, stood a truly great man, a genius, one of God's elect.... Everything he had done up to now was wonderful, fresh, unusual, and the work he would do in time, when his extraordinary talent had matured with the years, would be striking, immeasurably lofty, and all this could be seen in his face, in his way of expressing himself, and in his attitude to nature. He had his own special language for describing the shadows, the hues of evening, the brilliance of the moonlight, and the charm of his power over nature was almost irresistible. He was good-looking, too, and original, and his life, independent, free, without earthly ties, was like the life of a bird.

"It's getting chilly," said Olga Ivanovna, and she shivered.

Ryabovsky wrapped his coat round her, saying mournfully:

"I feel I am in your power. I am a slave. What makes you so fascinating today?"

He gazed at her all the time, never looking away, and there was something terrible in his eyes, she was afraid to look at him.

"I am madly in love with you..." he whispered,

breathing on her cheek. "Only say the word and I will stop living, throw up art..." he murmured, profoundly stirred. "Love me, love me...."

"Don't talk like that," said Olga Ivanovna, closing her eyes. "It's awful. And what about Dimov?"

"What does Dimov matter? Why Dimov? What have I to do with Dimov? The Volga, the moon, beauty, my love, my ecstasy, but no Dimov.... Oh, I know nothing.... I don't need the past, give me only one moment ... one little moment!"

Olga Ivanovna's heart beat violently. She tried to think of her husband, but the entire past, her wedding, Dimov, her Wednesday evenings, now seemed to her small, insignificant, dull, useless, and far, far away.... And after all—what did Dimov matter? Why Dimov? What had she to do with Dimov? Was there really such a person, wasn't he just a dream?

"The happiness he has had is quite enough for an ordinary man like him," she told herself, covering her face with her hands. "Let them judge *there,* let them curse me, I will go to my ruin, yes, to my ruin, just to spite them.... One should try everything once. Oh, God, how terrifying, and how lovely!"

"Well? Well?" murmured the artist, putting his arms round her and eagerly kissing the hands with which she was feebly trying to push him away. "Do you love me? Do you? Oh, what a night! What a divine night!"

"Yes, what a night!" she whispered, looking into his eyes, which were shining with tears, and then, looking away quickly, she put her arms round him and kissed him firmly on the lips.

"We'll be at Kineshma in a minute," said someone from the other side of the deck. Heavy steps were heard. It was the man from the refreshment-room passing.

"Listen," called Olga Ivanovna to him, laughing and crying from joy. "Bring us some wine."

The artist, pale with agitation, sat down on a bench, looking at Olga Ivanovna with adoring, grateful eyes, and then shut his own, and said with a weary smile:

"I am tired."

And he laid his head on the rail.

V

The second of September was a warm, still day, but misty. A light fog had hovered over the Volga in the early morning, and after nine o'clock it began to drizzle. And there was not the slightest hope of its clearing up. At breakfast Ryabovsky had told Olga Ivanovna that painting was the most ungrateful and tedious of the arts, that he was no artist, that no one but fools believed in his talent, and suddenly, without the faintest warning, seized a knife and slashed at his most successful sketch. After breakfast he sat moodily at the window and looked out at the river. And the Volga, no longer shining, was dimmed, dull, cold-looking. Everything spoke of the approach of the sad, bleak autumn. It seemed as if the lush green carpets on the banks, the diamond-like reflections of the sun-rays, the transparent, blue distance, and all the elegant show of nature had been taken from the Volga and laid away in a chest till next spring, and the crows flew over the river, teasing it: "Bare! Bare!" Ryabovsky listened to their cawing and told himself that he had painted himself out and lost his talent, that everything in the world was conventional, relative, idiotic, and that he should never have got mixed up with this woman. . . . In a word he was dejected and depressed. . . .

Olga Ivanovna sat on the bed on the other side of the partition, passing her fingers through her beautiful flaxen hair, seeing herself in imagination in her drawing-room, in the bedroom, in her husband's study. Her imagination bore her to the theatre, to the dressmaker, to her celebrated friends. What were they doing at this moment? Did they ever think of her? The season had begun and it was time to think of her Wednesday evenings. And Dimov? Dear Dimov! How meekly and with what childish plaintiveness he kept begging her in his letters to come home. Every month he sent her 75 rubles, and when she wrote him that she had borrowed a hundred rubles from the artists he sent her another hundred. What a good, generous man! The journey had tired Olga Ivanovna, she was bored, she was longing to get away from these peasants, from the smell of damp rising from the river, to shake off the feeling of physical uncleanliness which never left her, while living in peasant huts and migrating from village to village. If Ryabovsky had not given the artists his word of honour that he would stay with them till the twentieth of September they could have gone away this very day. And wouldn't that have been nice!

"My God," groaned Ryabovsky. "Whenever will the sun come out? I can't go on with a sunlit landscape when there isn't any sun."

"You have a sketch with a cloudy sky," said Olga Ivanovna, coming out from behind the partition. "Don't you remember—with a wood in the right foreground and a herd of cows and geese on the left. You might finish it now."

"For God's sake!" The artist made a grimace of distaste. "Finish! Do you really consider me too much of a fool to know what I ought to do?"

"How you have changed to me," sighed Olga Ivanovna.

"And a good thing, too!"

Olga Ivanovna's features twitched, she crossed over to the stove, and stood there, crying.

"And now tears—if that isn't the limit! Stop it! I have a thousand reasons for crying, but I don't cry."

"Reasons!" sobbed Olga Ivanovna. "The chief reason of all is that you are sick of me. Yes, you are!" And her sobs increased. "The whole truth is that you are ashamed of our love. You are afraid of the artists noticing, though there's no concealing it, and they've known about it for ages."

"Olga, I ask you only one thing," said the artist in imploring tones, placing his hand on his heart. "Only one thing—leave me alone! That's all I want from you."

"But swear that you still love me!"

"This is torture!" the artist hissed through clenched teeth, and he leaped to his feet. "It'll end in my throwing myself into the Volga or going mad! Leave me alone!"

"Kill me, then, go on, kill me!" cried Olga Ivanovna. "Kill me!"

She burst out sobbing and went behind the partition again. The rain rustled on the straw thatch. Ryabovsky clutched at his head and paced up and down the room for a time, and then, an expression of determination on his face, as if he were clinching an argument with someone, he put on his cap, threw his gun over his shoulder, and went out of the hut.

After he had gone, Olga Ivanovna lay on her bed for a long time, crying. At first she thought how nice it would be to take poison, and for Ryabovsky to find her dead when he came back, but very soon her thoughts flew back to her drawing-room, to her husband's study, and she saw herself sitting quite still beside Dimov, enjoying the physical sensations of peace and cleanliness, and then seated in the theatre listening to Mazzini. And the yearning for civilisation, for the noises of the city, for celebrated men, struck a pang to her heart. A country-woman came into the hut and began heating the stove with leisured movements, in preparation for cooking dinner. There was a smell of smouldering wood, and the air turned blue with smoke. The artists came in in their muddy high-boots, their faces wet with rain, looked at one another's sketches and consoled themselves by the reflection that the Volga had its charm even in bad weather. And the pendulum of the cheap clock on the wall went tick-tock-tick. Chilly flies clustered in the corner next to the icons, buzzing faintly, and cockroaches crawled about in the bulging files under the benches.

Ryabovsky returned to the hut at sunset. He flung his cap on the table, sank on to the bench, pale, exhausted, still in his muddy boots, and closed his eyes.

"I'm tired," he said, his eyebrows twitching in the effort to lift his eyelids.

Olga Ivanovna, in her anxiety to ingratiate herself, and show him that she was not really angry, went over to him, kissed him in silence, and passed a comb through his fair hair. She felt a sudden desire to comb his hair.

"What's this?" he said, starting as if something clammy had touched him, and opening his eyes. "What's this? Leave me in peace, I beg you!"

He pushed her from him and moved away and she caught an expression of disgust and annoyance on his face. Just then the woman came up to him, holding a plate of cabbage soup carefully in both hands, and Olga Ivanovna noticed that her thick thumbs were wet with the soup. And the dirty woman with her skirt drawn tight over her stomach, the cabbage soup, which Ryabovsky fell upon eagerly, the hut, this life which had at first seemed so delightful in its simplicity and artistic disorder, now struck her as appalling. Suddenly affronted, she said coldly:

"We shall have to part for a time, or we shall quarrel outright, from sheer boredom. I'm sick of all this! I shall leave today."

"How? On a broomstick?"

"Today's Thursday, so the steamer will arrive at nine-thirty."

"Will it? Oh, yes.... Very well, go then," said Ryabovsky softly, wiping his lips with a towel, for want of a napkin. "It's dull for you here, and I'm not such an egoist as to try and detain you. Go, we'll meet again after the 20th."

Olga Ivanovna started packing with a light heart, her cheeks flaming with satisfaction. Could it really be, she asked herself, that she would soon be sitting in her drawing-room, painting, sleeping in a bedroom, and dining with a cloth on the table? A load seemed to fall from her shoulders, and she was no longer angry with the artist.

"I'll leave you my paints and brushes, Ryabusha," she called out. "If there are any left over you can bring them back.... Now mind you don't get lazy when I'm not here, don't indulge in the blues—work! You're a brick, Ryabusha!"

At nine o'clock Ryabovsky kissed her good-bye, so as not to have to kiss her on the deck in front of the artists, she was sure, and saw her to the landing-stage. The steamer soon hove in sight and bore her away.

She was home in two and a half days. Without removing her hat and waterproof, breathing heavily in her agitation, she went into the drawing-room, and from there to the dining-room. Dimov was seated at the table in his shirt-sleeves, his waistcoat unbuttoned, sharpening a knife on the prongs of a fork; on a plate before him was a roasted grouse. Olga Ivanovna had entered the flat with the conviction that she must conceal everything from her husband, and that she had the ability and strength to do this, but at the sight of his broad, meek, joyful smile and the happiness shining in his eyes she felt that it would be as base and detestable, as impossible for her to deceive such a man as it would be to slander, to steal, or to murder, and she then and there decided to tell him all that had occurred. Allowing him to kiss and embrace her, she sank down on her knees before him and covered her face with her hands.

"What is it? What is it, Mums?" he asked her tenderly. "Did you miss me so?"

She lifted her face, red with shame, and cast a guilty look, full of entreaty, at him, but shame and fear prevented her from telling him the truth.

"It's nothing..." she said. "I'm just...."

"Let's sit down," he said, raising her, and seating her at the table. "That's the way.... Have some grouse. You're hungry, poor darling."

She inhaled the familiar atmosphere eagerly, and ate some grouse, while he gazed at her affectionately, laughing with delight.

VI

It was apparently some time in the middle of the winter that Dimov began to suspect that he was being deceived. He could no longer look his wife in the eyes, as if it were he whose conscience was not clear, no longer smiled joyfully when he met her, and in order to be as little alone with her as possible often brought home to dinner his friend Korostelev, a crop-headed little man with puckered features, who started buttoning and unbuttoning his coat from sheer embarrassment whenever Olga Ivanovna addressed him, and then fell to tweaking the left side of his moustache with his right hand. During dinner the doctors remarked that when the diaphragm was too high up, palpitations sometimes occurred, or that there had been a great deal of nervous disease lately, or that Dimov, the evening before, performing a post-mortem on a patient said to have died of pernicious anemia, had discovered cancer of the pancreas. And they seemed to carry on this medical conversation just to give Olga Ivanovna an excuse not to talk, that is, not to lie. After dinner Korostelev would sit down at the piano, and Dimov would sigh and call out:

"Come on, old boy! What are you waiting for? Give us something nice and sad."

His shoulders raised and his fingers outspread, Korostelev would strike a few chords and begin singing in a tenor voice: "Show me, show me the place in our country, where the Russian muzhik does not groan!" and Dimov would give another sigh, prop his head on his fist and plunge into thought.

Olga Ivanovna had now begun to behave extremely incautiously. She woke up every morning in the worst possible spirits, to the thought that she no longer loved Ryabovsky, and that it was all over between them, thank God. But after she had had a cup of coffee she would remind herself that Ryabovsky had robbed her of her husband and that she was now left without a husband, and without Ryabovsky. Then she would remember that her friends were speaking of some marvellous picture Ryabovsky was finishing for a show, a kind of mixture of landscape and problem picture, in the style of Polenov, and that everyone who visited his studio was in ecstasies about it. But he had created this picture under her influence, she told herself, he had improved enormously, thanks to her influence. Her influence had been so beneficial, so real, that if she were to leave him he might go all to pieces. She remembered, moreover, that the last time he had come to see her he had worn a grey coat with silvery threads in it and a new tie, and had asked her in languishing tones: "Do I look nice?". And he had certainly looked very nice, in his smart coat, with his long curls and blue eyes (or at least she had thought so), and he had been very affectionate with her.

Remembering all this and more, and forming her own conclusions, Olga Ivanovna would dress and go in a state of great excitement to Ryabovsky's studio. She usually found him in excellent spirits and full of admiration for his picture, which really was very good. When he was in a playful mood, he would fool about and parry serious questions with a joke. Olga Ivanovna was jealous of the picture and detested it, but always stood in front of it in polite silence for five minutes, and then would say, sighing as people sigh in a shrine:

"Yes, you never painted anything like it before. You know, it quite frightens me."

Then she would implore him to love her, not to throw her over, to pity her, poor, unhappy thing. She would weep, kiss his hands, try to drag an assurance of love out of him, pointing out that without her good influence he would stray from the path and be lost. Then, having thoroughly upset him and humiliated herself, she would go to the dressmaker or to an actress friend about a theatre-ticket.

On the days when she did not find him in his studio she left him a note threatening to take poison if he did not come to see her that very day. Alarmed, he would go to her and stay to dinner. Unabashed by the presence of her husband, he would make insulting remarks to her, she repaying him in his own coin. They both felt that they were in each other's way, that they were tyrants and enemies, and this infuriated them, and in their fury they did not notice how indecent their behaviour was and that even the crop-headed Korostelev could not fail to understand everything. After dinner Ryabovsky would bid them a hasty farewell and go.

"Where are you going?" Olga Ivanovna would ask him in the hall, looking at him with hatred.

Frowning and narrowing his eyes he would name some lady whom they both knew, and it was obvious that he was making fun of her jealousy and wanted to annoy her. She would go to her bedroom and lie down. In her jealousy, rage, humiliation and shame she would bite the pillow and sob loudly. Then Dimov would leave Korostelev in the drawing-room and step into the bedroom, looking shy and embarrassed, and say in a low voice:

"Don't cry so, Mums! What's the good? You ought to keep quiet about it. You mustn't let people see. . . . What's done can't be undone, you know."

Unable to control her jealousy, which made her very temples throb, and telling herself that it was not too late

to put things right, she would get up and wash, powder
her tear-stained face, and rush off to the lady he had
mentioned. Not finding Ryabovsky there, she would drive
to another, and another.... At first she felt shame in
these journeys, but she soon got used to them, and sometimes visited all the women she knew in a single evening,
in her search for Ryabovsky, and they all understood her
motive.

Once she said to Ryabovsky of her husband:

"That man oppresses me with his magnanimity."

This phrase pleased her so much that whenever she
met any of the artists who were in the secret of her affair
with Ryabovsky, she would mention her husband, saying,
with a powerful gesture:

"That man oppresses me with his magnanimity."

Their routine of life went on just the same as the pre-
ceding year. On Wednesday evenings there were the at-
homes. The actor recited, the artists drew, the 'cellist
played, the singer sang, and invariably at half past eleven
the door into the dining-room opened and Dimov said,
smiling: "Come to supper, gentlemen."

As before, Olga Ivanovna sought out great men, found
them, and, still not satisfied, went to look for others. As
before, she came home late every night, but Dimov was
never asleep when she returned, as he had been the year
before, but sat working at something in his study. He
went to bed at three and got up at eight.

One evening when she was taking a last look at herself
in the glass before going to the theatre, Dimov came into
the bedroom in a frock-coat and white tie. He smiled
meekly and looked straight into her eyes, as he used to
formerly. His face was radiant.

"I've just presented my thesis," he said, sitting down
and smoothing the knees of his trousers.

"Was it a success?" asked Olga Ivanovna.

"Wasn't it just!" he laughed, craning his neck to catch
sight of his wife's face in the mirror, for she still stood
with her back towards him putting the finishing touches
to her hair. "Wasn't it just!" he repeated. "And it's
highly probable, you know, that they'll make me docent
in general pathology. It looks very like it."

It was obvious from his blissful, radiant expression that if Olga Ivanovna had shared his joy and triumph he would have forgiven her all, both present and future, and would have forgotten all, but she understood neither what a docent was nor what general pathology meant, besides she was afraid of being late for the theatre, and so she said nothing.

He sat on for a few minutes, and then, smiling apologetically, went away.

VII

It had been a most restless day.

Dimov had a violent headache. He had no breakfast and did not go to the hospital, but lay all day on the couch in his study. Olga Ivanovna went off as usual to Ryabovsky soon after twelve, to show him a sketch for a still life that she had made, and ask him why he had not been to see her the day before. She knew her sketch was poor, and had only painted it so as to have an excuse to go and see the artist.

She went in without ringing and while she was taking off her galoshes in the hall she thought she heard soft steps in the studio, accompanied by the rustle of a woman's dress, and when she glanced hastily in she was just in time to catch a glimpse of a brown skirt, which flashed by one moment and disappeared the next behind a large canvas over which a sheet of black calico was draped, covering the easel and reaching to the floor. There could be no doubt that a woman was hiding there. How often had Olga Ivanovna found herself a hiding place behind this canvas! Ryabovsky, obviously profoundly embarrassed, stretched out both his hands towards her, as if astonished to see her, and said with a strained smile:

"A-a-ah! Glad to see you! What's your news?"

Olga Ivanovna's eyes filled with tears. She felt ashamed and wretched, and would not for anything in the world have spoken in front of that other woman, her rival, that liar, who was now standing behind the canvas and no doubt laughing up her sleeve.

"I just wanted to show you my sketch," she said, in a high, timid voice, and her lips quivered. "It's a *nature morte*."

"A-a-ah, a sketch. . . ."

The artist took the sketch in his hands, and, his eyes fixed on it, strolled as it were absent-mindedly into the next room.

Olga Ivanovna followed him submissively.

"*Nature morte*, of the very best sort," he muttered, mechanically seeking rhymes, "kur-ort, sport, port, short. . . ."

The sound of hasty steps and the rustling of skirts came from the studio. This meant *she* had gone. Olga Ivanovna felt an impulse to cry out, to hit the artist over the head with something heavy, and run away, but she was blinded with tears, crushed with shame, and felt she was no longer Olga Ivanovna, the artist, but some wretched little pigmy.

"I'm tired," said the artist in languishing tones, looking at the sketch and trying to shake off his fatigue with a toss of his head. "It's quite nice, of course, but it's a sketch today, and a sketch last year and in a month's time another sketch. . . . Aren't you sick of them? In your place I would give up art and go in for music or something seriously. You're not an artist, you know, you're a musician. But if you only knew how tired I am! I'll tell them to bring us some tea, shall I?"

He went out of the room and Olga Ivanovna could hear him speaking something to his man-servant. To avoid a leave-taking and a scene, above all to prevent herself from bursting out crying, she ran out into the hall before Ryabovsky had time to get back, put on her galoshes, and went out. Once in the street she breathed more freely, feeling that she had shaken off Ryabovsky, art, and the unendurable sense of humiliation she had undergone in the studio, for good and all. This was the end.

She went to her dressmaker, then to Barnai, who had only just come back, from Barnai to a music-shop, thinking all the time of the cold, ruthless and dignified letter she would write to Ryabovsky, and of how she would go

to the Crimea with Dimov in the spring or summer, there
to shake off the past for ever, and begin a new life.

She got home quite late, but instead of going to her
room to undress she went straight to the drawing-room to
compose her letter. Ryabovsky had told her she was not
an artist, and in revenge she would now tell him that he
painted the same picture year after year, that he said the
same things day after day, that he had gone off, that he
would never achieve any more than he had already
achieved. She intended to add that he was greatly indebted
to her good influence and that if he was now behaving
badly it was because her influence had been stultified by
all sorts of disreputable creatures, like the one who had
hidden behind the picture today.

"Mums," called Dimov from his study, without opening the door. "Mums."

"What d'you want?"

"Don't come near me, Mums, but just come to the door.
That's right. I caught diphtheria a day or two ago in the
hospital and . . . I feel very bad. Send for Korostelev."

Olga Ivanovna always called her husband by his sur-
name, as she did all her men friends. His name was
Ossip, and she did not like it, for it reminded her of
Gogol's Ossip and a silly pun on the names Ossip and
Arkhip. But now she exclaimed:

"Oh, Ossip, it can't be true!"

"Send for him. I feel bad. . ." said Dimov from inside
the room, and she could hear him walk over to the sofa
and lie down. "Send for him." His voice sounded hollow.

"Can it really be?" thought Olga Ivanovna, cold with
horror. "Why, it's dangerous!"

Without knowing why she lit a candle and took it to
her bedroom, and while trying to decide what she ought
to do, she caught sight of herself in the looking-glass.
With her pale, frightened face, in her jacket with the
high, puffy sleeves, and yellow flounces in front, and the
eccentric diagonal stripes on her skirt, she saw herself
as an awful fright, a revolting creature. An infinite pity
for Dimov surged up within her, for his boundless love
for her, his young life and even his lonely bed, in which
he had not slept for so long, and she remembered his

invariable meek, submissive smile. She wept bitterly and
wrote an imploring note to Korostelev. It was two o'clock
in the morning.

VIII

When Olga Ivanovna, her head heavy from lack of
sleep, her hair not done, a guilty expression on her face,
and looking quite plain, came out of her bedroom soon
after seven the next morning, a gentleman with a black
beard, a doctor apparently, passed her in the hall. There
was a smell of medicaments. Korostelev was standing at
the door in the study, tweaking the left side of his moustache with his right hand.

"Sorry, but I can't let you go to him," he said morosely
to Olga Ivanovna. "You might catch it. And besides,
there's no point in your going to him. He's delirious."

"Has he really got diphtheria?" whispered Olga Ivanovna.

"I would have everyone who courts danger needlessly
sent to prison," muttered Korostelev, not answering her
question. "D'you know how he got infected? He sucked
up pus from the throat of a little boy with diphtheria.
And what for? Sheer folly, imbecility!"

"Is it very dangerous?" asked Olga Ivanovna.

"Yes, they say it's a very bad case. What we ought to
do is to send for Shreck."

A red-haired little man with a long nose and a Jewish
accent came, and after him a tall, stooping, shaggy man,
rather like an archdeacon, and then a younger man, stout
and red-faced, wearing spectacles. They were all doctors
who came to take turns at the bed-side of their comrade.
Korostelev, who did not go home when his watch was
over, wandered about the rooms like a ghost. The maid
made tea for the doctors and was always running to the
chemist's, so there was no one to do the rooms. It was
very quiet, very dreary.

Olga Ivanovna sat in her bedroom telling herself that
God was punishing her for deceiving her husband. The
silent, unmurmuring, enigmatic being, his individuality

sapped by good-nature, yielding, weakened by excess of kindness, now lay on the couch, suffering in silence. If he had complained, if he had even raved in delirium, the doctors keeping watch over him would have discovered that it was not only diphtheria that was to blame. They might have asked Korostelev, he knew all, and it was not for nothing that he regarded his friend's wife with eyes which seemed to say that it was she who was the evil genius, and that the diphtheria was merely her ally. She forgot the moonlit night on the Volga, the assurances of love, the poetic life in the peasant hut, and remembered only that she had plunged head and shoulders into something foul and sticky, from which she would never be able to wash herself clean—and all out of sheer caprice, for the sake of trivial amusement.

"What a liar I have been!" she said to herself, remembering the restless love which had existed between Ryabovsky and herself. "A curse on it all!"

At four o'clock she had dinner with Korostelev. He ate nothing, only drinking some red wine and frowning. She, too, ate nothing. She prayed silently, promising God that if Dimov recovered, she would love him again and be a faithful wife. And then, forgetting her troubles for a moment, she would look at Korostelev and wonder: "Surely it must be a bore to be such an insignificant, obscure person, with such a puckered-up face and such bad manners!" And again it seemed to her that God might strike her down this very moment for, in her fear of infection, never once having been in her husband's study. Her prevailing mood was a feeling of dull misery and the conviction that her life was ruined and spoilt beyond repair....

After dinner the dusk soon fell. When Olga Ivanovna went into the drawing-room she found Korostelev asleep on the sofa, his head on a silk cushion embroidered in gilt thread. "Hup-wah," he snored. "Hup-wah."

The doctors, coming and going on their visits to the bed-side, were quite unaware of all this irregularity. The strange man snoring in the drawing-room, the pictures on the walls, the eccentric furniture, the mistress of the house going about with the hair not done and her dress in disarray, all this was now incapable of arousing the slightest interest. One of the doctors happened to laugh at something, and the laugh sounded strangely timid, making everyone feel uneasy.

When Olga Ivanovna next went into the drawing-room Korostelev was awake sitting up on the sofa, smoking.

"The diphtheria has settled in the nasal cavities," he said in an undertone. "His heart is already beginning to show the strain. Things look bad, bad."

"Why don't you send for Shreck?" asked Olga Ivanovna.

"He's been. It was he who noticed that the diphtheria had gone into the nose. And who's Shreck, anyhow? Shreck is nothing special, really. He's Shreck and I'm Korostelev, and that's all."

Time passed with agonising slowness. Olga Ivanovna, fully dressed, lay dozing on her bed, unmade since the morning. The whole flat seemed to be filled from floor to ceiling by a huge block of iron, and she felt that if only this block could be removed, everyone would cheer up. Waking with a start, she realised that it was not a block of iron but Dimov's illness.

"*Nature morte,* port," she said to herself, again falling into a doze, "sport, kur-ort. . . . And who's Shreck? Shreck, treck . . . wreck . . . kreck. And where are all my friends? Do they know we are in trouble? Oh, God, save us, have mercy. . . . Shreck, treck. . . ."

And again the block of iron. . . . Time dragged on endlessly, though the clock on the floor below seemed to be always striking the hour. And every now and then there came rings at the bell: the doctors coming to Dimov. . . . The maid came into the room holding a tray with an empty glass on it.

"Shall I do your bed, Ma'am?" she asked.

Getting no reply she went out again. The clock downstairs struck the hour, Olga Ivanovna dreamed it was raining on the Volga, and again someone came into her room, a stranger apparently. But the next moment she recognised Korostelev, and sat up in bed.

"What's the time?" she asked.

"About three."

"How is he?"

"How is he? I came to tell you he's dying."

He swallowed a sob, and sat down on the bed beside her, wiping away his tears with his cuff. She did not take it in at first, but went suddenly cold and crossed herself slowly.

"Dying," he repeated in a high voice and again sobbed. "Dying, because he sacrificed himself. What a loss to science!" he said with bitter emphasis. "In comparison with all the rest of us he was a great man, a remarkable man. What a gift! What hopes he inspired in us all!" went on Korostelev, wringing his hands. "My God, my God, he would have been such a scientist, such a rare scientist! Ossip Dimov, Ossip Dimov, what have you done? Oh, God!"

In his despair Korostelev covered his face with both hands.

"And what moral force!" he continued, getting more and more angry with someone. "Kind, pure, affectionate soul—crystal-clear! He served science and he died in the cause of science. Worked like a horse, day and night, nobody spared him, and he, young, learned, a future professor, had to look for private practice, sit up at night doing translations, to pay for those—miserable rags!"

Korostelev looked at Olga Ivanovna with loathing, seized the sheet in both his hands and tore angrily at it, as if it were to blame.

"He did not spare himself and nobody spared him. But what's the good of talking?"

"Yes, he was a remarkable man," came in deep tones from the drawing-room.

Olga Ivanovna went back in memory over her whole life with him, from beginning to end, in the utmost detail, and suddenly realised that he really had been a remarkable man, an unusual man, a great man, in comparison with all the others she had known. And remembering the attitude to him of her late father, and of all his colleagues, she realised that they had all seen in him a future celebrity. The walls, the ceiling, the lamp and the carpet on the floor winked mockingly at her, as if trying to say: "You've missed your chance!" She rushed weeping out of the bedroom, almost running into a strange man in the drawing-room, and burst into the study to her husband. He lay motionless on the couch, a blanket covering him up to the waist. His face was terribly drawn and thin and had that greyish yellow tinge never seen on the living. Only his forehead, his black eyebrows and his familiar smile showed that it was Dimov. Olga Ivanovna touched his breast, his brow and his hands with rapid movements. The breast was still warm, but the brow and hands were unpleasantly cold. And the half-shut eyes gazed, not at Olga Ivanovna, but at the blanket.

"Dimov!" she called out loud. "Dimov!"

She wanted to explain to him that it had all been a mistake, that everything was not yet lost, that life might yet be beautiful and happy, that he was an unusual, a remarkable, a great man, and that she would worship him all her life, would kneel before him, would feel a sacred awe of him. . . .

"Dimov!" she called, shaking him by the shoulder, unable to believe that he would never again wake up. "Dimov, Dimov, I say!"

And in the drawing-room Korostelev was saying to the maid:

"What is there to ask about? Go round to the church and ask where the almswomen live. They'll wash the body and put everything in order—they'll do all that is necessary."

1892

THE HOUSE WITH THE MANSARD

AN ARTIST'S STORY

I

All this happened six or seven years ago when I was living in the province of T., on the estate of a landed proprietor called Belokurov, a young man who rose very early, went about in a full-skirted peasant coat, drank beer of an evening, and was always complaining that he never met with sympathy anywhere. He lived in an annexe in the garden, and I took up my quarters in the old mansion, in a huge pillared ball-room, with no furniture but a wide sofa on which I slept, and a table at which I played patience. All the time, even in still weather, the ancient stoves hummed, and during thunderstorms the whole house shook as if it were on the point of falling to pieces; this was rather alarming, especially on stormy nights, when the ten great windows were lit up by lightning.

Doomed as I was to a life of idleness, I did nothing whatever. For hours at a time I looked out of the window at the sky, the birds, the garden walks, read whatever the post brought me, and slept. Sometimes I left the house and roamed about till late at night.

On my way home from one of these rambles, I happened upon an estate I had never seen before. The sun was setting and the shades of evening lay over the flowering rye. Two rows of ancient, towering fir-trees, planted close together so that they formed almost solid walls, enclosed a walk of sombre beauty. I climbed easily over some railings and made my way along this walk, my feet slipping on the carpet of pine-needles which lay an inch thick on the ground. It was still and dark but for the brilliant gold of the sunlight shimmering rainbow-like in the spiders' webs. The fragrance spread by the fir-trees was almost overpowering. I soon turned into a long avenue of lime-trees. Here, too, everything spoke of neglect and age. Last year's leaves rustled mournfully underfoot, and shadows lurked in the twilight between the trunks of the trees. On my right, in an ancient orchard, an oriole warbled feebly and listlessly—the bird, like everything else here, was probably old. And then the lime-trees came to an end in front of an old house with a verandah and a mansard, and suddenly I had a view of the courtyard, a big pond with a bathing-place on the bank, a huddle of green willows, and, in the midst of a village on the other side of the pond, a high, narrow belfry, the cross on its top lit up in the last rays of the departing sun.

For a moment I was under the spell of something familiar, something I had known long ago, as if I had seen this panorama before, at some time during my childhood.

A sturdy white stone gateway, adorned with lions, led from the courtyard into the open fields, and in this gateway stood two girls. The older of the two, slender, pale, very pretty, with a great knot of auburn hair on the top of her head and a small, obstinate mouth, looked very severe, and scarcely took any notice of me; the other, who looked extremely young, hardly more than seventeen or eighteen, was pale and slender, too, but her mouth was large and she looked shy, gazing at me from great wondering eyes and dropping out a word or two in English as I passed by; and it seemed to me that I had known these charming faces, too, at some distant time. I returned home, feeling as if I had had a delightful dream.

One afternoon, a few days later, Belokurov and I were walking about in front of the house, when the tall grass rustled beneath the wheels of a light carriage turning into the yard. In it sat one of the girls I had seen, the older one. She had brought a subscription list for aid to the victims of a fire. Not looking at us, she told us gravely, and in much detail the number of houses burned in the village of Siyanovo, the number of men, women and children rendered homeless, and the temporary measures proposed by the committee, of which she was a member, for rendering aid to the victims. After giving us the list to sign, she put it away and prepared to take her leave immediately.

"You've quite forgotten us, Pyotr Petrovich," she said to Belokurov, putting out her hand to him. "Come and see us, and if Monsieur N. (she named me) would like to make the acquaintance of some of his admirers, my mother and I would be very glad to see him."

I bowed.

When she had gone Pyotr Petrovich began telling me about her. He said she came from a good family, and was called Lydia Volchaninova, and both the estate on which she lived with her mother and sister, and the village on the other side of the pond, were called Shelkovka. Her father had occupied a prominent post in Moscow, and had died with the rank of privy councillor. Though quite well off, the Volchaninovs lived in the country all the year round, and Lydia taught in the Zemstvo school in her home village of Shelkovka, receiving a monthly salary of twenty-five rubles. She made this money suffice for her personal expenditure, and was proud to earn her own living.

"A very interesting family," said Belokurov. "We must pay them a visit. They would be very pleased if you went."

One day after dinner—it was some saint's day—we remembered the Volchaninovs, and set off to Shelkovka. We found the mother and both daughters at home. The mother, Yekaterina Pavlovna, must once have been good-looking, but had grown stouter than her age warranted, was short-winded, melancholy and absent-minded. She tried to entertain me with talk about art. Having learned from her daughter that I might visit Shelkovka, she had hastily recalled two or three landscapes of mine which she had seen at exhibitions in Moscow, and now asked me what I had intended to express by them. Lydia, or, as she was called at home, Leda, spoke more to Belokurov than to me. Her face grave and unsmiling, she asked him why he did not work in the Zemstvo, and why he had never been at a single one of its meetings.

"It's not right, Pyotr Petrovich," she said reproachfully. "Really it isn't—you ought to be ashamed of yourself."

"Quite true, Leda, quite true," agreed her mother. "It's not right."

"Our whole district is in the hands of Balagin," continued Leda, turning to me. "He is the chairman of the local board and has put his nephews and sons-in-law into all the district posts, and does whatever he likes. We must resist. We young people ought to make up a strong party, but you see what our young people are like. It's too bad, Pyotr Petrovich!"

Zhenya, the younger sister, said nothing while the Zemstvo was being discussed. She took no part in serious conversation, not being considered as a grown-up person by the family, among whom she went under the childish pet name of Missie, because that was what she had called her governess when she was a little girl. She kept looking at me with curiosity, telling me all about the originals of the family album I was looking through. "That's my uncle ... that's my godfather," she said, touching the portraits with her finger, her shoulder brushing artlessly against mine, giving me a clear view of her slight undeveloped breasts, her slender shoulders, her plait, and her whole thin figure, tightly drawn in at the waist by her belt.

We played croquet and tennis, walked about the garden, drank tea, and afterwards sat a long time over supper. After the huge empty pillared ball-room I felt quite at ease in the comfortable little house in which there were no oleograph pictures on the walls, and they said "you" and not the familiar "thou" to the servants. Leda and Missie made the atmosphere seem pure and youthful, and everything breathed integrity. At supper Leda again talked to Belokurov about the Zemstvo, Balagin, and school libraries. She was lively, sincere, strong in her convictions. She was an interesting talker, though she spoke a great deal, and very loud—perhaps because she was accustomed to addressing classes. My friend Pyotr Petrovich, on the other hand, still clung to the habit of his student days—the habit of turning every conversation into an argument. He held forth listlessly, tediously, and at length, with an obvious desire to show off his intelligence and his progressive views. He gesticulated and knocked a sauce-boat over with his cuff, and a large pool formed on the table-cloth, but no one but myself seemed to notice it.

When we set off for home it was dark and still.

"Good breeding does not consist in not upsetting sauce on the table, but in not noticing if someone else does," sighed Belokurov. "Yes, they're a delightful, cultured family. I've lost touch with nice people—I've deteriorated. There's so much to do, so much!"

He spoke of the work to be done if you wanted to be a model landlord. And I thought what a lazy, unmanageable fellow he was. When he spoke of serious things he interspersed his speech with painfully emphatic "er-er's" and he did everything in the same way as he spoke—slowly, always getting behind, never finishing anything in time. I did not believe he was a bit practical, if only because when I gave him letters to post he kept them in his pocket for weeks.

"And the worst of it is," he muttered, as he walked by my side, "you work and work, and meet with no sympathy from anyone. No sympathy whatever."

II

I got into the habit of visiting the Volchaninovs. My usual place there was on the lowest of the steps leading to the verandah. I was devoured by remorse, deploring my life which was passing so rapidly and trivially, and continually telling myself that it would be a good thing if I could tear out my heart, which was such a heavy burden to me. And all the time there was talk going on on the verandah, the sound of skirts rustling, and pages being turned. I soon grew accustomed to the knowledge that Leda received patients, gave out books and went often to the village with a parasol over her uncovered head in the day-time, and in the evening talked in a loud voice about the Zemstvo and schools. Whenever this girl, slender, good-looking, invariably severe, with her small, daintily curved mouth, began talking about practical things, she would preface her remarks by saying to me coldly:

"This won't interest you."

Me she disliked. She disliked me for being a landscape painter and not trying to show the needs of the people in my pictures, and also because she felt I was indifferent to all in which she believed so firmly. I remember riding along the shores of the Lake of Baikal, and meeting a Buryat girl in a shirt and blue denim trousers, riding astride. I asked her to sell me her pipe, but she only glanced contemptuously at my European features and hat, and, too bored to spend more than a minute talking to me, galloped past with a wild whoop. And Leda, too, felt there was something alien in me. She gave no outward signs of her dislike, but I could feel it, and, seated on the lowest step of the verandah, gave way to my irritation and said that to treat the peasants without being oneself a doctor was to deceive them, and that when one had any amount of broad acres, it was easy to be charitable.

But her sister Missie had not a care in the world, and, like myself, passed the time in complete idleness. The moment she got up of a morning she began reading, seated in a deep arm-chair on the verandah, her feet scarcely reaching the floor, or secluded herself with her book in the lime-tree walk, or passed through the gate into the fields. She read all day, scanning the pages avidly, and only an occasional weary and listless glance and the extreme pallor of her face showed that this reading was a mental strain. When I arrived and she caught sight of me, she would blush faintly, eagerly relinquish her book, and, fixing her great eyes on my face, begin to tell me what had happened since she last saw me—that the chimney had been on fire in the servants' quarters, that one of the workmen had caught a big fish in the pond, and so on. On week-days she usually wore a coloured blouse and a dark blue skirt. She and I used to stroll about, pick cherries for jam or go rowing, and when she jumped up to reach a cherry, or bent over the oars, her thin, delicate arms showed through her wide sleeves. Or

I would sketch, and she would stand by, watching admiringly.

One Sunday in the end of July, I set off for the Volchaninovs at about nine o'clock in the morning. I walked about the park, keeping as far from the house as possible, looking for mushrooms, which were very plentiful that summer, and marking the places where I found them with sticks, so as later to gather them with Zhenya. A warm wind was blowing. I could see Zhenya and her mother, both in light-coloured Sunday dresses, coming home from church, Zhenya holding her hat on against the wind. Then I heard sounds which meant they were having tea on the verandah.

For a carefree individual like myself, always seeking an excuse to be idle, these summer Sunday mornings on our country-estates hold a special charm. When the garden, green and sparkling with dew, lies radiant and happy in the rays of the sun, when the oleanders and the mignonette in the flower-beds near the house spread their perfume, and the young folk, just returned from church, are having tea in the garden, and everyone is so cheerful and so charmingly dressed; when I remind myself that all these healthy, well-nourished, good-looking people will do nothing at all the livelong day, I long for life to be always like this. This particular morning I was thinking these same thoughts and walking about the garden, ready to stroll about aimlessly, with nothing to do, the whole day, the whole summer.

Zhenya appeared with a basket over her arm. Her expression showed that she had known, or at any rate felt, that she would find me in the garden. We gathered mushrooms and talked, and when she put a question to me she went in front, so as to see my face.

"There was a miracle in the village yesterday," she said. "Lame Pelageya has been ill a whole year, no doctors or medicine were any use, and yesterday a wise woman whispered over her, and she isn't ill any more."

"That's nothing," I said. "We ought not to look for miracles only when people are ill or old. Isn't health a miracle in itself? And life? Everything we don't understand is a miracle."

"And aren't you frightened by things you can't understand?"

"No. I approach phenomena I don't understand boldly, I don't give in to them. I am above them. A human being should rate himself higher than lions, tigers and stars, higher than the whole of nature, even higher than things which we cannot understand and regard as miraculous, otherwise he is not a man, but a mouse, afraid of everything."

Zhenya supposed that, being an artist, I knew a great deal, and could divine accurately what I did not know. She wanted me to waft her to some exquisite eternal sphere, to that higher world where, she believed, I was quite at home, and she spoke to me of God, of life everlasting, of miracles. And I, unwilling to admit that myself and my imagination would perish altogether after death, would reply: "Yes, human beings are immortal," "Yes, life everlasting awaits us." And she would listen, believing me without demanding proofs.

As we were going back to the house she suddenly came to a halt and said:

"Isn't Leda splendid? I adore her and would sacrifice my life for her at a moment's notice. But why—" Zhenya put a finger on my coat-sleeve, "why do you always argue with her? Why are you so irritable?"

"Because she's wrong."

Zhenya shook her head disapprovingly, and tears came into her eyes.

"How hard that is to understand," she said.

At that moment Leda, who had just returned from somewhere or other, stood by the porch with a riding-crop in her hand—slender, pretty, lit up by the rays of the sun—giving orders to a workman. She received two or three patients, in great haste, talking loudly, and then went from room to room looking extremely business-like and preoccupied, opening one wardrobe after another, and going to the mansard. They looked for her to call her to dinner for a long time, and by the time she came we had finished our soup. Somehow I recall all these trivial details affectionately, and I have the liveliest remembrance of this day, though nothing particular happened on it. After dinner Zhenya read, reclining in a deep arm-chair, and I sat on the lowest step of the verandah. Nobody spoke. The sky was enveloped in clouds, and there was a light drizzle. It was warm, the wind had long fallen, and it seemed as if this day would go on for ever. Yekaterina Pavlovna, who was still heavy with sleep, came on to the verandah, holding a fan.

"Oh, Mamma," said Zhenya, kissing her hand. "It's bad for you to sleep in the day-time!"

They adored each other. When one of them went into the garden, the other was sure to appear on the verandah, and call out, her glance travelling among the trunks of the trees: "Cooee, Zhenya!" or "Mamma, where are you?" They always said their prayers together, and they were equally devout, understanding each other perfectly, even when they said nothing. And their opinions of other people were the same. Yekaterina Pavlovna very soon got fond of me, too, and when I did not come for two or three days she would send to know if I was well. She, too, inspected my sketches admiringly, and told me everything that happened as freely and frankly as Missie, not infrequently confiding her domestic secrets in me.

She went in awe of her eldest daughter. Leda had no caressing ways, and only talked about serious things. She lived her own special life and was for her mother and her sister the sacred, somewhat enigmatic figure that the admiral, sequestered in his cabin, is for sailors.

"Our Leda is a fine person, isn't she?" the mother often said.

And now, while the rain fell gently, we talked about Leda.

"She's marvellous," said the mother, adding in conspiratorial undertones, glancing timidly around, "there are very few like her, but, you know, I begin to be rather alarmed. Schools, dispensaries, books—are all very well, but why go to extremes? She's nearly twenty-four, it's time for her to be thinking seriously about her future. All those books and dispensaries make one blind to the passage of time.... It's time for her to get married."

Zhenya, pale from her reading, her hair rumpled, raised her head and said, as if to herself, but looking at her mother:

"We are all in the hands of God, Mummie."

And plunged into her book again.

Belokurov appeared in his peasant jacket and embroidered shirt. We played croquet and tennis, and when it got dark, sat long round the supper-table, Leda again talking about schools and about Balagin, who had got the whole district into his hands. When I left the Volchaninovs that evening I carried away an impression of a long, long, idle day, and told myself mournfully that everything comes to an end in this world, however long it is. Zhenya saw us to the gate, and, perhaps because I had spent the whole day with her from morn till eve, I began to feel I should be lonely without her, to realise how dear this whole charming family was to me. And for the first time that summer the desire to paint a picture rose in me.

"Why should *your* life be so dull and colourless?" I asked Belokurov, as we walked home together. "*My* life is dull, boring, monotonous, because I'm an artist, a crank, I have been eaten up with envy, remorse, and disbelief in my own work from my youth up. I shall always be poor, I am a tramp, but you—you are a healthy, normal man, a landowner, a gentleman—why is your life so dreary, why do you get so little out of it? What is there to prevent you from falling in love with Leda or Zhenya, for instance?"

"You forget I love another woman," replied Belokurov.

I knew he meant Lyubov Ivanovna, the woman who lived with him in the annexe. Every day I saw this lady, stout, chubby-faced, pompous, rather like a Michaelmas goose, walking about the garden, wearing Russian national costume and bead necklaces, always carrying an open parasol, and always being called by the servant to have a meal, or take tea. Three years before she had rented one of the annexes for the summer, and had remained there with Belokurov, apparently for the rest of her life. She was about ten years older than Belokurov,

and kept him well in hand, so that before going anywhere he had to ask her permission. She often sobbed, in
hoarse, masculine tones, and I had to send and tell her
that if she did not stop I would give up my room; and
then she would stop sobbing.

When we got home Belokurov sat on my sofa, thinking, his brows knitted, while I paced up and down the
room, a prey to soft agitation, for all the world as if I
were in love. I felt a desire to talk about the Volchaninovs.

"Leda is only capable of loving some member of the
Zemstvo, somebody as keen on hospitals and schools as
herself," I said. "But for a girl like that a man should
be willing to walk about in iron boots, like the lover in
the fairy-tale, not to speak of becoming a member of
the Zemstvo. And Missie? What a darling that Missie
is!"

With many an "er", Belokurov embarked upon pro-
tracted reflections on pessimism—the disease of our
times. He spoke confidently, and by his tone it might
have been thought that I was arguing with him. An
endless, monotonous, sun-bleached steppe is not more
dreary than a single individual who sits in one's room
talking and talking, as if he never meant to stop.

"It's not a matter of pessimism or optimism," I said
irately. "The point is that ninety per cent of people have
no brains."

Belokurov took this remark as a personal affront, and
went away offended.

III

"The Prince is staying at Malozemovo, and sends you
greetings," said Leda to her mother. She had just come
back from some visit and was taking off her gloves. "He
was very interesting. He promised to raise the question
of a medical post at Malozemovo at the next meeting of
the council, but he says there's not much hope. Excuse
me," she said, turning to me. "I keep forgetting this sort
of thing can't be very interesting to you."

I felt a surge of irritation.

"Why not?" I asked, shrugging my shoulders. "You don't care to know my opinion, but I assure you this question interests me intensely."

"Does it?"

"Yes, it does. In my opinion a medical post is not required in Malozemovo."

My irritation communicated itself to her. Looking at me from narrowed eyes, she said:

"What is required then—landscape paintings?"

"Landscapes are not required, either. Nothing is required."

She had drawn off her gloves and was opening the newspaper which had just been brought from the post-office. A minute after she said quietly, obviously trying to keep her feelings under control:

"Last week Anna died in childbirth; if there had been a medical-aid post in the neighbourhood she would be alive now. I can't help thinking that even landscape-painters should deign to have some convictions in this respect."

"I have extremely definite convictions in this respect, I assure you," I replied, but she hid from me behind the newspaper, as if not wishing to hear me. "In my opinion medical-aid posts, schools, libraries, dispensaries only serve the cause of enslavement under existing circumstances. The people are fettered by heavy chains, and you do nothing to break them asunder, only add new links—there you have my convictions."

She raised her eyes to my face and smiled scornfully, but I went on, endeavouring to pin down my basic idea.

"What matters is not that Anna died in childbirth, but that Anna, Martha, and Pelageya must stoop over their work from morning to night, fall sick from onerous toil, spend their whole lives worrying over their hungry, sickly children, in fear of death and disease, dose themselves all their lives, fade early, age early, and die in filth and stench. As soon as their children grow up, they follow the example of their mothers, and hundreds of years pass like this, millions of people living in worse conditions than animals, merely to gain a crust of bread, to live in perpetual fear. And the true horror of their situation is that they never have time to think of their souls, of themselves as images of God. Hunger, cold, physical terror, perpetual toil are like snow-drifts cutting off all paths to spiritual activities, to everything distinguishing human beings from animals and making life worth living. You go to their aid with hospitals and schools, but this does not deliver them from their chains, on the contrary, it enslaves them still more, since, by introducing fresh superstitions into their lives, you increase their demands, not to mention the fact that they have to pay the Zemstvo for their leeches and their books, and, consequently, to work still harder."

"I shall not argue with you," said Leda, lowering the newspaper. "I have heard all this before. I will only say one thing—one can't just sit and do nothing. True, we are not saving humanity and perhaps we make many mistakes, but we do what we can, and—we are right. The loftiest and most sacred task of a cultured person is to serve his neighbours, and we endeavour to do so to the best of our abilities. You don't like what we do, but one can't please everyone, after all."

"True, Leda, true," said her mother.

She was always timid in the presence of Leda, glancing nervously at her when she spoke, afraid of saying something foolish or inappropriate. And she never contradicted her, always agreeing with her: "True, Leda, true."

"Peasant literacy, books full of wretched moralisings and popular maxims, and medical-aid posts can no more lessen their ignorance or their mortality rate than the light from your windows can light up this huge garden," I said. "You give them nothing, merely by your interference in the lives of these people creating fresh demands, fresh motives for working."

"But goodness me, something must be done!" said Leda irately, and the tone in which she spoke showed that she considered my arguments trifling and contemptible.

"People must be freed from heavy physical labour," I said. "Their burden must be lightened, they must be given a breathing-space, so that they do not have to spend their whole lives at the stove and the wash-tub, or working in the fields, but have time to think of their souls, too, and of God, and get a chance to display their spiritual abilities. Every individual has a spiritual vocation—the continual search for the truth and significance of life. Free them from coarse, physical toil, let them feel that they have liberty, then you will see the mockery that these books and dispensaries really are. When a person feels his true vocation, the only things that can satisfy him are religion, science, art—and not such trifles."

"Free them from toil!" mocked Leda. "As if that were possible!"

"Yes. Undertake some of their work yourself. If we all, town and country dwellers, all without exception, agreed to take our part in the labour on which the mass of humanity spend their time for the satisfaction of physical requirements, perhaps each one of us would not have to work more than two or three hours a day. Think how it would be if we all, rich and poor alike, worked only three hours a day, and had the rest of the time to ourselves! And think what it would mean if, in order to depend still less on our bodies and work still less, we were to invent machinery to substitute toil, and try to reduce the number of our requirements to a minimum! We would harden ourselves and our children, so that they need not fear hunger and cold, and we need not worry constantly over their health, as Anna, Martha, and Pelageya do. Just think, if we did not take medicine and did not maintain dispensaries, tobacco factories and distilleries—what a lot of spare time we should have as a result! We could devote this time in united work on science and art. Just as the peasants sometimes repair the roads in a body, we could, all together, by general con- sent, search for the truth and meaning of life, and—of this I am sure—the truth would very soon be discovered, humanity would be freed from the perpetual, agonising, oppressive fear of death—and even from death itself."

"But you contradict yourself," said Leda. "You preach science, and reject the idea of literacy."

"The literacy which enables a person to do no more than spell out tavern-signs, and every now and then real books he cannot understand, has existed in our country since the time of Rurik; Gogol's Petrushka has long been able to read, and yet the countryside is just as it was in Rurik's time. It is not literacy that we need, but leisure for the full display of our spiritual abilities. It is not schools, but universities that we need."

"You deny medicine."

"Yes. It would only be required for the study of disease as a natural phenomenon, and not for its cure. If treatment is required, let it be, not of disease, but of its causes. Remove the main cause—physical labour, and there will be no more diseases. I do not recognise that science which aspires to heal," I continued excitedly. "True science and art aim not at temporary, partial measures, but at what is eternal and general. They seek for the truth and meaning of life, they seek God, the soul, and when they are fastened down to the needs of the moment, to dispensaries and libraries, they can only complicate and burden life. We have plenty of doctors, chemists and lawyers, and there are plenty of literate persons now, but no biologists, mathematicians, philosophers, poets. Our brains, our spiritual energy, are wasted on the satisfaction of temporary, passing needs.... Scientists, writers and painters work with a will; thanks to them the comforts of life increase daily, our physical demands multiply, and yet we are far from the truth, and man still remains the most predatory, the uncleanest of animals, and everything tends towards the degeneracy of humanity as a whole and the irreparable loss of vitality. In such conditions the life of the artist is meaningless and the more talented he is the worse and the more incomprehensible his function, since superficially it would appear that he works for the entertainment of a predatory, unclean animal, by supporting the existing order of things. And I don't want to work, and I won't.... Nothing is wanted, let the world rattle to smithereens...."

"Go away, Missie," said Leda to her sister, apparently considering my words unsuited to the hearing of so young a girl.

Zhenya glanced mournfully from her sister to her mother, and went away.

"People usually say nice things like that when they wish to justify their own indifference," said Leda. "It's much easier to deny the usefulness of hospitals and schools, than to cure and to teach...."

"True, Leda, true," said her mother.

"You say you will throw up painting," continued Leda. "Apparently you rate your work very high. Let's stop arguing, we shall never agree, for I rate the most imperfect of those libraries and dispensaries, you have just referred to so contemptuously, higher than all the landscape paintings in the world." And she turned abruptly to her mother, and began speaking in quite a different voice. "The Prince has got very thin and has changed greatly since he was last here. They're sending him to Vichy."

She talked to her mother about the Prince, to avoid talking to me. Her face was flushed, and to conceal her agitation, she bent low over the table as if she were shortsighted, and pretended to be reading the paper. My presence was evidently disagreeable to her. I took my leave and went home.

IV

It was very still in the courtyard. The village on the other side of the pond was already asleep, not a light was to be seen, but for the pale reflections of the stars shimmering almost imperceptibly on the surface of the pond. At the gates with the lions Zhenya stood motionless, waiting to see me out. "They're all asleep in the village," I said, trying to make out her features in the darkness, but only seeing a pair of dark, mournful eyes fixed on my face. "The inn-keeper and the horse-thieves are peacefully asleep, but we, respectable folk, irritate one another and argue."

It was a melancholy August night, melancholy, because there was a hint of autumn in the air. The moon was rising from behind a crimson cloud, but it scarcely lit up the road, on either side of which extended the autumn fields. Shooting stars darted continually about the sky. Zhenya walked beside me along the road and tried not to look up, so as not to see the shooting stars, which for some reason or other frightened her.

"I think you are right," she said, shivering in the evening dampness. "If all of us, all together, were to devote ourselves to spiritual activities, we would soon discover everything."

"Of course. We are higher beings, and if we really appreciated the power of human genius and lived only for higher aims, we should at last become like gods. But that will never be—humanity is degenerating, and soon there will not be a trace of genius left."

When we were out of sight of the gates, Zhenya stood still and hastily pressed my hand.

"Good night," she said, shivering. She had nothing but a thin blouse over her shoulders, and cringed with cold. "Come tomorrow."

The thought of being alone, in this irritated state of dissatisfaction with myself and others, terrified me. I, too, began trying not to look at the shooting stars.

"Stay with me a little longer," I said. "Do!"

I was in love with Zhenya. Perhaps I had fallen in love with her for her way of meeting me and seeing me off, for the tender, admiring glances she cast at me. Her pale face, thin neck and arms, her delicacy, her idleness, her books, held a wistful appeal for me. And her mind? I suspected her of having an unusual brain, I admired her broad-mindedness, perhaps because she thought differently from the severe beauteous Leda, who did not like me. Zhenya liked me as an artist, I had conquered her heart by my talent, and I desired passionately to paint for her alone, dreaming of her as my little queen, who would, together with me, hold sway over these villages, fields, this mist, and evening glow, this countryside, so delightful, so exquisite, amidst which I had till now felt so hopelessly lonely and superfluous.

"Wait a little longer," I pleaded. "Only a few minutes."

I took off my coat and put it over her chilly shoulders. Afraid of looking funny and ugly in a man's coat, she laughed and threw it off, and I put my arms round her and began showering kisses on her face, shoulders and hands.

"Till tomorrow," she whispered, embracing me cautiously, as if afraid to disturb the stillness of the night. "We have no secrets from one another, I shall have to tell my mother and sister everything, immediately.... Oh, dear, I'm so frightened! Mamma's all right, Mamma is fond of you—but Leda!"

She ran back towards the gate.

"Good-bye!" she cried.

I stood listening to her retreating footsteps for a minute or two. I did not want to go home, and there was no reason for going there. I stood deep in thought for a short time, and then sauntered slowly back, to have another look at the house in which she lived, the dear innocent old house, with its mansard windows looking down at me as if they were eyes, as if they understood everything. I passed the verandah, sat on a bench near the tennis-court, in the darkness beneath an ancient willow, and looked at the house from there. In the windows of the mansard, where Missie's room was, a light shone brilliantly, and then turned a sober green—someone had put a shade on the lamp. Shadows moved.... My heart was filled with tenderness, calm and content—delighted to discover that I was capable of falling in love—and yet at the same time I was worried by the thought that at this moment, a few paces away, Leda lived in one of the rooms of this house, Leda who disliked, perhaps detested me. I sat there waiting for Zhenya to appear, straining my ears, and it seemed to me I could hear talking in the mansard.

About an hour passed. The green light went out and the shadows could no longer be seen. The moon now rode high over the house and lit up the sleeping garden and deserted walks. The dahlias and roses in the bed in front of the house stood out distinctly, but they all looked the same colour. It grew really cold. I went out of the garden, picked up my coat from the road, and wandered slowly homewards.

When I went to the Volchaninovs the next afternoon,

the glass door into the garden was wide open. I sat down on the verandah, hoping Zhenya would suddenly appear on the tennis-court, or on one of the paths, listening for the sound of her voice from the house. Then I went into the drawing-room and after that the dining-room. Not a soul was in sight. From the dining-room I made my way through the long passage into the hall, and back again. There were several doors opening into the passage, and from one of the rooms could be heard the voice of Leda:

"The crow had somewhere found a bit of—" she was saying loudly, in a singsong voice—dictating probably. "...a bit of cheese.... The crow— Who's there?" she cried suddenly, hearing my steps.

"It's me."

"Oh. Excuse me, I can't come to you just now, I'm giving Dasha her lesson."

"Is Yekaterina Pavlovna in the garden?"

"No. She and my sister left this morning on a visit to my aunt in the Penza province. And in the winter they'll probably go abroad," she added, after a short pause.

"The crow had ... somewhere ... found ... a bit of cheese.... Written that down?"

I went into the hall and stood there, staring vacantly at the pond and the distant village, my ears still assailed by the words: "... a bit of cheese.... The crow had somewhere found a bit of cheese...."

I went off the estate by the road I had approached it from the first time, but in reverse—from the courtyard to the garden, past the house, till I got to the lime-tree avenue.... Here a small boy ran after me and gave me a note. "I told my sister everything and she insists that we part," I read. "I had not the heart to grieve her by disobedience. May God send you happiness—forgive me! If you only knew how bitterly Mamma and I are crying."

Then came the fir walk, the broken railings.... In the field where the rye had been in bloom and the quail had given its cries, there now wandered cows and hobbled horses. Here and there on hillocks the winter crops showed green. A prosaic everyday mood enveloped me and I was ashamed of all I had said at the Volchaninovs', and once more life became a tedious affair. When I got home I packed up my things, and left for St. Petersburg that evening.

I never saw the Volchaninovs again. Not so long ago I met Belokurov in the train on my way to the Crimea. He was still wearing his peasant coat and embroidered shirt, and when I asked him how he was, he replied: "Quite well, thanks to your prayers!" We had a talk. He had sold his estate and bought another, a smaller one, in the name of Lyubov Ivanovna. He could not tell me much about the Volchaninovs. Leda still lived at Shelkovka and taught in the village school. She had gradually contrived to gather round her a circle of people in sympathy with her ideas, and these composed a powerful party, and at the last Zemstvo meetings they had blackballed Balagin, who till then had kept the whole district in his hands. All he could tell me of Zhenya was that she did not live at home, and he did not know where she was.

I have begun to forget the house with the mansard, but every once in a while, painting or reading, I recall for no apparent reason the green light in the window, the sound of my own steps echoing in the nocturnal fields, that night I returned home, in love, chafing my cold hands. Still less frequently, in moments of loneliness and melancholy, I yield to vague memories, till I gradually begin to feel that I, too, am remembered, that I am being waited for, and that we shall meet. . . .

Missie . . . where are you?

1896

THE MAN WHO LIVED IN A SHELL

The sportsmen, overtaken by darkness on the outskirts of the village of Mironositskoye, decided to spend the night in a shed belonging to Prokofy, the village elder. There were two of them, Ivan Ivanich, the veterinary surgeon, and Burkin, the high-school teacher. Ivan Ivanich bore a strange, hyphenated name: Chimsha-Himalaisky; the name did not seem to suit him, and everyone called him simply by his name and patronymic—Ivan Ivanich; he lived at a stud-farm not far from the town, and was now hunting for the sake of an outing in the fresh air. The high-school teacher Burkin spent every summer on the estate of Count P. and was regarded by the inhabitants of those parts as quite one of themselves.

Neither of them slept. Ivan Ivanich, a tall, lean old man with a long moustache, sat outside the door, in the moonlight, smoking his pipe. Burkin lay inside, on the hay, concealed by the darkness.

They whiled away the time by telling each other stories. They spoke of Mavra, the wife of the village elder, a perfectly healthy and by no means unintelligent woman, who had never been out of her native village in her life. She had never seen a town or a railway, and had spent the last ten years sitting by her stove, only venturing out at night.

"Is it so very strange, though?" said Burkin. "There are plenty of people in this world who are recluses by nature and strive, like the hermit-crab or the snail, to retreat within their shells. Perhaps this is just a manifestation of atavism, a return to the times when our forbears had not yet become social animals, and inhabited solitary caves. Or perhaps such people are one of the varieties of the human species, who knows? I am no naturalist, and it is not for me to attempt to solve such problems; all I want to say is that people like Mavra are by no means rare phenomena. Why, only a month or two ago there died in our town a colleague of mine, Belikov, a teacher of Greek. You must have heard of him. He was famous for never stirring out of his house, even in the best weather, without an umbrella, galoshes and a wadded coat. His umbrella he kept in a case, he had a case of grey suède for his watch, and when he took out his pen-knife to sharpen a pencil, he had to draw it out of a case, too; even his face seemed to have a case of its own, since it was always hidden in his turned-up coat-collar. He wore dark glasses, and a thick jersey, and stopped up his ears with cotton wool, and when he engaged a droshky, made the driver put up the hood. In fact, he betrayed a perpetual, irrepressible urge to create a covering for himself, as it were a case, to isolate him and protect him against external influences. Reality irritated and alarmed him and kept him in constant terror, and, perhaps to justify his timidity, the disgust which the present aroused in him, he always praised the past and things which had never had any existence. Even the dead languages he taught were merely galoshes and umbrellas between himself and real life.

" 'How beautiful, how sonorous is the Greek language!' he would say with a beatific expression; and by way of proof he would half-close his eyes, raise a finger and murmur: 'An-thropos!'

"Belikov tried to keep his thoughts in a case, too. Only those circulars and newspaper articles in which something was prohibited were comprehensible to him. When instructions were circulated forbidding school-boys to be in the streets after 9 p. m., or an article was published in which indulgence in carnal love was condemned, everything was clear and definite for him—these things were prohibited once and for all. In his eyes permission and indulgence always seemed to contain some doubtful element, something left unsaid, vague. If a dramatic society or a reading-room or a café were allowed to be opened, he would shake his head and say gently:

" 'It's a very fine thing no doubt, but ... let's hope no evil will come of it.'

"The slightest infringement or deviation from the rules plunged him in dejection, even when it could not possibly concern him. If one of his colleagues were late for prayers, or rumours of a trick played by some school-boys reached his ears, if a *dame de classe* were seen late at night in the company of an officer, he would be profoundly agitated, repeating constantly that he was afraid it would lead to no good. At the meetings of the teachers' council he fairly tormented us with his circumspection and suspicions, his apprehensions and suggestions (typical of a mind encased): the young people in both the girls' and boys' schools behave disgracefully, make a terrible noise in the class-rooms—supposing the authorities get to hear of it, he hoped no evil would come of it, and wouldn't it help matters if we expelled Petrov from the second form, and Yegorov from the fourth? And what do you think? With his sighs and moans, his dark glasses on his little, white face—a ferrety sort of face, you know—he managed to depress us all to such an extent that we yielded, gave Petrov and Yegorov low marks for behaviour, had them put in the lock-up, and, finally, expelled. He had an old habit of visiting us in our homes. Going to the rooms of a fellow-teacher, he would sit down and say nothing, with a watchful air. After an hour or so of this, he would get up and go. He called this 'keeping on friendly terms with one's colleagues', and it was obvious that he found it an uncongenial task and only came to see us because he considered it his duty as a fellow-teacher. We were all afraid of him. Even the headmaster was. Just think! Our teachers are on the whole a decent, intelligent set, brought up on Turgenev and Shchedrin, and yet this mite of a man, with his eternal umbrella and galoshes, managed to keep the whole school under his thumb for fifteen years! And not only the school, but the entire town! Our ladies gave up their Saturday private theatricals for fear of his finding out about them; the clergy were afraid of eating meat or playing cards in his presence. Under the influence of men like Belikov the people in our town have begun to be afraid of everything. They are afraid to speak loudly, write letters, make friends, read books, help the poor, teach the illiterate. . . ."

Ivan Ivanich cleared his throat as if in preparation for some weighty remark, but first he relit his pipe and glanced up at the moon, and only then said, in unhurried tones:

"Quite right. A decent, intelligent set, reading Turgenev, Shchedrin and Buckle and all those, and yet they submitted, they bore with him. . . . That's just it."

"Belikov and I lived in the same house," went on Burkin, "on the same floor; his door was just opposite mine, we saw quite a lot of one another, and I had a pretty good idea of what his home-life was like. It was the same story: dressing-gown, night-cap, shutters, bolts and bars, a long list of restrictions and prohibitions, and the same adage— let's hope no evil will come of it! Lenten fare did not agree with him, but he could not eat meat or people might say that Belikov did not. observe Lent. So he ate pike fried in butter—it was not fasting but neither could it be called meat. He never kept female servants for fear of people getting 'notions', but employed a male cook, Afanasy, an old man of about sixty, drunken and crazy, who knew how to cook from having served as a batman some time in his life. This Afanasy was usually to be seen standing outside the door with folded arms always muttering the same thing over and over again with a deep sigh:

"'Ah, there's a sight of *them* about, nowadays!'

"Belikov's tiny bedroom was like a box, and there was a canopy over the bed. Before going to sleep he always drew the bedclothes over his head; the room was hot and stuffy, the wind rattled against the closed doors and moaned in the chimney; sighs were heard in the kitchen, ominous sighs. . . .

"And he would lie trembling under his blanket. He was afraid that some evil would come, that Afanasy .would murder him, that thieves would break in, and his very dreams were haunted by these fears; and in the mornings, when we walked side by side to the school, he was always pale and languid and it was obvious that the crowded school he was approaching was the object of his terror and aversion, and that it was distasteful for him, a recluse by nature, to have to walk by my side.

" 'They make such a noise in the class-rooms,' he would say, as if trying to find an explanation for his heaviness of heart. 'It's quite disgraceful.'

"And what do you think? This teacher of Greek, this hermit-crab, once nearly got married."

Ivan Ivanich turned his head sharply towards the shed.

"You don't mean it!" he said.

"Yes, he nearly got married, strange as it may sound. We were sent a new teacher for history and geography, one Kovalenko, Mikhail Savvich, a Ukrainian. He brought his sister Varya with him. He was young, tall, dark-complexioned, with enormous hands and the sort of face that goes with a deep voice; as a matter of fact he had a deep, booming voice, as if it came from a barrel.... His sister, who was not so young, thirty or thereabouts, was also tall; willowy, black-browed, red-cheeked, she was a peach of a girl, lively and noisy, always singing Ukrainian songs, always laughing. On the slightest provocation she would burst out into a ringing ha-ha-ha! The first time we became really acquainted with brother and sister, if I am not mistaken, was at our headmaster's name-day party. Suddenly, among the severe, conventional, dull teachers who make even going to parties a duty, a new Venus rose from the foam, one who walked about with arms akimbo, laughed, sang, danced.... She sang with great feeling 'The Winds Are Blowing', following it with another song, then another, and we were all charmed, even Belikov. He sat beside her, and said, with a honeyed smile:

" 'The Ukrainian tongue in its sweetness and delightful sonority is reminiscent of the ancient Greek.'

"The lady was flattered, and began telling him with sincere feeling about her farmstead in the Gadyachi uyezd, where her Mummie lived and where there were such pears, such melons and such pumpkins! Pumpkins are called marrows in the Ukraine, and they make a delicious *borshch* with blue egg-plant and red capsicum, ever so good, you know!

"We sat round her, listening, and the same thought struck us all.

" 'Why shouldn't these two get married?' said the head-master's wife to me in a low voice.

"For some reason everyone suddenly realised that our Belikov was a bachelor and we wondered how it was that we had never remarked, had completely overlooked, so important a detail in his life. What was his attitude to women, how did he solve this vital problem for himself? We had never thought about it before; perhaps none of us could admit the idea that a man who wore galoshes all the year round and slept under a canopy was capable of loving.

" 'He's well over forty, and she's thirty...' the head-master's wife went on. 'I think she would take him.'

"The things one does out of sheer boredom in the prov-inces, the absurd, useless things! And all because what ought to be done, never is done. Why, why did we feel we had to marry off this Belikov, whom nobody could imagine in the role of a married man? The headmaster's wife, the inspector's wife, and all the ladies who had anything to do with the school, brightened up, and actu-ally became handsomer, as if they had at last found an object in life. The headmaster's wife took a box in the theatre, and whom do we behold in this box but Varya, fanning herself with an enormous fan, radiant, happy, and at her side Belikov, small and huddled up, as if he had been extracted from his room with pincers. I myself gave a party, to which the ladies insisted on my inviting Belikov and Varya. In a word, we started the ball rolling. The idea of marriage, it appeared, was by no means dis-agreeable to Varya. Her life with her brother was far from happy, they did nothing but wrangle all day long. I'll give you a typical scene in their lives: Kovalenko stalks along the street, tall and massive, wearing an em-broidered shirt, his forelock tumbling over his brow from beneath the peak of his cap; a parcel of books in one hand, a gnarled walking-stick in the other. He is followed by his sister, also carrying books.

" 'But, Misha, you haven't read it!' she shouts. 'You haven't, I tell you, I am absolutely certain you never read it!'

" 'And I tell you I have!' Kovalenko shouts back, knocking with his stick on the pavement.

" 'For goodness' sake, Misha! What makes you so cross? It's only a matter of principle, after all!'

" 'And I tell you I *have* read it!' shouts Kovalenko, still louder.

"And at home, whenever anyone came to see them, they would start bickering. She was probably sick of such a life, and longing for a home of her own, and then—her age: there was no time for picking and choosing, the girl would marry anyone, even a teacher of Greek. It's the same with all our girls, by the way—they'd marry anyone, simply for the sake of getting married. However that may be, Varya was beginning to show a marked liking for this Belikov of ours.

"And Belikov? He visited Kovalenko in the same way that he visited the rest of us. He would go to see him, and sit saying nothing. And there he would sit in silence, while Varya sang 'The Winds Are Blowing', gazing at him from her dark eyes, or suddenly breaking out into her 'ha-ha-ha!'

"In affairs of the heart, especially when matrimony is involved, suggestion is all-powerful. Everyone—his colleagues, the ladies—began assuring Belikov that he ought to marry, that there was nothing left for him in life but marriage; we all congratulated him, uttering with solemn countenances various commonplaces to the effect that marriage was a serious step, and the like; besides, Varenka was by no means plain, she might even be considered handsome, and then she was the daughter of a councillor of state, she had a farmstead of her own and, still more important, was the first woman who had ever treated him with affection. So he lost his head and persuaded himself it was his duty to marry."

"That was the moment to take his umbrella and overshoes away from him!" put in Ivan Ivanich.

"Ah, but that proved to be impossible! He placed Varenka's photograph on his desk, kept coming to me to talk about Varenka, family life, and the seriousness of marriage, went often to the Kovalenkos, but did not change his way of living in the least. On the contrary, the decision to marry seemed to have a painful effect on him, he grew thinner, paler and seemed to retreat still further into his shell.

" 'I find Varvara Savvishna an agreeable girl,' he said to me with his faint, crooked smile, 'and every man ought to get married, I know, but ... it's all so sudden, you know.... One must think....'

" 'What's there to think about?' I answered. 'Get married, that's all.'

" 'No, no, marriage is a serious step, one ought to weigh one's future duties and responsibilities first ... so's to make sure no evil will come of it.... It worries me so, I can't sleep at night. And to tell you the truth, I am somewhat alarmed—they have such a strange way of thinking, she and her brother, their outlook, you know, is so strange, and then she is so sprightly. Supposing I marry and get mixed up in something....'

"And he put off proposing to her, putting it off from day to day, much to the disappointment of the head-master's wife and the other ladies; he kept weighing his future duties and responsibilities, walking out with Varenka almost every day, probably thinking the situation demanded it of him, and coming to me to discuss family life in all its aspects. Very likely he would have proposed in the end, contracting another of those stupid, unnecessary marriages, which are made here by the thousand, out of sheer boredom and for want of something better to do, if *ein kolossalische Skandal* had not suddenly broken out. I must tell you that Varenka's brother, Kovalenko, had contracted a hatred for Belikov from the very first day of their acquaintance, and could never stand him.

" 'I can't understand you,' he would say, shrugging his shoulders, 'how can you tolerate that sneak of a man, that mug? How can you live here, gentlemen? The atmosphere is stifling, poisonous. Do you call yourselves teachers, pedagogues? You're nothing but a pack of place-hunters. Your school is not a temple of science, but a charitable institution, there's a sickly smell about it, like in a policeman's booth. No, my friends, I shan't be long with you, I'll be going back to my farmstead, to catch crayfish and teach the Ukrainian lads. Yes, I'll go away, and you may stay with your Judas, and be damned to him!'

"Another time he would roar with laughter first in a deep bass, and then in a shrill soprano till the tears came to his eyes.

" 'Why does he sit there? What does he want—sitting and staring?'

"He gave Belikov a nickname of his own: vampire-spider.

"Naturally we avoided mentioning to him that his sister was about to marry this 'spider'. When the headmaster's wife hinted to him that it would be nice to see his sister settled down with such a solid and respected person as Belikov, he knitted his brows and said:

" 'It's none of my business. She may marry a snake for all I care. I'm not one to meddle in other people's affairs.'

"Now, hear what happened later. Some wag drew a caricature: Belikov in his galoshes, the ends of his trousers turned up, his umbrella open over his head and Varya walking arm-in-arm with him; beneath the drawing there was an inscription: 'The Anthropos in Love'. The expression of his face, you know, was very true to life. The artist must have sat up several nights over his work, for the teachers of both the schools, the girls' and the boys', and of the seminary, and all the town officials received a copy. Belikov received one, too. The caricature had the most depressing effect on him.

"One day we went out of the house together, it happened to be the first of May and a Sunday and the whole school, pupils and masters, were to meet in front of the school and walk to a wood outside the town—well, we went out, he looking very green about the gills and as black as thunder.

" 'What cruel, malicious people there are in the world,' he said, and his lips quivered.

"I could not help feeling sorry for him. We walked on, when who should we see but Kovalenko riding a bicycle, followed by Varenka, also on a bicycle, panting, red-faced, but very jolly and happy.

" 'We'll be there before all of you!' she cried. 'Isn't it a glorious day? Wonderful!'

"They were soon out of sight. My Belikov, no longer green but deathly pale, was struck dumb. He stopped and stared at me.

"'What can the meaning of this be?' he asked. 'Or do my eyes deceive me? Is it proper for schoolteachers and women to ride bicycles?'

"'There's nothing improper about it,' I said. 'Why shouldn't they ride bicycles?'

"'But it is insufferable!' he cried. 'How can you talk like that?'

"The shock he had received was too great; refusing to go any further, he turned homewards.

"All the next day he kept nervously rubbing his hands together and starting, and you could see by his face that he was not well. He left school before lessons were over —a thing he had never done before. And he did not eat any dinner. Towards evening he dressed warmly, though it was a real summer day, and shuffled off to the Kovalenkos. Varenka was not in, but her brother was.

"'Take a seat, please,' said Kovalenko coldly, knitting his brows; he had just got up from his afternoon nap, his face was still heavy with sleep, and he felt awful.

"After sitting in silence for about ten minutes, Belikov began:

"'I have come to relieve my mind. I am very, very unhappy. A certain unknown lampoonist has made a drawing in which he ridicules me and a certain other person near to us both. I consider it my duty to assure you that it is not my fault. I have done nothing to give grounds for such ridicule, on the contrary, I have behaved like a thorough gentleman all the time.'

"Kovalenko sat silent and lowering. After a short pause Belikov went on in his low plaintive voice:

"'And there's something else I have to say to you. I am a veteran and you are only beginning your career, and it is my duty as an older colleague of yours to warn you. You ride a bicycle and this is a highly reprehensible amusement for one who aspires to educate the young.'

"'Why?' asked Kovalenko in his deep bass voice.

"'Does it require explanation, Mikhail Savvich, I should have thought it was self-evident. If the master is to go about riding a bicycle, there is nothing left for the pupils but to walk on their heads. And since no circular permitting this has been issued, it is wrong. I was astounded yesterday! I nearly fainted when I saw your sister. A young lady on a bicycle—preposterous!'

" 'What exactly do you want from me?'

" 'I only want to warn you, Mikhail Savvich. You are young, you have your life before you, you must be very, very careful, and you are so reckless, so very reckless! You go about in embroidered shirts, are constantly seen carrying all sorts of books about the streets, and now this bicycle. The fact that you and your sister have been seen riding bicycles will be made known to the headmaster, it will reach the patron's ears.... And that's no good.'

" 'It is no man's business whether my sister and I ride bicycles or not!' said Kovalenko, flushing up. 'And if people stick their noses into my domestic and family affairs they can go to hell.'

"Belikov turned pale and rose to his feet.

" 'Since you assume such a tone with me, I cannot go on,' he said. 'And I would beg you to be careful what you say about our superiors in my presence. The authorities must be treated with deference.'

" 'And did I say anything wrong about the authorities?' asked Kovalenko, looking at him with hatred. 'Leave me alone, Sir. I am an honest man, and have nothing to say to a person like you. I abhor snakes.'

"Belikov fidgeted nervously and began hastily putting on his coat, an expression of horror on his face. Never in his life had anyone spoken so rudely to him.

" 'You may say what you like,' he said as he passed on to the landing. 'But I must warn you: somebody may have overheard us, and to prevent our conversation from being misrepresented, and the possible consequence of this, I shall have to report the purport of our conversation to the headmaster ... its main points. It is my duty.'

" 'What? Report? Go on, then!'

"Kovalenko grasped him by the collar and gave him a push, and Belikov rolled down the stairs, his galoshes knocking against the steps. The staircase was long and steep, but he arrived at the bottom unhurt, rose to his

feet and felt the bridge of his nose to see if his glasses
were unbroken. But while he was rolling down the steps,
Varenka, accompanied by two other ladies, entered the
porch; they all three stood at the bottom of the stairs,
looking at him—and for Belikov that was the worst of all
his sufferings. He would a great deal sooner have broken
his neck, and both legs, than appear in a ridiculous light.
Now the whole town would know of it, the headmaster
would be told, and probably the patron, too. And who
knows what that would lead to! Someone might draw
another caricature and it would end in his having to re-
sign. . . .

"When he got up, Varya recognised him, and looking
at his ridiculous face, his rumpled coat, his overshoes,
without the faintest idea what had happened, but supposing that he must have slipped, she could not help bursting out with her loud 'ha-ha-ha!'

"This buoyant resonant 'ha-ha' was the end: the end
of Belikov's courting and of his earthly existence. He
never again saw Varenka. The first thing he did when
he got home was to remove her photograph from the
top of his desk, then he lay down on his bed, never to
leave it.

"Three days later Afanasy came to ask me whether he
should send for the doctor, for his master was behaving
very strangely. I went to see Belikov. He was lying under
his canopy, covered by a blanket, mute; he answered my
questions with a monosyllabic 'yes' or 'no', and not a word
more. There he lay, while Afanasy, morose and frowning,
stumped round the bed, heaving deep sighs and reeking
of spirits like a tavern.

"A month went by and Belikov died. Everybody, that
is to say, the two schools and the seminary, went to his
funeral. Now, as he lay in his coffin, the expression on
his face was gentle, pleasing, even cheerful, as if he were
glad at last to be put into a case which he would never
have to leave. Yes, he had achieved his ideal! As if in his
honour the day was cloudy and wet, and we all wore
galoshes and carried umbrellas. Varya was at the funeral,
too, and shed a tear when the coffin was lowered into the
grave. I have noticed with Ukrainian women that they

must either laugh or weep, they do not admit of any intermediate moods.

"I must confess that it is a great pleasure to bury individuals like Belikov. But we returned from the cemetery with long, 'lenten' faces; none of us wished to show our relief, a relief like that we felt long ago, in childhood, when the grown-ups went away and we could run about the garden for an hour or two enjoying perfect freedom. Ah, freedom! A hint of it, the faintest hope of attaining it, gives wings to our souls, doesn't it?

"We returned from the cemetery in good spirits. But hardly a week passed before everyday life, bleak, fatiguing, meaningless life, neither forbidden in one circular nor sanctioned in another, resumed its usual course; and things were no better than they had been before. After all, when you come to think of it, though we have buried Belikov, there are still plenty of men who live in a shell, and there are plenty as yet unborn."

"Yes, indeed," said Ivan Ivanich as he lit his pipe.

"And plenty as yet unborn!" repeated Burkin.

The high-school teacher came out of the shed. He was short, corpulent, quite bald, with a long black beard reaching nearly to his belt; two dogs came out with him.

"What a moon!" he said, looking up.

It was past midnight. The whole of the village was visible on the right, the long street extending for five versts or so. Everything was plunged in profound, calm sleep; not a sound, not a stir, it seemed incredible that nature could be so calm. When we gaze upon a wide village street on a moonlit night, with its dwellings and hayricks and sleeping willows, a great peace descends on our souls; in its serenity, sheltered by the shadows of the night from all toil, cares and grief, the village seems gentle, melancholy and beautiful, the very stars seem to look down upon it kindly, and there seems to be no more evil in the world, and all is well. To the left, where the village ended, stretched the fields; one could look far into them, to the very horizon, and all was silent and motionless there, too, and the vast plain was flooded with moonlight.

"Yes, indeed," repeated Ivan Ivanich. "And is not our living in towns, in our stuffy, cramped rooms, writing our useless papers, playing vint, isn't that living in an oyster-shell, too? And the fact that we spend all our life among drones, litigious boors, silly, idle women, talk nonsense and listen to nonsense, is not that our oyster-shell, too? I could tell you a highly instructive yarn, if you'd care to listen. . . ."

"I think it's time we went to sleep," said Burkin. "Keep it for tomorrow."

They went to the shed and lay down. They snuggled into the hay and began to doze when a light footstep was heard outside. Somebody was walking about not far from the shed; a few steps, then a stop, and then again the light steps. The dogs growled.

"It's Mavra having a walk," said Burkin.

The steps were heard no more.

"To have to look on and listen to people lying," said Ivan Ivanich as he turned on his side, "and then to be called a fool for tolerating all those lies; to swallow insults, humiliations, not dare to speak up and declare yourself on the side of honest, free men, to lie yourself, to smile, and all for the sake of a crust of bread and a snug corner to live in, for the sake of some miserable rank—no, no, life is intolerable!"

"This is quite another theme, Ivan Ivanich," said the school-master. "Let's go to sleep."

In ten minutes Burkin was asleep. But Ivan Ivanich kept sighing and tossing on the hay; then he got up, went out again, and sitting down by the door, lit his pipe.

1898

GOOSEBERRIES

The sky had been covered with rain-clouds ever since the early morning; it was a still day, cool and dull, one of those misty days when the clouds have long been lowering overhead and you keep thinking it is just going to rain, and the rain holds off. Ivan Ivanich, the veterinary surgeon, and Burkin, the high-school teacher, had walked till they were tired, and the way over the fields seemed endless to them. Far ahead they could just make out the windmill of the village of Mironositskoye, and what looked like a range of low hills at the right extending well beyond the village, and they both knew that this range was really the bank of the river, and that further on were meadows, green willow-trees, country-estates; if they were on the top of these hills, they knew they would see the same boundless fields and telegraph-posts, and the train, like a crawling caterpillar in the distance, while in fine weather even the town would be visible. On this still day, when the whole of nature seemed kindly and pensive, Ivan Ivanich and Burkin felt a surge of love for this plain, and thought how vast and beautiful their country was.

"The last time we stayed in Elder Prokofy's hut," said Burkin, "you said you had a story to tell me."

"Yes. I wanted to tell you the story of my brother."

Ivan Ivanich took a deep breath and lighted his pipe as a preliminary to his narrative, but just then the rain came. Five minutes later it was coming down in torrents and nobody could say when it would stop. Ivan Ivanich and Burkin stood still, lost in thought. The dogs, already soaked, stood with drooping tails, gazing at them wistfully.

"We must try and find shelter," said Burkin. "Let's go to Alekhin's. It's quite near."

"Come on, then."

They turned aside and walked straight across the newly reaped field, veering to the right till they came to a road. Very soon poplars, an orchard, and the red roofs of barns came into sight. The surface of the river gleamed, and they had a view of an extensive reach of water, a windmill and a whitewashed bathing-shed. This was Sofyino, where Alekhin lived.

The mill was working, and the noise made by its sails drowned the sound of the rain; the whole dam trembled. Horses, soaking wet, were standing near some carts, their heads drooping, and people were moving about with sacks over their heads and shoulders. It was wet, muddy, bleak, and the water looked cold and sinister. Ivan Ivanich and Burkin were already experiencing the misery of dampness, dirt, physical discomfort, their boots were caked with mud, and when, having passed the mill-dam, they took the upward path to the landowner's barns, they fell silent, as if vexed with one another.

The sound of winnowing came from one of the barns; the door was open, and clouds of dust issued from it. Standing in the doorway was Alekhin himself, a stout man of some forty years, with longish hair, looking more like a professor or an artist than a landed proprietor. He was wearing a white shirt greatly in need of washing, belted with a piece of string, and long drawers with no trousers over them. His boots, too, were caked with mud and straw. His eyes and nose were ringed with dust. He recognised Ivan Ivanich and Burkin, and seemed glad to see them.

"Go up to the house, gentlemen," he said, smiling. "I'll be with you in a minute."

It was a large two-storey house. Alekhin occupied the ground floor, two rooms with vaulted ceilings and tiny windows, where the stewards had lived formerly. They were poorly furnished, and smelled of rye-bread, cheap vodka, and harness. He hardly ever went into the upstairs rooms, excepting when he had guests. Ivan Ivanich and Burkin were met by a maid-servant, a young woman of such beauty that they stood still involuntarily and exchanged glances.

"You have no idea how glad I am to see you here, dear friends," said Alekhin, overtaking them in the hall. "It's quite a surprise! Pelageya," he said, turning to the maid, "find the gentlemen a change of clothes. And I might as well change, myself. But I must have a wash first, for I don't believe I've had a bath since the spring. Wouldn't you like to go and have a bathe while they get things ready here?"

The beauteous Pelageya, looking very soft and delicate, brought them towels and soap, and Alekhin and his guests set off for the bathing-house.

"Yes, it's a long time since I had a wash," he said, taking off his clothes. "As you see I have a nice bathing-place, my father had it built, but somehow I never seem to get time to wash."

He sat on the step, soaping his long locks and his neck, and all round him the water was brown.

"Yes, you certainly..." remarked Ivan Ivanich, with a significant glance at his host's head.

"It's a long time since I had a wash..." repeated Alekhin, somewhat abashed, and he soaped himself again, and now the water was dark blue, like ink.

Ivan Ivanich emerged from the shed, splashed noisily into the water, and began swimming beneath the rain spreading his arms wide, making waves all round him and the white water-lilies rocked on the waves he made. He swam into the very middle of the river and then dived, a moment later came up at another place and swam further, diving constantly, and trying to touch the bottom. "Ah, my God" he kept exclaiming in his enjoyment. "Ah, my God...." He swam up to the mill, had a little talk with some peasants there and turned back, but when he got to the middle of the river, he floated, holding his face up to the rain. Burkin and Alekhin were dressed and ready to go, but he went on swimming and diving.

"God! God!" he kept exclaiming. "Dear God!"

"Come out!" Burkin shouted to him.

They went back to the house. And only after the lamp was lit in the great drawing-room on the upper floor, and Burkin and Ivan Ivanich, in silk dressing-gowns and warm slippers, were seated in arm-chairs, while Alekhin,

washed and combed, paced the room in his new frock-
coat, enjoying the warmth, the cleanliness, his dry clothes
and comfortable slippers, while the fair Pelageya, smiling benevolently, stepped noiselessly over the carpet with
her tray of tea preserves, did Ivan Ivanich embark
upon his yarn, and the ancient dames, young ladies and
military gentlemen looking down at them severely from
their gilded frames, as if they, too, were listening.

"There were two of us brothers," he began. "Ivan Ivanich (me), and my brother Nikolai Ivanich, two years
younger than myself. I went in for learning and became
a veterinary surgeon, but Nikolai started working in a
government office when he was only nineteen. Our father,
Chimsha-Himalaisky, was educated in a school for the
sons of private soldiers, but was later promoted to officer's
rank, and was made a hereditary nobleman and given a
small estate. After his death the estate had to be sold for
debts, but at least our childhood was passed in the freedom of the countryside, where we roamed the fields and
the woods like peasant children, taking the horses to
graze, peeling bark from the trunks of lime-trees, fishing,
and all that sort of thing. And anyone who has once in
his life fished for perch, or watched the thrushes fly south
in the autumn, rising high over the village on clear, cool
days, is spoilt for town life, and will long for the countryside for the rest of his days. My brother pined in his government office. The years passed and he sat in the same
place every day, writing out the same documents and thinking all the time of the same thing—how to get back to the
country. And these longings of his gradually turned into a
definite desire, into a dream of purchasing a little estate
somewhere on the bank of a river or the shore of a lake.

"He was a meek, good-natured chap, I was fond of
him, but could feel no sympathy with the desire to lock
oneself up for life in an estate of one's own. They say
man only needs six feet of earth. But it is a corpse, and
not man, which needs these six feet. And now people are
actually saying that it is a good sign for our intellectuals
to yearn for the land and try to obtain country-dwellings.
And yet these estates are nothing but those same six feet
of earth. To escape from the town, from the struggle,

from the noise of life, to escape and hide one's head on a country-estate, is not life, but egoism, idleness, it is a sort of renunciation, but renunciation without faith. It is not six feet of earth, not a country-estate, that man needs, but the whole globe, the whole of nature, room to display his qualities and the individual characteristics of his soul.

"My brother Nikolai sat at his office-desk, dreaming of eating soup made from his own cabbages, which would spread a delicious smell all over his own yard, of eating out of doors, on the green grass, of sleeping in the sun, sitting for hours on a bench outside his gate, and gazing at the fields and woods. Books on agriculture and all those hints printed on calendars were his delight, his favourite spiritual nourishment. He was fond of reading newspapers, too, but all he read in them was advertisements of the sale of so many acres of arable and meadowland, with residence attached, a river, an orchard, a mill, and ponds fed by springs. His head was full of visions of garden paths, flowers, fruit, nesting-boxes, carp-ponds, and all that sort of thing. These visions differed according to the advertisements he came across, but for some reason gooseberry bushes invariably figured in them. He could not picture to himself a single estate or picturesque nook that did not have gooseberry bushes in it.

" 'Country life has its conveniences,' he would say. 'You sit on the verandah, drinking tea, with your own ducks floating on the pond, and everything smells so nice, and... and the gooseberries ripen on the bushes.'

"He drew up plans for his estate, and every plan showed the same features: a) the main residence, b) the servants' wing, c) the kitchen-garden, d) gooseberry bushes. He lived thriftily, never ate or drank his fill, dressed anyhow, like a beggar, and saved up all his money in the bank. He became terribly stingy. I could hardly bear to look at him, and whenever I gave him a little money, or sent him a present on some holiday, he put that away, too. Once a man gets an idea into his head, there's no doing anything with him.

"The years passed, he was sent to another gubernia, he was over forty, and was still reading advertisements in the papers, and saving up: At last I heard he had married. All for the same purpose, to buy himself an estate with gooseberry bushes on it, he married an ugly elderly widow, for whom he had not the slightest affection, just because she had some money. After his marriage he went on living as thriftily as ever, half-starving his wife, and putting her money in his own bank account. Her first husband had been a post-master, and she was used to pies and cordials, but with her second husband she did not even get enough black bread to eat. She began to languish on this diet and three years later yielded up her soul to God. Of course my brother did not for a moment consider himself guilty of her death. Money, like vodka, makes a man eccentric. There was a merchant in our town who asked for a plate of honey on his deathbed and ate up all his bank-notes and lottery tickets with the honey, so that no one else should get them. And one day when I was examining a consignment of cattle at a railway station, a drover fell under the engine and his leg was severed from his body. We carried him all bloody into the waiting-room, a terrible sight, and he did nothing but beg us to look for his leg, worrying all the time—there were twenty rubles in the boot, and he was afraid they would be lost."

"You're losing the thread," put in Burkin.

Ivan Ivanich paused for a moment, and went on: "After his wife's death my brother began to look about for an estate. You can search for five years, of course, and in the end make a mistake and buy something quite different from what you dream of. My brother Nikolai bought three hundred acres, complete with gentleman's house, servants' quarters, and a park, on a mortgage to be paid through an agent, but there were neither an orchard, gooseberry bushes, nor a pond with ducks on it. There was a river, but it was as dark as coffee, owing to the fact that there was a brick-works on one side of the estate, and bone-kilns on the other. Nothing daunted, however, my brother Nikolai Ivanich ordered two dozen gooseberry bushes and settled down as a landed proprietor.

"Last year I paid him a visit. I thought I would go and see how he was getting on there. In his letters my brother gave his address as Chumbaroklova Pustosh or

Himalaiskoye. I arrived at Himalaiskoye in the afternoon.
It was very hot. Everywhere were ditches, fences, hedges,
rows of fir-trees, and it was hard to drive into the yard
and find a place to leave one's carriage. As I went a fat
ginger-coloured dog, remarkably like a pig, came out to
meet me. It looked as if it would have barked if it were
not so lazy. The cook, who was also fat and like a pig,
came out of the kitchen, barefoot, and said her master
was having his after-dinner rest. I made my way to my
brother's room, and found him sitting up in bed, his knees
covered by a blanket. He had aged, and grown stout and
flabby. His cheeks, nose and lips protruded—I almost expected him to grunt into the blanket.

"We embraced and wept—tears of joy, mingled with
melancholy—because we had once been young and were
now both grey-haired and approaching the grave. He put
on his clothes and went out to show me over his estate.

"'Well, how are you getting on here?' I asked.

"'All right, thanks be, I'm enjoying myself.'

"He was no longer the poor, timid clerk, but a true
proprietor, a gentleman. He had settled down, and was
entering with zest into country life. He ate a lot, washed
in the bath-house, and put on flesh. He had already got
into litigation with the village commune, the brick-works
and the bone-kilns, and took offence if the peasants failed
to call him 'Your Honour'. He went in for religion in a
solid, gentlemanly way, and there was nothing casual
about his pretentious good works. And what were these
good works? He treated all the diseases of the peasants
with bicarbonate of soda and castor-oil, and had a special
thanksgiving service held on his name-day, after which
he provided half a pail of vodka, supposing that this was
the right thing to do. Oh, those terrible half pails! Today
the fat landlord hauls the peasants before the Zemstvo
representative for letting their sheep graze on his land,
tomorrow, on the day of rejoicing, he treats them to half
a pail of vodka, and they drink and sing and shout hurrah,
prostrating themselves before him when they are drunk.
Any improvement in his conditions, anything like satiety
or idleness, develops the most insolent complacency in a
Russian. Nikolai Ivanich, who had been afraid of having

an opinion of his own when he was in the government service, was now continually coming out with axioms, in the most ministerial manner: 'Education is essential, but the people are not ready for it yet', 'corporal punishment is an evil, but in certain cases it is beneficial and indispensable'.

" 'I know the people and I know how to treat them,' he said. 'The people love me. I only have to lift my little finger, and the people will do whatever I want.'

"And all this, mark you, with a wise, indulgent smile. Over and over again he repeated: 'We the gentry', or 'speaking as a gentleman', and seemed to have quite forgotten that our grandfather was a peasant, and our father a common soldier. Our very surname—Chimsha-Himalaisky—in reality so absurd, now seemed to him a resounding, distinguished, and euphonious name.

"But it is of myself, and not of him, that I wish to speak. I should like to describe to you the change which came over me in those few hours I spent on my brother's estate. As we were drinking tea in the evening, the cook brought us a full plate of gooseberries. These were not gooseberries bought for money, they came from his own garden, and were the first fruits of the bushes he had planted. Nikolai Ivanich broke into a laugh and gazed at the gooseberries in tearful silence for at least five minutes. Speechless with emotion, he popped a single gooseberry into his mouth, darted at me the triumphant glance of a child who has at last gained possession of a longed-for toy, and said:

" 'Delicious!'

"And he ate them greedily, repeating over and over again:

" 'Simply delicious! You try them.'

"They were hard and sour, but, as Pushkin says: 'The lie which elates us is dearer than a thousand sober truths.' I saw before me a really happy man, one whose dearest wish had come true, who had achieved his aim in life, got what he wanted, and was content with his lot and with himself. There had always been a tinge of melancholy in my conception of human happiness, and now, confronted by a happy man, I was overcome by a feeling of sadness bordering on desperation. This feeling grew strongest of all in the night. A bed was made up for me in the room next to my brother's bedroom, and I could hear him moving about restlessly, every now and then getting up to take a gooseberry from the plate. How many happy, satisfied people there are, after all, I said to myself. What an overwhelming force! Just consider this life—the insolence and idleness of the strong, the ignorance and bestiality of the weak, all around intolerable poverty, cramped dwellings, degeneracy, drunkenness, hypocrisy, lying.... And yet peace and order apparently prevail in all those homes and in the streets. Of the fifty thousand inhabitants of a town, not one will be found to cry out, to proclaim his indignation aloud. We see those who go to the market to buy food, who eat in the day-time and sleep at night, who prattle away, marry, grow old, carry their dead to the cemeteries. But we neither hear nor see those who suffer, and the terrible things in life are played out behind the scenes. All is calm and quiet, only statistics, which are dumb, protest: so many have gone mad, so many barrels of drink have been consumed, so many children died of malnutrition.... And apparently this is as it should be. Apparently those who are happy can only enjoy themselves because the unhappy bear their burdens in silence, and but for this silence happiness would be impossible. It is a kind of universal hypnosis. There ought to be a man with a hammer behind the door of every happy man, to remind him by his constant knocks that there are unhappy people, and that happy as he himself may be, life will sooner or later show him its claws, catastrophe will overtake him—sickness, poverty, loss—and nobody will see it, just as he now neither sees nor hears the misfortunes of others. But there is no man with a hammer, the happy man goes on living and the petty vicissitudes of life touch him lightly, like the wind in an aspen-tree, and all is well.

"That night I understood that I, too, was happy and content," continued Ivan Ivanich, getting up. "I, too, while out hunting, or at the dinner table, have held forth on the right way to live, to worship, to manage the people. I, too, have declared that without knowledge there can be no light, that education is essential, but that bare literacy is sufficient for the common people. Freedom is a blessing, I have said, one can't get on without it, any more than without air, but we must wait. Yes, that is what I said, and now I ask: In the name of what must we wait?" Here Ivan Ivanich looked angrily at Burkin. "In the name of what must we wait, I ask you? What is there to be considered? Don't be in such a hurry, they tell me, every idea materialises gradually, in its own time. But who are they who say this? What is the proof that it is just? You refer to the natural order of things, to the logic of facts, but according to what order, what logic do I, a living, thinking individual, stand on the edge of a ditch and wait for it to be gradually filled up, or choked with silt, when I might leap across it or build a bridge over it? And again, in the name of what must we wait? Wait, when we have not the strength to live, though live we must and to live we desire!

"I left my brother early the next morning, and ever since I have found town life intolerable. The peace and order weigh on my spirits, and I am afraid to look into windows, because there is now no sadder spectacle for me than a happy family seated around the tea-table. I am old and unfit for the struggle, I am even incapable of feeling hatred. I can only suffer inwardly, and give way to irritation and annoyance, at night my head burns from the rush of thoughts, and I am unable to sleep.... Oh, if only I were young!"

Ivan Ivanich began pacing backwards and forwards, repeating:

"If only I were young still!"

Suddenly he went up to Alekhin and began pressing first one of his hands, and then the other

"Pavel Konstantinich," he said in imploring accents. "Don't *you* fall into apathy, don't *you* let your conscience be lulled to sleep! While you are still young, strong, active, do not be weary of well-doing. There is no such thing as happiness, nor ought there to be, but if there is any sense or purpose in life, this sense and purpose are to be found not in our own happiness, but in something greater and more rational. Do good!"

Ivan Ivanich said all this with a piteous, imploring smile, as if he were asking for something for himself.

Then they all three sat in their arm-chairs a long way apart from one another, and said nothing. Ivan Ivanich's story satisfied neither Burkin nor Alekhin. It was not interesting to listen to the story of a poor clerk who ate gooseberries, when from the walls generals and fine ladies, who seemed to come to life in the dark, were looking down from their gilded frames. It would have been much more interesting to hear about elegant people, lovely women. And the fact that they were sitting in a drawing-room in which everything—the swathed chandeliers, the arm-chairs, the carpet on the floor—proved that the people now looking out of the frames had once moved about here, sat in the chairs, drunk tea, where the fair Pelageya was now going noiselessly to and fro, was better than any story.

Alekhin was desperately sleepy. He had got up early, at three o'clock in the morning, to go about his work on the estate, and could now hardly keep his eyes open. But he would not go to bed, for fear one of his guests would relate something interesting after he was gone. He could not be sure whether what Ivan Ivanich had just told them was wise or just, but his visitors talked of other things besides grain, hay, or tar, of things which had no direct bearing on his daily life, and he liked this, and wanted them to go on. ...

"Well, time to go to bed," said Burkin, getting up. "Allow me to wish you a good night."

Alekhin said good night and went downstairs to his own room, the visitors remaining on the upper floor. They were allotted a big room for the night, in which were two ancient bedsteads of carved wood, and an ivory crucifix in one corner. There was a pleasant smell of freshly laundered sheets from the wide, cool beds which the fair Pelageya had made up for them.

Ivan Ivanich undressed in silence and lay down.

"Lord have mercy on us, sinners," he said, and covered his head with the sheet.

There was a strong smell of stale tobacco from his pipe, which he put on the table, and Burkin lay awake a long time, wondering where the stifling smell came from.

The rain tapped on the window-panes all night.

1898

I

When fresh arrivals to the town of S. complained of boredom and the monotony of life there, the old-established inhabitants pointed out in its favour that S. was a most interesting town, that it had a library, a theatre, and a club, that balls were given there, and, finally, that there were many clever, interesting and pleasant families whose acquaintance could be made. And they would point to the Turkin family as an example of all that was cultured and talented.

The Turkins lived in the main street, next door to the Governor's residence, in a house which was their own property. The head of the family, Ivan Petrovich, a stout, handsome, dark-haired man with side-whiskers, got up private theatricals for charitable purposes and took the part of old generals, and coughed to extremely humourous effect. He had a store of anecdotes, charades, and proverbs, was fond of a joke, indeed, was quite a wag, and it was impossible to tell from his expression whether he was serious or joking. His wife, Vera Yosifovna, was a gaunt, pleasant-faced lady who wore pince-nez and wrote stories and novels, which she was always ready to read aloud to visitors. They had a daughter called Yekaterina Ivanovna, a young lady who played the piano. In a word, each member of the family had some gift or other. The Turkins were the soul of hospitality and showed off their talents light-heartedly, with frank simplicity. The big stone-built house was always cool in the summer, its back windows looking out on an old, shady garden, where nightingales sang in the spring. When there was company the house would ring with the sound of knives being sharpened in the kitchen, and the smell of fried onions would perfume the yard, giving promise of an abundant and tasty supper.

And Dr. Dmitri Yonich Startsev, the newly appointed Zemstvo medical officer, was told, as soon as he took up his residence in Dyalizh, some nine versts from S., that, as a cultured man, he simply must make the acquaintance of the Turkins. He was introduced to Ivan Petrovich in the street one winter day. They discussed the weather, the theatre, and the cholera epidemic, and an invitation followed. So on one of the spring church-holidays—the Ascension it was—Startsev, having seen all his patients for the day, set off for the town in search of relaxation and to make some necessary purchases while he was about it. He went on foot, at a leisurely pace (he had not yet set up his own carriage), singing to himself the whole way:

"Ere I had learned to drink of tears from the chalice of life."

He dined in town, walked about the park, and, the invitation of Ivan Petrovich coming into his head, decided to go to the Turkins and see what sort of people they were.

"Howdy! Howdy!" said Ivan Petrovich, who met him in the porch. "Delighted to see such a welcome visitor! Come in, I'll introduce you to my better half. I was telling him, Vera," he went on, after introducing the doctor to his wife, "I was telling him he has no earthly right to stick in his hospital, it's his duty to bestow his leisure on society. I'm right, darling, aren't I?"

"Sit here," said Vera Yosifovna, pointing to a chair next to herself. "You can make up to me. My husband is as jealous as Othello, but we will try to be discreet, won't we?"

"Little witch!" murmured Ivan Petrovich tenderly, imprinting a kiss on her brow. "You've chosen a very good moment for your visit," he said, turning to his visitor again. "My better half has just finished a great enormous novel, and she's going to read it aloud to us this evening."

"Jean, ducky," said Vera Yosifovna to her husband. *"Dites que l'on nous donne du thé."*

Startsev was next introduced to Yekaterina Ivanovna, an eighteen-year-old damsel, strikingly like her mother, and equally thin and pleasant-faced. Her expression was still childish, and she had a slender delicate frame. And her virginal breasts, already beginning to develop, held in their beauty and healthiness, a suggestion of spring, the genuine spring. Afterwards they sat down to have tea, with jam, honey, sweets, and some wonderful biscuits which fairly melted in the mouth. With the approach of dusk visitors began dropping in, and Ivan Petrovich, his eyes smiling, said to every one of them: "Howdy! Howdy!"

When everybody had come they seated themselves in the drawing-room with grave faces and Vera Yosifovna read her novel. It began with the words: "'Twas bitter cold. . . ." The windows were wide-open and the sound of knives clanging in the kitchen came through them, together with the smell of frying onions. . . . It was very peaceful sitting in the soft arm-chairs, with the lights blinking lazily in the semi-dark of the drawing-room. And it was hard to realise, on this summer evening, with the sound of voices and laughter coming from the street, and the fragrance of lilac wafted in from the garden, that "'twas bitter cold" and that the setting sun could be lighting up with its cold rays the snowy plain and the solitary wayfarer. Vera Yosifovna read how the young and beautiful countess got up schools, hospitals and libraries in her native village, and how she fell in love with the roving artist, describing things that never happen in real life, and yet it was so pleasant and comforting to listen to her, while calm, delightful thoughts passed through one's mind, that nobody wanted to get up. . . .

"Not badsome!" said Ivan Petrovich softly.

And one of the visitors, who had been listening, with his thoughts somewhere far, far away, said almost inaudibly:

"Yes, indeed. . . ."

An hour passed, and another. In the town park, nearby, an orchestra was playing, and a choir was singing. When Vera Yosifovna closed her note-book nobody spoke for five minutes, all listening to "Luchinushka", which the choir was singing, and the song spoke to them of what was lacking in the novel but what was present in real life.

"Do you publish your works in the periodicals?" Startsev asked Vera Yosifovna.

"No," she replied. "I don't publish them at all. I write them and put them away in a cupboard. Why should I publish them? We have enough to live on," she added by way of explanation.

And for some reason or other everyone sighed.

"And now you play us something, Kitten," Ivan Petrovich said to his daughter.

The lid of the grand piano was raised, the music-sheets were in readiness, on the music rack, and the instrument was opened. Yekaterina Ivanovna sat down and struck the keys with both hands. Then she struck them again with all her might, and again, and yet again. Her shoulders and breasts quivered, and she went on pertinaciously striking the keys in the same place, as if she did not mean to stop till she had driven them inside the piano. The drawing-room filled with thunder; everything thundered —the floor, the ceiling, the furniture.... Yekaterina Ivanovna played an intricate passage, the whole interest of which lay in its difficulty. It was long and monotonous, and Startsev, as he listened, pictured to himself rocks tumbling from the summit of a high mountain; they kept tumbling, tumbling, one after the other, and he wished they would stop, though he found Yekaterina Ivanovna, rosy with the exertion, strong, energetic, a lock of hair falling over her forehead, exceedingly attractive. After a winter in Dyalizh, amongst sick people and peasants, it was very pleasant, very novel, to be sitting in a drawing-room, looking at this youthful, elegant, and, no doubt, pure creature, and listening to these loud, tiresome, but nevertheless cultured sounds....

"Well, Kitten, you surpassed yourself today," said Ivan Petrovich with tears in his eyes, when his daughter, finishing her piece, got up. "You'll never improve upon that, Denis, if you die in the attempt."

Everyone surrounded her, congratulating her, marvelling, vowing that they had not heard such music for ages, while she listened in silence, with a slight smile on her face, her whole figure expressing triumph.

"Splendid! Wonderful!"

And Startsev, too, yielding to the general enthusiasm, cried: "Splendid!"

"Where did you study?" he asked Yekaterina Ivanovna. "At the conservatoire?"

"No, I'm only preparing for the conservatoire, in the meantime I'm taking lessons here, from Madame Zavlovskaya."

"Did you graduate from the high school here?"

"Oh, no," Vera Yosifovna answered for her. "We had teachers for her at home, you will agree that there might be bad influences in the high school or at a boarding-school. While a girl is growing she ought to be under the influence of no one but her mother."

"But I intend to go to the conservatoire," said Yekaterina Ivanovna.

"Oh, no, our Kitten loves her mamma. Our Kitten would not grieve her papa and mamma."

"I will go, I will!" said Yekaterina Ivanovna, with humorous petulance, stamping her foot.

At supper-time it was the turn of Ivan Petrovich to show off his talents. Smiling with his eyes alone, he related anecdotes, joked, set comic problems which he solved himself, all the time speaking in his own peculiar language, which he had acquired by long practice in waggishness, and which had apparently now become a habit with him: *splendiferous, not badsome, I thank thee humblesomely.*

But this was not all. When the guests, sated and happy, flocked into the hall to look for their coats and walking-sticks, the footman Pavel, or, as they called him, Pava, a fourteen-year-old boy with a cropped head and chubby cheeks, hovered around them.

"Perform, Pava, perform!" said Ivan Petrovich.

Pava threw himself into an attitude, raised one hand and uttered in tragic accents:

"Perish, unhappy female!"

And everyone laughed.

"Amusing!" thought Startsev, as he went out of the house.

He went to a restaurant for a drink of beer, and then walked back to Dyalizh. All the way home he hummed:

"The melting accents of your tender voice...."

After his six-mile walk he went to bed without the slightest sensation of fatigue, telling himself that he could have walked another six miles with pleasure.

"Not badsome!" he remembered, laughing, as he fell asleep.

II

Startsev kept meaning to visit the Turkins again, but he had a great deal to do in the hospital and could never find an hour or two to spare. Over a year passed thus in work and solitude. And one day a letter in a blue envelope came to him from the town....

Vera Yosifovna had long suffered from headaches, but of late, with Kitten threatening every day to go to the conservatoire, the attacks had become more and more frequent. All the doctors in the town visited the Turkins, and at last the turn of the Zemstvo doctor had come. Vera Yosifovna wrote him a touching letter, asking him to come and ease her sufferings. Startsev visited her, and after this began to be often, very often at the Turkins.... He really did manage to help Vera Yosifovna a little, and all visitors were told that he was an extraordinary, a marvellous doctor. But it was no longer on account of her headaches that he went to the Turkins....

It was a holiday. Yekaterina Ivanovna had finished her long, tedious exercises on the piano. Then they all sat long at the dining-room table, drinking tea. Ivan Petrovich was in the middle of a funny story when there was a ring at the front door, and he had to go out to meet some visitor. Startsev took advantage of the moment of bustle to whisper, in great agitation, in the ear of Yekaterina Ivanovna:

"Do not torture me, for God's sake, I implore you. Let's go into the garden."

She shrugged her shoulders as if she were surprised and did not understand what he wanted, but she got up and went out.

"You practise three or four hours," he said, following her. "Then you sit with your mamma, and there's never a chance to speak to you. Give me just one quarter of an hour, I implore you!"

Autumn was approaching, and the old garden was still and melancholy, the walks strewn with dark leaves. The days were drawing in.

"I haven't seen you for a whole week," continued Startsev. "And if you only knew what suffering that is for me! Let's sit down. I want to speak to you."

They had their favourite place in the garden—a bench beneath an ancient spreading maple. And now they sat down on this bench.

"What is it you want?" Yekaterina Ivanovna asked in a cold, business-like voice.

"I haven't seen you for a whole week, it's ages since I heard your voice! I long passionately, I thirst for your voice! Speak!"

He was captivated by her freshness, by the innocent expression in her eyes, her naive cheeks. Even in the fit of her dress he found something extraordinarily sweet, something in its simple and innocent grace that was touching. And at the same time, despite this innocence, she seemed to him very clever, wise beyond her years. He could talk to her about literature, art, or anything he liked, could complain to her about life and people, despite the fact that she sometimes started laughing in a very disconcerting manner in the middle of a serious conversation, or ran back to the house. Like almost all the girls in S., she was a great reader (there was very little reading done in S., and the local librarians declared that but for the girls and the young Jews they might as well close the library), and this caused Startsev infinite delight. Every time he saw her he asked her eagerly what she had been reading the last few days, and listened entranced when she told him.

"What have you been reading this week, since we last met?" he now asked her. "Do tell me."

"I've been reading Pisemsky."

"Which of his books?"

"*A Thousand Souls*," replied Kitten. "And what a funny name Pisemsky has—Alexei Feofilaktich!"

"Where are you going?" cried Startsev in alarm, when she suddenly got up and went towards the house. "I simply must have a talk with you, there's something I must tell you. . . . Stay with me—if only five minutes, I implore you!"

She halted as if intending to speak, then thrust a note awkwardly into his hand and ran into the house, where she immediately sat down to the piano again.

"Be in the cemetery at Demetti's tomb, at eleven tonight," read Startsev.

"Now that really is silly," he thought, when he had recovered from his surprise. "Why the cemetery? What-ever for?"

It was all perfectly clear: Kitten was trying to fool him. Nobody in his senses would make an appointment at night, a long way from town, when they could so easily meet in the street, or in the municipal park. And did it become him, a Zemstvo medical officer, an intelligent, highly-respected individual, to be sighing after a girl, receiving notes, roaming about cemeteries, committing follies which a modern schoolboy would laugh at? What would this affair lead to? What would his colleagues say, if they discovered it? Such were the thoughts of Startsev, as he threaded his way among the tables in the club, and yet at half past ten he suddenly started off for the cemetery.

He now had his own carriage and pair, and a coach-man named Panteleimon, who sported a velveteen waist-coat. The moon was shining. It was still and warm, but with an autumnal warmth. In the suburb of the town, near the slaughter-house, dogs were howling. Startsev left his carriage at the outskirts of the town, in a side-street, and went on foot to the cemetery. "Everyone has his peculiarities," he told himself. "Kitten is a queer girl, and who knows?—perhaps she really meant it, perhaps she'll be there." And he yielded to the intoxication of this vain, feeble hope.

The last part of the way was across a field. The cemetery was a dark strip in the distance, like a belt of woods, or a great park. A white stone wall came into sight, and then a gate.... In the moonlight the inscription over the gate could be read: "Your hour, too, will strike." Startsev pushed open the wicket-gate, and found himself in a broad alley lined on either side by white crosses and monuments and tall poplars, all casting long black shadows across his path. Everything was black or white, the drowsy trees spreading their branches over the white stones. It seemed to be lighter here than in the field. The leaves of the maples looked like paws, and stood out in bold relief against the yellow sand of the alley and the white tombstones, and the inscriptions on the monuments were clearly visible. Startsev was struck by the thought that he was seeing for the first time in his life a thing which he would probably never again see—a world unlike any other world, a world in which the moonlight was as soft and sweet as if this place were its cradle, where there was no life, none at all, but where, in every darkling poplar, in every grave, could be felt the presence of mystery, fraught with the promise of eternal life—still and exquisite. From the tombstones, the fading flowers, and the autumnal smell of decaying leaves, sorrow and peace seemed to be wafted.

All round was silence. The stars gazed down from the sky as if in profound humility and Startsev's footsteps struck a harsh discordant note. It was only while the church clock was striking the hour, and he was imagining himself dead, buried for all time, that he felt as if somebody were looking at him, and fancied for a moment that this was not peace and stillness, but the profound melancholy of non-existence, suppressed despair....

Demetti's tomb was in the form of a chapel, with an angel on the roof. Some time in the past an Italian operatic troupe had visited the town of S., and one of the singers had died, and been buried here, and this monument erected to her memory. Nobody in the town remembered her any more, but the lamp hanging over the entrance to her tomb reflected the moonlight and seemed to be burning.

There was no one in sight. And who would be coming
here at midnight? But Startsev waited, and, as if the
moonlight had kindled his passion, waited ardently,
picturing to himself kisses, embraces.... He sat beside
the tomb about half an hour, and then began walking up
and down one of the side paths, his hat in his hands,
waiting, wondering how many of the women and girls in
these graves had been beautiful and fascinating, had
loved, burned with passion at nights, as they yielded to
their lovers' caresses. What a sorry jest Mother Nature
plays upon human beings, and how humiliating to have
to acknowledge this! Startsev, pondering all these things,
felt a desire to cry out that he must have love, that he
must have love at all costs! He no longer contemplated
white slabs of marble, but bodies, he saw their forms
hiding bashfully in the shadows of trees, he could feel
their warmth, and at last the amorous languor became
unbearable.

And suddenly, as if a curtain had been lowered, the
moon went behind a cloud and darkness fell on all
around. Startsev could hardly find the gateway, for it was
by now as dark as an autumn night, and he wandered
about for an hour and a half looking for the side-street
in which he had left his carriage.

"I'm so tired I can hardly stand," he told Panteleimon.
And sinking luxuriously into the seat he said to
himself:

"I shouldn't let myself get so fat."

III

The next day he went to the Turkins' in the evening
fully intending to propose. But the moment was unsuit-
able, since the hairdresser was in Yekaterina Ivanovna's
bedroom, doing her hair. She was going to a dance at
the club.

Once more a long time had to be spent in the dining-
room over tea. Ivan Petrovich, seeing that his guest was
pensive and dull, drew some papers from his waistcoat
pocket and read aloud a letter from a German steward,
written in excruciatingly funny, broken Russian.

"And they'd probably give her a pretty good dowry," thought Startsev, listening abstractedly.

After his sleepless night he was in a state of bewilderment, as if he had been given something sweet and soporific to drink. There was a sensation at once dreamy, joyful and warm in his heart, but a cold and heavy particle in his brain was arguing:

"Stop before it is too late. Is she a match for you? She is spoilt and wilful, sleeps till two in the afternoon, and you are a sexton's son, a Zemstvo doctor. . . ."

"Well, what about it?" he thought.

"Besides, if you marry her," continued the particle, "her relations will make you give up your work in the Zemstvo, and come to live in the town."

"Well," he thought, "and why not live in the town? They'll give her a dowry and we'll set up house. . . ."

At last Yekaterina Ivanovna came looking so fresh and pretty in her low-cut ball dress, and Startsev gazed his fill at her, falling into such an ecstasy that he could not utter a word and could only look at her and laugh.

She began saying good-bye all round and he—there was nothing for him to stay for—got up, saying it was time for him to go home. His patients were waiting for him.

"Too bad!" said Ivan Petrovich. "Off you go, then! And you might as well give Kitten a lift!"

Out of doors it was dark and drizzling, and they could only discover where the carriage was from the sound of Panteleimon's hoarse coughing. The hood of the carriage was raised.

Ivan Petrovich joked incessantly as he helped his daughter into the carriage and bade them a facetious farewell. "Off with you! Goodeebye!"

They drove off.

"I went to the cemetery yesterday," said Startsev. "How ungenerous and cruel of you it was. . . ."

"You were at the cemetery?"

"Yes, and I waited almost two hours. I suffered. . . ."

"Serve you right—can't you understand a joke?"

Yekaterina Ivanovna, delighted to have fooled her admirer so successfully and to be loved so ardently, laughed loudly, and the next moment cried out in alarm, for the horses turned sharply in at the club gates, and the carriage lurched. Startsev put his arm round her waist. In her fright she leaned against him, and he could not refrain from pressing passionate kisses on her lips and chin, and holding her still more tightly.

"That'll do," she said coldly.

And a moment later she was no longer in the carriage, and the policeman standing by the brightly lighted entrance to the club shouted brutally to Panteleimon:

"What are you waiting for, dolt? Move on!"

Startsev went home, but soon came out again. In another man's frock-coat, and a stiff white tie which puckered up and slipped to one side, he was sitting at midnight in the club drawing-room, and saying ecstatically to Yekaterina Ivanovna:

"Oh, how little do those know who have never loved! It seems to me that no one has ever yet described love faithfully, indeed it is practically impossible to describe this tender, joyous, torturing feeling, and whoever has experienced it, if only once, will never try to put it into words. Why go in for preliminaries, for descriptions? Why all this superfluous eloquence? My love is boundless.... I beg you, I implore you," Startsev ended up, getting it out at last, "to be my wife!"

"Dmitri Yonich," said Yekaterina Ivanovna, looking extremely grave, after a slight pause. "Dmitri Yonich, I am very grateful to you for the honour, I respect you, but..." she rose and went on speaking in a standing position, "but, forgive me, I cannot be your wife. Let us speak plainly. You know very well, Dmitri Yonich, that I love art most of all in life, I love music madly, I adore it, I have consecrated my whole life to it. I want to be a musician, I want fame, success, liberty, and you want me to go on living in this town, to continue this dull, futile life, which has become intolerable to me. Just somebody's wife? No, thank you! A person should aspire to some lofty, brilliant aim, and family life would bind me for ever. Dmitri Yonich" (she smiled faintly, for when she pronounced the name "Dmitri Yonich", she could not help remembering "Alexei Feofilaktich"),

"Dmitri Yonich, you are a kind, generous, clever man, you are better than all the rest—" here tears welled up in her eyes, "I feel for you with all my heart, but ... but, I'm sure you understand. ..."

She turned away to prevent herself from crying, and went out of the drawing-room.

Startsev's heart no longer fluttered nervously. Going out of the club into the street the first thing he did was to tear off his stiff tie and take a deep breath. He was somewhat abashed, his vanity had received an affront— he had not anticipated a refusal—and he could not believe that all his dreams, torments and hopes had come to such a banal end, like the final scene of some little comedy acted by amateurs. He was so sorry for his feelings, for this love of his, that he felt like sobbing, or bringing his umbrella down with all his strength on the broad shoulders of Panteleimon.

For three days everything went wrong with him, he neither ate nor slept, but when the news reached him that Yekaterina Ivanovna had gone to Moscow to enter the conservatoire he quieted down and lived as before.

Afterwards, when he happened to remember how he had roamed about the cemetery, or how he had driven all over the town looking for a frock-coat, he stretched lazily and said:

"What a to-do!"

IV

Four years passed. Startsev had a big practice in the town. Every morning he hastily examined his patients in Dyalizh, and then drove to his town patients, and now he drove not in a carriage-and-pair, but behind three horses with jingling bells, and returned home late at night. He had grown fat and ponderous and avoided walking, which gave him palpitations. Panteleimon had grown fat, too, and the broader his girth became, the more mournfully he sighed and complained of his bitter lot: "Always on the move."

Startsev visited many houses and met many people, but he never grew intimate with any of them. The conversation, views, the very look of the townsfolk, irritated him. He had gradually learned that so long as he played cards and supped with a man in the town of S., the latter would be peaceable, good-humoured and even comparatively intelligent, but the moment the conversation turned to anything but food, say to politics or science, he would either be utterly bewildered, or begin to air a philosophy so stupid and cruel that one could only leave him alone and go away.

When Startsev tried to talk even with a liberal-minded man about the fact that humanity, thank God, is progressing and that in time we shall be able to dispense with passports and capital punishment, his interlocutor would shoot him an oblique, mistrustful glance, and ask: "So people will be able to cut one another's throat in the street as much as they like, then?" And when Startsev said during supper or tea that everyone ought to work, that life without work was impossible, all present took it as a reproach, and began arguing insistently. And with it all, these ordinary people did nothing, nothing whatever, and interested themselves in nothing, and it was impossible to find anything to talk to them about. And Startsev evaded conversation, only eating and playing vint with them, and when he happened to be in a house where some domestic event was being celebrated, and they invited him to take part in it, he would sit down and eat in silence, staring at his plate. For everything said on these occasions was uninteresting, unjust, stupid, and he would be irritated and excite himself; but he held his tongue, and, because he always stared at his plate in severe silence, he was known in the town as a "jumped-up Pole", although there was not a drop of Polish blood in his veins.

He avoided such entertainments as the theatre and concerts, but played vint every evening for about three hours with complete enjoyment. There was yet another amusement into which he was gradually and imperceptibly drawn: this was to take out of his pockets of an evening all the bank-notes accumulated during his rounds; and these notes with which his pockets were crammed—some yellow, some green, some smelling of scent, some of vinegar, incense, or fish—sometimes amounted to as much as seventy rubles. When he had several hundred of them he paid the money into his account at the Mutual Credit Society.

In the four years since the departure of Yekaterina Ivanovna he had only been twice at the Turkins', on the invitation of Vera Yosifovna, who was still being treated for headaches. Yekaterina Ivanovna came back to stay with her parents every summer, but he never saw her—somehow it did not come about.

And now four years had passed. One still, warm morning a letter was brought to the hospital. Vera Yosifovna wrote to Dmitri Yonich that she missed him very much, and that he simply must come and see her and ease her sufferings, and that today happened to be her birthday. At the bottom of the letter was a postscript: "I join in Mamma's request. K."

Startsev thought it over and in the evening went to the Turkins. Ivan Petrovich greeted him with his usual "Hullo-ullo-ullo!" smiling with his eyes alone, and added: "Bon-joursky!"

Vera Yosifovna, who had aged considerably, and was now white-haired, pressed Startsev's hand, sighed affectedly, and said:

"You don't want to make up to me, Doctor, you never come to see us, I'm too old for you. But the young one is here now, perhaps she will be more fortunate."

And Kitten? She was thinner and paler, but still lovelier and more graceful. She was Yekaterina Ivanovna now, not a Kitten. Her freshness and expression of child-like innocence had vanished. There was something new, something timid and guilty in her glance, as if she no longer felt at home here, in the Turkin house.

"We haven't met for ages," she said, putting her hand into his, and it was obvious that her heart was beating violently. Looking fixedly and with curiosity into his face, she continued: "You've got quite stout! You're darker and more manly looking, but on the whole you haven't changed much."

He still found her attractive, extremely attractive, but there was something lacking in her now, or something superfluous, he could not say exactly what, but whatever it was it prevented him from feeling as he had before. He did not like her pallor, her new expression, her faint smile, her voice, and very soon he was disliking her dress, the chair in which she sat, disliking something in the past, when he had almost married her. He remembered his love, the hopes and dreams which had agitated him four years ago, and he felt awkward.

There was tea and a cream tart. Vera Yosifovna read her novel aloud, read of what never happens in real life, and Startsev listened, and sat looking at her beautiful grey head and waiting for her to finish.

"It is not the person unable to write stories who is mediocre," he said to himself, "but the person who writes them and is unable to conceal the fact."

But Ivan Petrovich said: "Not badsome!"

Then Yekaterina Ivanovna played long and noisily and when she stopped everybody took a long time thanking and applauding her.

"It's a good thing I didn't marry her, after all," thought Startsev.

She looked at him, obviously expecting him to ask her to go into the garden, but he said nothing.

"Let's talk," she said, going over to him. "How are you getting on? What kind of a life do you have? I've been thinking about you all these days," she continued nervously. "I wanted to write to you, to go to see you in Dyalizh, I had determined to, but then I changed my mind—goodness knows what you feel about me now! I waited so impatiently for you to come today. Do come out into the garden."

They went out into the garden and sat down on the bench under the ancient maple-tree, as they had done four years ago. It was dark.

"Well now, how are you getting on?" said Yekaterina Ivanovna.

"I'm all right, thanks," replied Startsev.

He could not think of anything else to say. They sat in silence.

"I'm all worked up," said Yekaterina Ivanovna, putting her hand over her face. "Take no notice! I'm so glad to be home, so glad to see everyone, and I can't get used to it. What memories! I thought you and I would talk our heads off all night!"

He could see her face and her brilliantly shining eyes, and here, in the dark, she seemed younger than in the room, even her former child-like expression seemed to have come back. He could see she was looking at him with a naive curiosity, as if she wanted to get closer to him, to understand this man who had once loved her so ardently, so tenderly, and so vainly. Her eyes thanked him for that love. And he, too, recalled all that had happened down to the most trifling detail, how he had roamed about the cemetery, and how, in the small hours, exhausted, he had gone back to his home; and suddenly he felt sad, regretting the past. A flame flickered in his soul.

"Do you remember that night I took you to the club?" he said. "It was raining, dark...."

The flame in his soul grew bigger, and now he felt a desire to talk, to bewail his life....

"Ah me!" he sighed. "You ask me about my life. How do we live here? We don't live. We grow old and fat, we let ourselves go. One day follows another, life passes, drab and dingy, without any striking impressions or thoughts.... The day goes in making money, the evenings at the club, in the company of card-players, drinkers, blusterers, all of whom I detest. What sort of a life is that?"

"But you have your work, a noble aim in life. You used to be so fond of talking about your hospital. I was an odd sort of creature then, fancying myself a great pianist. All young ladies play the piano nowadays, and I did, too, like everyone else, but there was nothing special about me. I'm as much a pianist as Mamma is a novelist. I did not understand you then, of course, but afterwards, in Moscow, I often thought of you. I never thought of anything else. What a joy to be a Zemstvo doctor, to help sufferers, to serve the people! What a joy!" repeated Yekaterina Ivanovna enthusiastically. "When I thought about you in Moscow you seemed to me an ideal, lofty character...."

Startsev remembered the notes he produced with such satisfaction from his pockets every evening, and the flame in his soul died down.

He got up to go back to the house. She took his arm.

"You're the best person I have ever known," she continued. "We will see one another and talk, won't we? Promise me that. I am not a real pianist, I am under no illusions about myself, and I will never play or talk about music in front of you."

When they re-entered the house and Startsev saw, in the lighted room, her face, the mournful, penetrating, grateful glance she bestowed on him, he felt a little uneasy, but assured himself once more:

"It's a good thing I didn't marry her."

He took his leave.

"You have no earthly right to leave before supper," said Ivan Petrovich, seeing him off. "It's extremely peekay-yulier on your part. Come on now, perform!" he cried, turning to Pava in the hall.

Pava, no longer a little boy, but a young man with a moustache, struck an attitude, raised his hand, and said in tragic accents:

"Perish, unhappy female!"

All this only irritated Startsev now. As he got into his carriage and looked out at the dark house and garden, once so dear to him, everything came back to him with a rush—Vera Yosifovna's novels, Kitten's noisy execution on the grand piano, Ivan Petrovich's witticisms, and Pava's tragic pose, and he asked himself, since the most talented people in the whole town were so mediocre, what was to be expected of the town itself?

Three days later Pava brought him a letter from Yekaterina Ivanovna.

"You never come to see us. Why?" she wrote. "I'm afraid you have changed towards us. I'm afraid, and the very thought terrifies me. Soothe me, come and tell me that everything is all right.

"I must see you. Your Y. T."

He read the letter, thought a moment, and said to Pava:

"Say I can't come today, my good man. I'm very busy. I'll come in a day or two."

But three days passed, and then a week, and still he did not go. Once, while driving by the Turkin house in his carriage, he told himself that he ought to look in, if only for a few minutes, but reflected a little ... and drove by.

He never went to the Turkins again.

V

A few more years passed. Startsev had become still stouter, quite obese, short of breath, and had to throw back his head when he walked. It was a sight to see him drive by, red-faced and chubby, his three horses jingling their bells, Panteleimon on the box seat, red-faced and chubby, too, with rolls of fat on the back of his neck. his arms extended straight in front of him as if they were of wood, shouting to drivers coming towards him: "Keep to the r-r-right!" Not a human being, but some heathen god seemed to be passing by. His practice in the town was now so extensive that he never had a breathing space; he had a country-estate, and two houses in the town, and had his eye on another, still more profitable. Whenever he heard, in the Mutual Credit Society, of a house soon to be sold at auction, he would enter it with scant ceremony, pass through all the rooms, quite regardless of the half-dressed women and children in them who looked at him in astonishment and terror, tap with his stick on each door, asking:

"Is this the study? Is this a bedroom? And what room is this?"

And all the while he would breathe heavily and mop his perspiring brow.

He had many cares, but he did not throw up his post as a Zemstvo doctor; the prey of avarice, he desired to get what he could everywhere. He was now always referred to as "Yonich", both in Dyalizh and the town.

"Where's Yonich off to?" or "Hadn't we better call in Yonich?"

His voice, no doubt owing to the layers of fat around his throat, had become shrill and squeaky. His disposition, too, had changed, he had become irritable and disagreeable. While examining his patients he would often lose his temper, bang impatiently on the floor with his stick, and exclaim, in his unpleasant voice:

"Kindly restrict yourself to answers to my questions. Don't talk unnecessarily."

He lives alone. His life is tedious, nothing interests him.

His love for Kitten was the only, probably the last joy he ever knew during the whole of his sojourn in Dyalizh. He plays vint at the club of an evening, and then sits at a big table all by himself and has supper. He is always waited on by Ivan, the oldest and most respected of all the club servants. They bring him Lafitte number 17, and everyone, the managing staff, the chef, the footmen know his likes and dislikes, and do their best to humour him, otherwise, which God forbid, he will suddenly fly into a rage and start knocking on the floor with his stick.

During supper he occasionally turns and joins in some conversation.

"What are you talking about? Eh? Who?"

And if the conversation at the next table should happen to turn on the Turkins, he asks:

"Are you talking about the Turkins? The ones whose daughter plays the piano?"

And that is about all there is to be said about him.

And the Turkins? Ivan Petrovich has not aged or altered in any way, he still jokes and relates funny stories. Vera Yosifovna reads her novels to her visitors with as much gusto and frankness as ever. And Kitten practises four hours a day. She has aged perceptibly, is often ill, and goes to the Crimea every autumn with her mother. When he sees them off, Ivan Petrovich wipes his eyes as the train draws out of the station, crying after it: "Goodeebyee!"

And he waves his handkerchief.

1898

THE LADY WITH THE DOG

I

People were telling one another that a newcomer had been seen on the promenade—a lady with a dog. Dmitri Dmitrich Gurov had been a fortnight in Yalta, and was accustomed to its ways, and he, too, had begun to take an interest in fresh arrivals. From his seat in Vernet's outdoor café, he caught sight of a young woman in a toque, passing along the promenade; she was fair and not very tall; after her trotted a white pomeranian.

Later he encountered her in the municipal park and in the square several times a day. She was always alone, wearing the same toque, and the pomeranian always trotted at her side. Nobody knew who she was, and people referred to her simply as "the lady with the dog".

"If she's here without her husband, and without any friends," thought Gurov, "it wouldn't be a bad idea to make her acquaintance."

He was not yet forty, but had a twelve-year-old daughter and two schoolboy sons. He had been talked into marrying in his second year at college, and his wife now looked nearly twice as old as he was. She was a tall, black-browed woman, erect, dignified, imposing, and, as she said of herself, a "thinker". She was a great reader, omitted the "hard sign"* at the end of words in her letters, and called her husband "Dimitri" instead of Dmitri; and though he secretly considered her shallow, narrow-minded, and dowdy, he stood in awe of her, and disliked being at home. It was long since he had first begun deceiving her and he was now constantly unfaith-

---

* Certain progressive intellectuals omitted the hard sign after consonants in writing, they anticipated the reform in the Russian alphabet introduced later on.—*Tr.*

ful to her, and this was no doubt why he spoke slightingly of women, to whom he referred as *the lower race.*

He considered that the ample lessons he had received from bitter experience entitled him to call them whatever he liked, but without this "lower race" he could not have existed a single day. He was bored and ill-at-ease in the company of men, with whom he was always cold and reserved, but felt quite at home among women, and knew exactly what to say to them, and how to behave, he could even be silent in their company without feeling the slightest awkwardness. There was an elusive charm in his appearance and disposition which attracted women and caught their sympathies. He knew this and was himself attracted to them by some invisible force.

Repeated and bitter experience had taught him that every fresh intimacy, while at first introducing such pleasant variety into everyday life, and offering itself as a charming, light adventure, inevitably developed, among decent people (especially in Moscow, where they are so irresolute and slow to move), into a problem of excessive complication leading to an intolerably irksome situation. But every time he encountered an attractive woman he forgot all about this experience, the desire for life surged up in him, and everything suddenly seemed simple and amusing.

One evening, then, while he was dining at the restaurant in the park, the lady in the toque came strolling up and took a seat at a neighbouring table. Her expression, gait, dress, coiffure, all told him that she was from the upper classes, that she was married, that she was in Yalta for the first time, alone and bored. . . . The accounts of the laxity of morals among visitors to Yalta are greatly exaggerated, and he paid no heed to them, knowing that for the most part they were invented by people who would gladly have transgressed themselves, had they known how to set about it. But when the lady sat down at a neighbouring table a few yards away from him, these stories of easy conquests, of excursions to the mountains, came back to him, and the seductive idea of a brisk transitory liaison, an affair with a woman whose very name he did not know, suddenly took possession of his mind.

He snapped his fingers at the pomeranian, and when it trotted up to him, shook his forefinger at it. The pomeranian growled. Gurov shook his finger again.

The lady glanced at him and instantly lowered her eyes.

"He doesn't bite," she said, and blushed.

"May I give him a bone?" he asked, and on her nod of consent added in friendly tones: "Have you been long in Yalta?"

"About five days."

"And I am dragging out my second week here."

Neither spoke for a few minutes.

"The days pass quickly, and yet one is so bored here," she said, not looking at him.

"It's the thing to say it's boring here. People never complain of boredom in God-forsaken holes like Belyev or Zhizdra, but when they get here it's: 'Oh, the dullness! Oh, the dust!' You'd think they'd come from Grenada to say the least of it."

She laughed. Then they both went on eating in silence, like complete strangers. But after dinner they left the restaurant together, and embarked upon the light, jesting talk of people free and contented, for whom it is all the same where they go, or what they talk about. They strolled along, remarking on the strange light over the sea. The water was a warm, tender purple, the moonlight lay on its surface in a golden strip. They said how close it was, after the hot day. Gurov told her he was from Moscow, that he was really a philologist, but worked in a bank; that he had at one time trained himself to sing in a private opera company, but had given up the idea; that he owned two houses in Moscow.... And from her he learned that she had grown up in St. Petersburg, but had got married in the town of S., where she had been living two years, that she would stay another month in Yalta, and that perhaps her husband, who also needed a rest, would join her. She was quite unable to explain whether her husband was a member of the gubernia council, or on the board of the Zemstvo, and was greatly amused at herself for this. Further, Gurov learned that her name was Anna Sergeyevna.

Back in his own room he thought about her, and felt sure he would meet her the next day. It was inevitable. As he went to bed he reminded himself that only a very short time ago she had been a schoolgirl, like his own daughter, learning her lessons, he remembered how much there was of shyness and constraint in her laughter, in her way of conversing with a stranger—it was probably the first time in her life that she found herself alone, and in a situation in which men could follow her and watch her, and speak to her, all the time with a secret aim she could not fail to divine. He recalled her slender, delicate neck, her fine grey eyes.

"And yet there's something pathetic about her," he thought to himself as he fell asleep.

II

A week had passed since the beginning of their acquaintance. It was a holiday. Indoors it was stuffy, but the dust rose in clouds out of doors, and people's hats blew off. It was a thirsty day and Gurov kept going to the outdoor café for fruit-drinks and ices to offer Anna Sergeyevna. The heat was overpowering.

In the evening, when the wind had dropped, they walked to the pier to see the steamer come in. There were a great many people strolling about the landing-place; some, bunches of flowers in their hands, were meeting friends. Two peculiarities of the smart Yalta crowd stood out distinctly—the elderly ladies all tried to dress very young, and there seemed to be an inordinate number of generals about.

Owing to the roughness of the sea the steamer arrived late, after the sun had gone down, and it had to manoeuvre for some time before it could get alongside the pier. Anna Sergeyevna scanned the steamer and passengers through her lorgnette, as if looking for someone she knew, and when she turned to Gurov her eyes were glistening. She talked a great deal, firing off abrupt questions and forgetting immediately what it was she had wanted to know. Then she lost her lorgnette in the crush.

The smart crowd began dispersing, features could no longer be made out, the wind had quite dropped, and Gurov and Anna Sergeyevna stood there as if waiting for someone else to come off the steamer. Anna Sergeyevna had fallen silent, every now and then smelling her flowers, but not looking at Gurov.

"It's turned out a fine evening," he said. "What shall we do? We might go for a drive."

She made no reply.

He looked steadily at her and suddenly took her in his arms and kissed her lips, and the fragrance and dampness of the flowers closed round him, but the next moment he looked behind him in alarm—had anyone seen them?

"Let's go to your room," he murmured.

And they walked off together, very quickly.

Her room was stuffy and smelt of some scent she had bought in the Japanese shop. Gurov looked at her, thinking to himself: "How full of strange encounters life is!" He could remember carefree, good-natured women who were exhilarated by love-making and grateful to him for the happiness he gave them, however short-lived; and there had been others—his wife among them—whose caresses were insincere, affected, hysterical, mixed up with a great deal of quite unnecessary talk, and whose expression seemed to say that all this was not just love-making or passion, but something much more significant; then there had been two or three beautiful, cold women, over whose features flitted a predatory expression, betraying a determination to wring from life more than it could give, women no longer in their first youth, capricious, irrational, despotic, brainless, and when Gurov had cooled to these, their beauty aroused in him nothing but repulsion, and the lace trimming on their underclothes reminded him of fish-scales.

But here the timidity and awkwardness of youth and inexperience were still apparent; and there was a feeling of embarrassment in the atmosphere, as if someone had just knocked at the door. Anna Sergeyevna, "the lady with the dog", seemed to regard the affair as something very special, very serious, as if she had become a fallen

woman, an attitude he found odd and disconcerting. Her
features lengthened and drooped, and her long hair hung
mournfully on either side of her face. She assumed a pose
of dismal meditation, like a repentant sinner in some
classical painting.

"It isn't right," she said. "You will never respect me
any more."

On the table was a water-melon. Gurov cut himself a
slice from it and began slowly eating it. At least half
an hour passed in silence.

Anna Sergeyevna was very touching, revealing the
purity of a decent, naive woman who had seen very
little of life. The solitary candle burning on the table
scarcely lit up her face, but it was obvious that her heart
was heavy.

"Why should I stop respecting you?" asked Gurov.
"You don't know what you're saying."

"May God forgive me!" she exclaimed, and her eyes
filled with tears. "It's terrible."

"No need to seek to justify yourself."

"How can I justify myself? I'm a wicked, fallen
woman, I despise myself and have not the least thought
of self-justification. It isn't my husband I have deceived,
it's myself. And not only now, I have been deceiving
myself for ever so long. My husband is no doubt an
honest, worthy man, but he's a flunkey. I don't know what
it is he does at his office, but I know he's a flunkey. I was
only twenty when I married him, and I was devoured by
curiosity, I wanted something higher. I told myself that
there must be a different kind of life. I wanted to live,
to live. . . . I was burning with curiosity . . . you'll never
understand that, but I swear to God I could no longer
control myself, nothing could hold me back, I told my
husband I was ill, and I came here. . . . And I started
going about like one possessed, like a madwoman . . . and
now I have become an ordinary, worthless woman, and
everyone has the right to despise me."

Gurov listened to her, bored to death. The naive
accents, the remorse, all was so unexpected, so out of
place. But for the tears in her eyes, she might have been
jesting or play-acting.

"I don't understand," he said gently. "What is it you want?"

She hid her face against his breast and pressed closer to him.

"Do believe me, I implore you to believe me," she said. "I love all that is honest and pure in life, vice is revolting to me, I don't know what I'm doing. The common people say they are snared by the devil. And now I can say that I have been snared by the devil, too."

"Come, come," he murmured.

He gazed into her fixed, terrified eyes, kissed her, and soothed her with gentle affectionate words, and gradually she calmed down and regained her cheerfulness. Soon they were laughing together again.

When, a little later, they went out, there was not a soul on the promenade, the town and its cypresses looked dead, but the sea was still roaring as it dashed against the beach. A solitary fishing-boat tossed on the waves, its lamp blinking sleepily.

They found a droshky and drove to Oreanda.

"I discovered your name in the hall, just now," said Gurov, "written up on the board. Von Diederitz. Is your husband a German?"

"No. His grandfather was, I think, but he belongs to the Orthodox Church himself."

When they got out of the droshky at Oreanda they sat down on a bench not far from the church, and looked down at the sea, without talking. Yalta could be dimly discerned through the morning mist, and white clouds rested motionless on the summits of the mountains. Not a leaf stirred, the grasshoppers chirruped, and the monotonous hollow roar of the sea came up to them, speaking of peace, of the eternal sleep lying in wait for us all. The sea had roared like this long before there was any Yalta or Oreanda, it was roaring now, and it would go on roaring, just as indifferently and hollowly, when we had passed away. And it may be that in this continuity, this utter indifference to life and death, lies the secret of our ultimate salvation, of the stream of life on our planet, and of its never-ceasing movement towards perfection.

Side by side with a young woman, who looked so exquisite in the early light, soothed and enchanted by the sight of all this magical beauty—sea, mountains, clouds and the vast expanse of the sky—Gurov told himself that, when you came to think of it, everything in the world is beautiful really, everything but our own thoughts and actions, when we lose sight of the higher aims of life, and of our dignity as human beings.

Someone approached them—a watchman, probably—looked at them and went away. And there was something mysterious and beautiful even in this. The steamer from Feodosia could be seen coming towards the pier, lit up by the dawn, its lamps out.

"There's dew on the grass," said Anna Sergeyevna, breaking the silence.

"Yes. Time to go home."

They went back to the town.

After this they met every day at noon on the promenade, lunching and dining together, going for walks, and admiring the sea. She complained of sleeplessness, of palpitations, asked the same questions over and over again, alternately surrendering to jealousy and the fear that he did not really respect her. And often, when there was nobody in sight in the square or the park, he would draw her to him and kiss her passionately. The utter idleness, these kisses in broad daylight, accompanied by furtive glances and the fear of discovery, the heat, the smell of the sea, and the idle, smart, well-fed people continually crossing their field of vision, seemed to have given him a new lease of life. He told Anna Sergeyevna she was beautiful and seductive, made love to her with impetuous passion, and never left her side, while she was always pensive, always trying to force from him the admission that he did not respect her, that he did not love her a bit, and considered her just an ordinary woman. Almost every night they drove out of town, to Oreanda, the water-fall, or some other beauty-spot. And these excursions were invariably a success, each contributing fresh impressions of majestic beauty.

All this time they kept expecting her husband to arrive. But a letter came in which he told his wife that he was having trouble with his eyes, and implored her to come home as soon as possible. Anna Sergeyevna made hasty preparations for leaving.

"It's a good thing I'm going," she said to Gurov. "It's the intervention of fate."

She left Yalta in a carriage, and he went with her as far as the railway station. The drive took nearly a whole day. When she got into the express train, after the second bell had been rung, she said:

"Let me have one more look at you.... One last look. That's right."

She did not weep, but was mournful, and seemed ill, the muscles of her cheeks twitching.

"I shall think of you ... I shall think of you all the time," she said. "God bless you! Think kindly of me. We are parting for ever, it must be so, because we ought never to have met. Good-bye—God bless you."

The train steamed rapidly out of the station, its lights soon disappearing, and a minute later even the sound it made was silenced, as if everything were conspiring to bring this sweet oblivion, this madness, to an end as quickly as possible. And Gurov, standing alone on the platform and gazing into the dark distance, listened to the shrilling of the grasshoppers and the humming of the telegraph wires, with a feeling that he had only just waked up. And he told himself that this had been just one more of the many adventures in his life, and that it, too, was over, leaving nothing but a memory.... He was moved and sad, and felt a slight remorse. After all, this young woman whom he would never again see had not been really happy with him. He had been friendly and affectionate with her, but in his whole behaviour, in the tones of his voice, in his very caresses, there had been a shade of irony, the insulting indulgence of the fortunate male, who was, moreover, almost twice her age. She had insisted in calling him good, remarkable, high-minded. Evidently he had appeared to her different from his real self, in a word he had involuntarily deceived her....

There was an autumnal feeling in the air, and the evening was chilly.

"It's time for me to be going north, too," thought Gurov, as he walked away from the platform. "High time!"

III

When he got back to Moscow it was beginning to look like winter, the stoves were heated every day, and it was still dark when the children got up to go to school and drank their tea, so that the nurse had to light the lamp for a short time. Frost had set in. When the first snow falls, and one goes for one's first sleigh-ride, it is pleasant to see the white ground, the white roofs; one breathes freely and lightly, and remembers the days of one's youth. The ancient lime-trees and birches, white with rime, have a good-natured look, they are closer to the heart than cypresses and palms, and beneath their branches one is no longer haunted by the memory of mountains and the sea.

Gurov had always lived in Moscow, and he returned to Moscow on a fine frosty day, and when he put on his fur-lined overcoat and thick gloves, and sauntered down Petrovka Street, and when, on Saturday evening, he heard the church bells ringing, his recent journey and the places he had visited lost their charm for him. He became gradually immersed in Moscow life, reading with avidity three newspapers a day, while declaring he never read Moscow newspapers on principle. Once more he was caught up in a whirl of restaurants, clubs, banquets, and celebrations, once more glowed with the flattering consciousness that well-known lawyers and actors came to his house, that he played cards in the Medical Club opposite a professor.

He had believed that in a month's time Anna Sergeyevna would be nothing but a vague memory, and that hereafter, with her wistful smile, she would only occasionally appear to him in dreams, like others before her. But the month was now well over and winter was in full swing, and all was as clear in his memory as if he had only parted with Anna Sergeyevna the day before. And his recollections grew ever more insistent. When the voices of his children at their lessons reached him in his study through the evening stillness, when he heard a song, or the sounds of a musical-box in a restaurant, when the wind howled in the chimney, it all came back to him: early morning on the pier, the misty mountains, the steamer from Feodosia, the kisses. He would pace up and down his room for a long time, smiling at his memories, and then memory turned into dreaming, and what had happened mingled in his imagination with what was going to happen. Anna Sergeyevna did not come to him in his dreams, she accompanied him everywhere, like his shadow, following him everywhere he went. When he closed his eyes, she seemed to stand before him in the flesh, still lovelier, younger, tenderer than she had really been, and looking back, he saw himself, too, as better than he had been in Yalta. In the evenings she looked out at him from the bookshelves, the fire-place, the corner, he could hear her breathing, the sweet rustle of her skirts. In the streets he followed women with his eyes, to see if there were any like her....

He began to feel an overwhelming desire to share his memories with someone. But he could not speak of his love at home, and outside his home who was there for him to confide in? Not the tenants living in his house, and certainly not his colleagues at the bank. And what was there to tell? Was it love that he had felt? Had there been anything exquisite, poetic, anything instructive or even amusing about his relations with Anna Sergeyevna? He had to content himself with uttering vague generalisations about love and women, and nobody guessed what he meant, though his wife's dark eyebrows twitched as she said:

"The role of a coxcomb doesn't suit you a bit, Dimitri."

One evening, leaving the Medical Club with one of his card-partners, a government official, he could not refrain from remarking:

"If you only knew what a charming woman I met in Yalta!"

The official got into his sleigh, and just before driving off, turned and called out:

"Dmitri Dmitrich!"

"Yes?"

"You were quite right, you know—the sturgeon was just a *leetle* off."

These words, in themselves so commonplace, for some reason infuriated Gurov, seemed to him humiliating, gross. What savage manners, what people! What wasted evenings, what tedious, empty days! Frantic card-playing, gluttony, drunkenness, perpetual talk always about the same thing. The greater part of one's time and energy went on business that was no use to anyone, and on discussing the same thing over and over again, and there was nothing to show for it all but a stunted, earth-bound existence and a round of trivialities, and there was nowhere to escape to, you might as well be in a mad-house or a convict settlement.

Gurov lay awake all night, raging, and went about the whole of the next day with a headache. He slept badly on the succeeding nights, too, sitting up in bed, thinking, or pacing the floor of his room. He was sick of his children, sick of the bank, felt not the slightest desire to go anywhere or talk about anything.

When the Christmas holidays came, he packed his things, telling his wife he had to go to St. Petersburg in the interests of a certain young man, and set off for the town of S. To what end? He hardly knew himself. He only knew that he must see Anna Sergeyevna, must speak to her, arrange a meeting, if possible.

He arrived at S. in the morning and engaged the best suite in the hotel, which had a carpet of grey military frieze, and a dusty ink-pot on the table, surmounted by a headless rider, holding his hat in his raised hand. The hall porter told him what he wanted to know: von Diederitz had a house of his own in Staro-Goncharnaya Street. It wasn't far from the hotel, he lived on a grand scale, luxuriously, kept carriage-horses, the whole town knew him. The hall porter pronounced the name "Drideritz".

Gurov strolled over to Staro-Goncharnaya Street and discovered the house. In front of it was a long grey fence with inverted nails hammered into the tops of the palings.

"A fence like that is enough to make anyone want to

run away," thought Gurov, looking at the windows of the house and the fence.

He reasoned that since it was a holiday, Anna's husband would probably be at home. In any case it would be tactless to embarrass her by calling at the house. And a note might fall into the hands of the husband, and bring about catastrophe. The best thing would be to wait about on the chance of seeing her. And he walked up and down the street, hovering in the vicinity of the fence, watching for his chance. A beggar entered the gate, only to be attacked by dogs, then, an hour later, the faint, vague sounds of a piano reached his ears. That would be Anna Sergeyevna playing. Suddenly the front door opened and an old woman came out, followed by a familiar white pomeranian. Gurov tried to call to it, but his heart beat violently, and in his agitation he could not remember its name.

He walked on, hating the grey fence more and more, and now ready to tell himself irately that Anna Sergeyevna had forgotten him, had already, perhaps, found distraction in another—what could be more natural in a young woman who had to look at this accursed fence from morning to night? He went back to his hotel and sat on the sofa in his suite for some time, not knowing what to do, then he ordered dinner, and after dinner, had a long sleep.

"What a foolish, restless business," he thought, waking up and looking towards the dark window-panes. It was evening by now. "Well, I've had my sleep out. And what am I to do in the night?"

He sat up in bed, covered by the cheap grey quilt, which reminded him of a hospital blanket, and in his vexation he fell to taunting himself.

"You and your lady with a dog ... there's adventure for you! See what you get for your pains."

On his arrival at the station that morning he had noticed a poster announcing in enormous letters the first performance at the local theatre of *The Geisha*. Remembering this, he got up and made for the theatre.

"It's highly probable that she goes to first-nights," he told himself.

The theatre was full. It was a typical provincial theatre, with a mist collecting over the chandeliers, and the
crowd in the gallery fidgeting noisily. In the first row of
the stalls the local dandies stood waiting for the curtain
to go up, their hands clasped behind them. There, in the
front seat of the Governor's box, sat the Governor's
daughter, wearing a boa, the Governor himself hiding
modestly behind the drapes, so that only his hands were
visible. The curtain stirred, the orchestra took a long time
tuning up their instruments. Gurov's eyes roamed eagerly
over the audience as they filed in and occupied their
seats.

Anna Sergeyevna came in, too. She seated herself in
the third row of the stalls, and when Gurov's glance fell
on her, his heart seemed to stop, and he knew in a flash
that the whole world contained no one nearer or dearer
to him, no one more important to his happiness. This little
woman, lost in the provincial crowd, in no way remarkable, holding a silly lorgnette in her hand, now filled his
whole life, was his grief, his joy, all that he desired. Lulled
by the sounds coming from the wretched orchestra,
with its feeble, amateurish violinists, he thought how
beautiful she was ... thought and dreamed....

Anna Sergeyevna was accompanied by a tall, round-
shouldered young man with small whiskers, who nodded
at every step before taking the seat beside her and seemed
to be continually bowing to someone. This must be her
husband, whom, in a fit of bitterness, at Yalta, she had
called a "flunkey". And there really was something of the
lackey's servility in his lanky figure, his side-whiskers,
and the little bald spot on the top of his head. And he
smiled sweetly, and the badge of some scientific society
gleaming in his buttonhole was like the number on a
footman's livery.

The husband went out to smoke in the first interval,
and she was left alone in her seat. Gurov, who had taken
a seat in the stalls, went up to her and said in a trembling
voice, with a forced smile: "How d'you do?"

She glanced up at him and turned pale, then looked at
him again in alarm, unable to believe her eyes, squeezing
her fan and lorgnette in one hand, evidently struggling

to overcome a feeling of faintness. Neither of them said a word. She sat there, and he stood beside her, disconcerted by her embarrassment, and not daring to sit down. The violins and flutes sang out as they were tuned, and there was a tense sensation in the atmosphere, as if they were being watched from all the boxes. At last she got up and moved rapidly towards one of the exits. He followed her and they wandered aimlessly along corridors, up and down stairs; figures flashed by in the uniforms of legal officials, high-school teachers and civil servants, all wearing badges; ladies, coats hanging from pegs flashed by; there was a sharp draught, bringing with it an odour of cigarette-stubs. And Gurov, whose heart was beating violently, thought:

"What on earth are all these people, this orchestra for?..."

The next minute he suddenly remembered how, after seeing Anna Sergeyevna off that evening at the station, he had told himself that all was over, and they would never meet again. And how far away the end seemed to be now!

She stopped on a dark narrow staircase over which was a notice bearing the inscription "To the upper circle".

"How you frightened me!" she said, breathing heavily, still pale and half-stunned. "Oh, how you frightened me! I'm almost dead! Why did you come? Oh, why?"

"But, Anna," he said, in low, hasty tones. "But, Anna.... Try to understand ... do try...."

She cast him a glance of fear, entreaty, love, and then gazed at him steadily, as if to fix his features firmly in her memory.

"I've been so unhappy," she continued, taking no notice of his words. "I could think of nothing but you the whole time, I lived on the thoughts of you. I tried to forget— why, oh, why did you come?"

On the landing above them were two schoolboys, smoking and looking down, but Gurov did not care, and drawing Anna Sergeyevna towards him, began kissing her face, her lips, her hands.

"What are you doing, oh, what are you doing?" she said in horror, drawing back. "We have both gone mad.

Go away this very night, this moment.... By all that is sacred, I implore you.... Somebody is coming."

Someone was ascending the stairs.

"You must go away," went on Anna Sergeyevna in a whisper. "D'you hear me, Dmitri Dmitrich? I'll come to you in Moscow. I have never been happy, I am unhappy now, and I shall never be happy—never! Do not make me suffer still more! I will come to you in Moscow, I swear it! And now we must part! My dear one, my kind one, my darling, we must part."

She pressed his hand and hurried down the stairs, looking back at him continually, and her eyes showed that she was in truth unhappy. Gurov stood where he was for a short time, listening, and when all was quiet, went to look for his coat, and left the theatre.

IV

And Anna Sergeyevna began going to Moscow to see him. Every two or three months she left the town of S., telling her husband that she was going to consult a specialist on female diseases, and her husband believed her and did not believe her. In Moscow she always stayed at the Slavyanski Bazaar, sending a man in a red cap to Gurov the moment she arrived. Gurov went to her, and no one in Moscow knew anything about it.

One winter morning he went to see her as usual (the messenger had been to him the evening before, but had not found him at home). His daughter was with him for her school was on the way, and he thought he might as well see her to it.

"It is three degrees above zero," said Gurov to his daughter, "and yet it is snowing. You see it is only above zero close to the ground, the temperature in the upper layers of the atmosphere is quite different."

"Why doesn't it ever thunder in winter, Papa?"

He explained this, too. As he was speaking, he kept reminding himself that he was going to a rendezvous and that not a living soul knew about it, or, probably, ever would. He led a double life—one in public, in the sight

10*

of all whom it concerned, full of conventional truth and conventional deception, exactly like the lives of his friends and acquaintances, and another which flowed in secret. And, owing to some strange, possibly quite accidental chain of circumstances, everything that was important, interesting, essential, everything about which he was sincere and never deceived himself, everything that composed the kernel of his life, went on in secret, while everything that was false in him, everything that composed the husk in which he hid himself and the truth which was in him—his work at the bank, discussions at the club, his "lower race", his attendance at anniversary celebrations with his wife—was on the surface. He began to judge others by himself, no longer believing what he saw, and always assuming that the real, the only interesting life of every individual goes on as under cover of night, secretly. Every individual existence revolves around mystery, and perhaps that is the chief reason that all cultivated individuals insisted so strongly on the respect due to personal secrets.

After leaving his daughter at the door of her school Gurov set off for the Slavyanski Bazaar. Taking off his overcoat in the lobby, he went upstairs and knocked softly on the door. Anna Sergeyevna, wearing the grey dress he liked most, exhausted by her journey and by suspense, had been expecting him since the evening before. She was pale and looked at him without smiling, but was in his arms almost before he was fairly in the room. Their kiss was lingering, prolonged, as if they had not met for years.

"Well, how are you?" he asked. "Anything new?"

"Wait, I'll tell you in a minute.... I can't...."

She could not speak, because she was crying. Turning away, she held her handkerchief to her eyes.

"I'll wait till she's had her cry out," he thought, and sank into a chair.

He rang for tea, and a little later, while he was drinking it, she was still standing there, her face to the window. She wept from emotion, from her bitter consciousness of the sadness of their life; they could only see one another in secret, hiding from people, as if they were thieves. Was not their life a broken one?

"Don't cry," he said.

It was quite obvious to him that this love of theirs would not soon come to an end, and that no one could say when this end would be. Anna Sergeyevna loved him ever more fondly, worshipped him, and there would have been no point in telling her that one day it must end. Indeed, she would not have believed him.

He moved over and took her by the shoulders, intending to fondle her with light words, but suddenly he caught sight of himself in the looking-glass.

His hair was already beginning to turn grey. It struck him as strange that he should have aged so much in the last few years. The shoulders on which his hands lay were warm and quivering. He felt a pity for this life, still so warm and exquisite, but probably soon to fade and droop like his own. Why did she love him so? Women had always believed him different from what he really was, had loved in him not himself but the man their imagination pictured him, a man they had sought for eagerly all their lives. And afterwards when they discovered their mistake, they went on loving him just the same. And not one of them had ever been happy with him. Time had passed, he had met one woman after another, become intimate with each, parted with each, but had never loved. There had been all sorts of things between them, but never love.

And only now, when he was grey-haired, had he fallen in love properly, thoroughly, for the first time in his life.

He and Anna Sergeyevna loved one another as people who are very close and intimate, as husband and wife, as dear friends love one another. It seemed to them that fate had intended them for one another, and they could not understand why she should have a husband, and he a wife. They were like two migrating birds, the male and the female, who had been caught and put into separate cages. They forgave one another all that they were ashamed of in the past and in the present, and felt that this love of theirs had changed them both.

Formerly, in moments of melancholy, he had consoled himself by the first argument that came into his head, but

now arguments were nothing to him, he felt profound
pity, desired to be sincere, tender.

"Stop crying, my dearest," he said. "You've had your
cry, now stop.... Now let us have a talk, let us try and
think what we are to do."

Then they discussed their situation for a long time, trying to think how they could get rid of the necessity for
hiding, deception, living in different towns, being so long
without meeting. How were they to shake off these intolerable fetters?

"How? How?" he repeated, clutching his head. "How?"

And it seemed to them that they were within an inch
of arriving at a decision, and that then a new, beautiful
life would begin. And they both realised that the end was
still far, far away, and that the hardest, the most com-
plicated part was only just beginning.

1899

IN THE GULLY

I

The village of Ukleyevo lay in a gully, and all that could be seen of it from the highroad and the railway station were the belfry and the chimneys of the cotton-printing works. When travellers asked what village that was, they were told: "It's the place where the sexton ate up all the caviare at the funeral."

At some funeral in the family of the mill-owner Kostyukov, an old sexton noticed, amidst other delicacies, a jar of caviare, and fell upon it with avidity. People nudged him, tugged at his sleeve, but he took no notice, only ate and ate in a kind of trance. There were four pounds in the jar and he ate it all. It happened ages ago, and the sexton had long been dead and buried, but everyone remembered how he ate up all the caviare. Whether it was that life here was so eventless, or that the only thing which ever made an impression on the villagers was this insignificant incident, which occurred ten years before, nothing else was ever related of the village of Ukleyevo.

Fevers raged here, and even in the summer sticky mud lingered, especially at the foot of the fences, over which bowed ancient willows, spreading wide shadows. There was always a smell of factory refuse, and of the acetic acid used in finishing the prints. The factories—three cotton mills and a tanning works—were not situated in the village itself, but on its outskirts and even beyond. They were small enterprises, employing not more than four hundred workers altogether. The water in the river stank continually from the tannery discharges; the meadowlands were polluted by refuse, the peasants' cattle suffered from anthrax, and the tannery was condemned. It was considered as closed, but worked in secret, with the connivance of the head of the rural police and district medical officer, each of whom the owner paid ten rubles a month. There were only two decent brick-built houses with iron roofs in the whole village; one of them belonged to the volost board of administration, in the other, a two-storey building, lived Tsibukin, Grigory Petrovich, who came from a lower middle-class family of the town of Yepifanovo.

Grigory kept a grocery shop, but that was merely a blind, his real occupation was the sale of vodka, cattle, hides, grain, hogs, in a word anything that came his way; thus, for instance, when magpie's wings for ladies' hats were in vogue abroad, he got thirty kopeks a pair for them; he bought up timber, lent money on interest, and was altogether a resourceful old man.

He had two sons. The elder, Anisim, was in the detective division of the police forces, and was away most of the time. The younger, Stepan, went in for trade and helped his father; but his help was not much depended on, for he was deaf and sickly. His wife Aksinya was a handsome, agile woman who wore a bonnet and carried an umbrella on Sundays and saints' days, rose early and went to bed late, rushing about all day long, her skirt tucked up and a bunch of keys jingling at her belt, from the store-house to the cellar, and from the cellar to the shop, and old Tsibukin watched her with joy, his eyes lighting up whenever he saw her, at the same time deploring that she had not married his elder son instead of the younger, the deaf one, who could hardly be expected to appreciate feminine loveliness.

The old man was of a domestic turn, prizing his family above everything in the world, especially his elder son, the detective, and his daughter-in-law. As soon as she became the wife of the deaf man, Aksinya showed herself an exceedingly business-like woman; she knew whom to allow credit for goods purchased, and whom to refuse it, kept the keys herself, not even trusting her husband with them, clicked away at the abacus, looked the horses in the mouth like a proper farmer, and was always either laughing or shouting; and whatever she did, or said, the old man could only admire, murmuring:

"There's a daughter-in-law for you! There's a beauty!"

He had been a widower for some time, but a year after his son's marriage had not been able to stand it any longer, and had married, too. A girl who lived thirty versts from Ukleyevo was chosen for him; her name was Varvara Nikolayevna, and she came of a good family. She was not very young, but still good-looking and attractive. The moment she was settled in her little room on the top floor, the whole house seemed to light up, as if new panes had been put in the windows. Lamps were lighted in front of the icons, table-cloths, white as snow, were spread on every table, red flowers appeared on window-sills and in the front garden, and at dinner everyone had a plate to himself instead of eating out of a common bowl. Varvara Nikolayevna had a sweet, affectionate smile, and everything in the house seemed to smile back at her. For the first time beggars, pilgrims, and pious mendicants were seen in the yard, beneath the windows were heard the piteous wails of Ukleyevo women, the apologetic coughs of sickly, hollow-cheeked men, sacked from the factory for drinking. Varvara relieved their sufferings with money, bread, and old clothes, and later, when she began to feel more sure of herself, even smuggled various articles from the shop for them. The deaf son saw her take two packets of tea from the shop, and this upset him greatly.

"Mother has taken two ounces of tea," he told his father afterwards. "Where shall I enter it?"

The old man did not answer him, but stood silent for a few moments, his brows twitching; then he went upstairs to speak to his wife.

"Varvara dear," he said affectionately, "if you ever want anything from the shop, take it. Take anything you like, don't think twice about it."

And the next day, the deaf son shouted to her as he was running across the yard:

"If you need anything, Mother, take it!"

There was something novel in her alms-giving, something as cheerful and bright as the lamps before the icons and the red flowers. At Shrovetide, or on the three-day holiday of the local patron-saint, when the peasants were sold tainted beef from a barrel which stank so that one could hardly stand beside it, and drunken men handed scythes, caps and their wives' shawls over the counter, when the mill-hands, bemused by bad vodka, wallowed in the mud, and sin seemed to rise over everything in a thick mist, it was nice to think that somewhere in the house was a quiet, cleanly woman who had nothing to do with tainted beef or vodka; on such dreary, foggy days her alms acted as a safety valve in machinery.

The days in the Tsibukin household passed in perpetual cares. Before the sun rose, Aksinya could be heard puffing and blowing in the entry as she washed her face, the samovar would be boiling in the kitchen, droning away as if warning of evil to come. The old man, Grigory Petrovich, natty and small in his long black coat, print trousers and shining high-boots, stumped about the rooms like the father-in-law in the popular song. Then the shop would be unlocked. As soon as it was light a racing sulky was brought up to the porch, and the old man jumped briskly into it, pulling his big peaked cap over his ears; to look at him, no one would have said he was fifty-six. His wife and daughter-in-law went out to see him off, and at such moments, in his good, well-brushed coat, with the enormous black stallion, which had cost him three hundred rubles, harnessed to the sulky, the old man did not like to have the peasants coming up to him with their complaints and requests; he had a fastidious dislike for peasants, and when he saw one waiting for him by the gate, he would shout angrily:

"What are you standing there for? Get out!"

Or if it happened to be a beggar, he would shout:

"The Lord will provide!"

Then he would drive off on his own business. His wife, a black apron over her dark dress, would put the rooms in order, or help in the kitchen. Aksinya stood behind the counter in the shop, and the clinking of bottles and coins, Aksinya's laughing and scolding, the angry retorts of the customers when she cheated them, could be heard from the yard; and it was obvious that a secret trade in vodka was already going on in the shop. The deaf son either sat in the shop, or walked about the street without his cap, glancing absently from the huts to the sky. Tea was drunk about six times during the day, and at least four meals were served. And in the evening, after the day's takings had been counted and entered in the books, everyone went to bed and slept soundly.

The three cotton mills in Ukleyevo were linked by telephone with the houses of the owners—Khrimins Senior, Khrimins Junior, and Kostyukov. The line had been extended to the volost board as well, but very soon ceased to work, owing to bugs and cockroaches in the apparatus. The volost elder could scarcely read and write and began every word with a capital letter, but when the telephone went out of order, he said:

"Yes, yes, it will be hard to do without a telephone."

The Khrimins Senior were constantly at law with the Khrimins Junior, while the Khrimins Junior often quarrelled among themselves and also went to law; during their quarrels the mills would stop working for a month or two, until they made it up again; this afforded much entertainment to the people of Ukleyevo, for every quarrel caused a great deal of talk and gossip. On holidays Kostyukov and the Khrimins Junior went for drives, tearing about Ukleyevo and running over calves. On those days Aksinya, dressed in her best, would walk up and down in front of the shop, her starched petticoats rustling; the Juniors would whisk her into their carriage, pretending to carry her off against her will. Then old Tsibukin would drive out to show off his new steed, taking Varvara with him.

In the night, after the drive, when other people had gone to bed, the strains of an expensive concertina could be heard in the yard of the Juniors, and if there was a moon, the music stirred and rejoiced people's hearts, and Ukleyevo no longer seemed such a hole.

II

The eldest son, Anisim, visited his home very seldom, only on special holidays, but he often sent gifts, and letters, penned in a stranger's exquisite hand, always cover-

ing a whole sheet of notepaper, and written in the form
of a petition. These letters were full of expressions which
Anisim would never have used in talking: "Honoured
Parents, I hereby transmit a packet of herb tea for the
satisfaction of your physical requirements." Every letter
was signed *Anisim Tsibukin*, in a scrawl which looked as
if written with a spoilt nib, and under the signature, in the
same excellent handwriting, was the word "Agent".

The letters were read aloud several times over, and
the old man, deeply affected and flushed with emotion,
would say:

"There, he wouldn't stay at home, but went in for
learning! Well, never mind! Each to his own, I say!"

One day, just before Shrovetide, a hard sleety rain
began to fall; the old man and Varvara went to the
window to look out, when whom should they see but
Anisim driving up in a sleigh from the station! Nobody
had expected him. He came into the room in a state of
anxiety and concealed dread which never seemed to abate
for a moment; but he bore himself with a kind of airy
familiarity. He was in no hurry to leave, and it looked
as if he had lost his job. Varvara seemed to be glad of his
visit; she cast him sly glances, sighing and wagging her
head:

"How's this, for goodness' sake!" she exclaimed. "Okh-
ch'k-ch'k, the lad is twenty-seven if he is a day, and still
a bachelor!"

From the next room it sounded as if she were saying
nothing but "okh-ch'k-ch'k, okh-ch'k-ch'k" over and over
again in her low monotonous voice. She held whispered
conferences with the old man and Aksinya, and they, too,
assumed a sly, mysterious expression, as if they were
conspirators.

It was decided that Anisim should marry.

"Your youngest brother has been married a long time,"
said Varvara, "and you go about alone, like a cock at the
market. That won't do, you know. God willing, you'll
marry, then you can go back to your work if you like, and
your wife will stay at home and help us. There's no order
in your life, my boy, you've forgotten what it is to have
order in your life. Oh, you town lads!"

When any of the Tsibukins decided to get married, the most beautiful brides were sought out for them, for they were rich people. This time, too, a beautiful girl was found for Anisim. He himself was insignificant and unattractive; short of stature, with a weak rickety frame; he had fat puffy cheeks, which he seemed to be always blowing out, a pair of unblinking, sharp eyes, and a reddish, sparse beard, and when he fell into a reverie, he would stuff it into his mouth and chew at the ends; and by way of a finishing touch he was a constant drinker, as both his face and gait betrayed. Nevertheless, when told that a wife was chosen for him, and that she was very beautiful, he said:

"Well, I'm not such a fright myself, am I? Nobody will deny that we Tsibukins are a good-looking lot."

Hard by the town lay the village of Torguyevo. One half of it had lately become part of the town, while the other half remained a village. In the town half there lived, in her own house, a widow-woman; she had a sister who was very poor and went out to work by the day, and this sister had a daughter Lipa, who worked by the day, too. Lipa's beauty was already being talked about in the town, and it was nothing but her appalling poverty that put people off; the general opinion was that some elderly man, perhaps a widower, would marry her despite her poverty, or simply take her to live with him, and then her mother would be fed, too. Varvara made enquiries about Lipa among the match-makers, and then set out for Torguyevo.

The showing of the bride was duly held in the house of Lipa's aunt, with food and drink served, and Lipa in a new pink gown, specially made for the occasion; and she wore a crimson ribbon like a tongue of flame in her hair. She was thin, fragile, pale, with tender, delicate features, and her skin was tanned from working in the fields; a timid melancholy smile hovered round her lips, and she had the child's glance, trustful and inquisitive.

She was very young, just a little girl with unformed breasts, but old enough to be wedded. She was beautiful—there was no gainsaying that. The only thing that could be said against her was that she had big, masculine hands, which now hung idle at her sides like great red claws.

"We can overlook the dowry," said the old man to the aunt, "we took a wife for our son Stepan from a poor family, too, and now we can't praise her enough. She does everything well, both in the house and in the shop."

Lipa stood by the door, her whole attitude expressing: "You may do what you like with me, I trust you", while her mother, the charwoman, hid in the kitchen, overcome by timidity. Once, in her youth, a merchant, whose floors she was washing, stamped his foot at her, so that she was almost numb with terror, and ever since had been unable to shake off her fear. Her hands and knees, her very cheeks would shake with fear. She sat in the kitchen, trying to hear what the visitors were saying, and kept crossing herself, pressing her fingers to her forehead and glancing at the icon. Anisim, slightly drunk, opened the door into the kitchen now and then, calling out negligently:

"Why don't you come out to us, dear Mother of ours? We miss you!"

And Praskovya, pressing her hands to her lean, shrivelled breast, answered every time:

"Oh, Sir, you are very kind. . . ."

After the bride-show a day was fixed for the wedding. Anisim walked about the rooms of his home, whistling. Then he would suddenly remember something, fall into a deep reverie and stare at the floor with a fixed, penetrating gaze, as if trying to see through it and deep into the earth below. He expressed neither satisfaction that he was to be wed—and that very soon, at Easter—nor a desire to see his betrothed, but only went about whistling softly. And it was obvious that he was only marrying to please his father and stepmother, and because it was the custom of the village that a son should marry, so that there should be someone to help in the house. When the time came for him to leave, he seemed to be in no hurry, and his behaviour as a whole was not what it had been during his former visits—he spoke with more airy familiarity than ever, and was always saying the wrong things.

III

In the village of Shikalovo lived two dressmakers, sisters, both belonging to the Khlysty sect. They were given the order to make the wedding-clothes and often came to the Tsibukin home to try on the dresses, sitting long over their tea afterwards. Varvara had a brown dress with black lace and bugles, and Aksinya, a light green one with a yellow front and a long train. When the dressmakers had finished their work, Tsibukin paid them, not in money but with goods from the shop, and they departed with sad countenances, carrying away in their bundles tallow candles and tins of sardines for which they had no use at all, and when they got to the fields outside the village, they sat down on a mound and wept.

Anisim arrived three days before the wedding all dressed in new clothes. He wore shiny rubber galoshes and a red cord with beads at the ends instead of a tie, and had flung his new coat over his shoulders without putting his arms into the sleeves.

After praying gravely in front of the icons, he greeted his father and gave him ten silver rubles and ten half-rubles; he gave the same to Varvara, but Aksinya he gave twenty quarter-ruble coins. The main charm of these presents lay in the fact that every coin was new and shone brightly in the sun. In his efforts to appear grave and dignified, Anisim strained the muscles of his face, puffing out his cheeks; he smelt strongly of spirits, he had evidently visited the refreshment-room at every station. And again, there was the airy familiarity, the something superfluous about the man. Anisim and his father had tea and a bite of food, while Varvara played with the brand-new rubles in her hands, and asked after friends from her village who had gone to live in the town.

"All are well, thanks be to God," answered Anisim. "True, there was an incident in the domestic life of Ivan Yegorov; his old woman, Sofia Nikiforovna, died. Consumption. They ordered the funeral feast at the confectioner's—two and a half rubles per head. There was wine, too. There were a few muzhiks from our parts, you know, and they were fed for two and a half rubles each, too.

But they ate nothing. As if a muzhik could appreciate sauces!"

"Two and a half rubles!" exclaimed the old man, shaking his head.

"Of course! It's not the village, you know. You step into a restaurant for a snack, order a dish or two, others drop in, you take a drop with them, and suddenly it's the dawn, and there you are—kindly pay up three or four rubles each! And if Samorodov's there, he likes to wind up with coffee and brandy, and brandy costs sixty kopeks a glass."

"How he lies!" exclaimed the old man admiringly.

"Oh, I always go about with Samorodov now. He's the one who writes my letters for me. He's a wonderful writer! And if I were to tell you, Mother," Anisim went on cheerfully, addressing Varvara, "what sort of man this Samorodov is, you wouldn't believe me. We all call him Mukhtar, he's just like an Armenian, dark all over. I can see right through him, I know all his affairs as well as I know the palm of my hand, Mother, and he feels it, and sticks to me, we are inseparable, him and me. He's a bit afraid of me, and yet he can't live without me. Wherever I go, he goes. I have a wonderful eye, Mother. For instance, a peasant is selling a shirt at the rag-market. 'Stop!' I cry. 'It's stolen goods!' And I'm quite right—it turns out to be stolen goods."

"How d'you know?" asked Varvara.

"I don't know, I have an eye, I suppose, I know nothing about the shirt, but it kind of draws me. Ha! It's stolen, and that's all! They always say at the office when they see me go out: 'There goes Anisim to shoot snipe!' That's what they call looking for stolen goods. Oh, yes, anyone can steal, it's keeping the things that's hard! The world is large, but there's no place for stolen goods in it."

"They stole a ram and two lambs last week from the Guntorevs in our village," said Varvara with a sigh. "And there's no one to look for the thief."

"Why, I might look into this. I don't say I won't."

The day of the wedding came, a chilly April day, but bright and cheerful. From early in the morning troikas and two-horse vehicles tore about Ukleyevo, bells jingling and bright-coloured ribbons streaming from the shaft-bows and the horses' manes. The rooks, disturbed by the noise, cawed among the willow-trees, and the starlings sang incessantly, as if they were delighted that the Tsibukins were having a wedding.

In the house the tables were already laden with enormous fishes, hams, stuffed game, tins of sprats, and pickles of every kind, and innumerable bottles of wine and vodka; a smell of smoked sausage and musty tinned lobster hung over it all. And the old man stumped round the tables sharpening the blade of one knife against another. Everyone was calling for Varvara, asking for this and that, and she, breathing heavily, and looking thoroughly flustered, kept running in and out of the kitchen, where the chef from Kostyukov and the headcook from the Khrimins Junior had been working since day-break. Aksinya, her hair curled, wearing nothing over her stays, her new boots squeaking, rushed about the yard like a whirlwind, so swiftly that all people saw was an occasional flash of her bare knees and exposed bosom. Oaths and imprecations could be heard amidst the din; passers-by stopped at the wide-open gate; and underlying everything was the sense that something out-of-the-way was in preparation.

"They've gone to fetch the bride!"

The jingling of bells was heard, gradually receding beyond the village. Soon after two the crowd pressed forward, and the jingling of the bells was again heard—they were bringing the bride. The church was full, the candles in the overhead sconces were lighted, and the choir, by special request of old Tsibukin, sang with the music in their hands. The glare of the lamps and the coloured dresses almost blinded Lipa, who felt as if the loud voices of the singers were tapping on her skull like little hammers; the stays which she was wearing for the first time in her life squeezed her, and her new boots were tight, and she looked as if she had just come out of a swoon and did not yet understand where she was. Anisim, in his black coat, with the red cord he wore in place of a tie, seemed to be deep in thought, gazing fixedly at one place, and when the choir started singing in loud voices, he crossed himself hastily. He was deeply moved and he would have liked to cry. He had known this church ever since he was a little boy; his mother used to take him in her arms to receive the holy sacrament here, and later he used to sing in the choir-stalls with the boys; how well he knew every nook, every icon! And now he was being married here, being married because it was the right thing to do, but he was not thinking of that just now, the fact that this was his wedding had somehow quite escaped his mind. He could hardly see the icons for tears, he felt a weight at his heart; he prayed, imploring God to allow the disaster hanging over his head and ready at any moment to burst out, to pass away, as rain-clouds during a drought sometimes pass over a village, without letting a drop of rain spill. He had committed so many sins in the past, so many sins, everything was so hopeless, so irrevocably spoilt, that it seemed incongruous to ask for forgiveness. And yet he did ask to be forgiven, too, and even sobbed aloud once, but no one took any notice, for they thought he was drunk.

A child's frightened voice cried out:

"Mummie dear, do take me away, please do!"

"Quiet, there!" shouted the priest.

The crowd ran after the wedding party as it left the church; near the shop, by the gate, in the yard, and pressing against the walls beneath the windows there was a crowd, too. The women came to congratulate the young couple. The moment the newly-wed couple crossed the threshold, the singers, who stood ready in the entry with their music, began singing loudly; the musicians, sent for from the town for the occasion, struck up. The Don champagne was being handed round in tall glasses, and the carpenter and building-contractor Yelisarov, a tall, lean old man with brows so thick that his eyes were hardly visible, addressed the couple:

"Anisim—and you, child—love one another, walk in the sight of God, and the Divine Mother will never abandon you." He buried his face in old Tsibukin's shoulder and gave a sob. "Let us weep, Grigory Petrovich, let us weep for joy!" he piped out in his high voice, and suddenly laughed and went on in a loud bass: "Ho-ho-ho! This bride of yours is beauteous, too! Everything is as it should be, all smooth, no rattling, the mechanism in order, all the screws in their places."

He was from the Yegoryevsk district, but had worked in the mill at Ukleyevo and in the neighbourhood from his youth, and felt he belonged to the place. It seemed to those who knew him that he had always been as old and lean and lanky as he was now, no one remembered calling him by any other name but Spike. Perhaps it was owing to his forty years of work in the factories on nothing but repairs that he judged both human beings and inanimate objects according to a single standard—their durability: were they in need of repair? This time, too, before sitting down to the table, he tried several chairs to see whether they were strong enough; he even touched the salmon before eating it.

After tossing off the champagne they all sat down to table. The guests talked as they drew their chairs in. The choir sang in the passage, the band played, and at the same time the women gathered in the yard began singing the ritual-song in unison, and there was a wild, appalling mixture of sounds, enough to make one's head go round.

Spike fidgeted in his chair, shoving his elbows into his neighbours, interrupting everyone, laughing and weeping by turns.

"Children, dear children," he muttered hurriedly. "Aksinya dear, Varvara, let us live in peace with one another, peace and quiet, my beloved little axes...."

He was not accustomed to drinking and the first glass of gin made him drunk. This bitter, nauseating drink, brewed of goodness knows what, stupefied everyone who drank it, like a blow on the head. Speech became thick and incoherent.

Round the table were assembled the local clergy, the foremen from the factories with their wives, merchants and tavern-keepers from neighbouring villages. The volost elder and volost clerk, who had been working together these fourteen years and had never signed a single paper or let a single person leave their office, without deceiving or injuring him, were both here, sitting side by side,

fat and sleek, and they seemed to be so saturated with lies
that the very skin on their faces looked like the skin of
swindlers. The clerk's wife, a meagre, cross-eyed woman,
had brought all her children with her and sat there like
some bird of prey, glancing from plate to plate, pounc-
ing on whatever came her way, and cramming into her
own and her children's pockets.

Lipa sat as if petrified, her face wearing the same
expression as it had in the church. Anisim had not exchanged a single word with her since they had made one
another's acquaintance, so that he did not even know what
her voice was like; and now he sat next to her, silently
drinking gin, and when he got drunk, addressed Lipa's
aunt across the table.

"I have a friend, his name is Samorodov. He's not
like anyone else. An honorary citizen, and knows how to
talk. But I see right through him. Auntie, and he knows
it. Let us drink the health of Samorodov, Auntie!"

Varvara walked round the table, pressing the guests
to eat; she was bewildered and exhausted, but pleased
that there was such a lot of food and everything was so
grand—nobody could say anything now. The sun went
down, but the feasting went on; the guests hardly knew
what they were putting into their mouths, nobody could
hear what was said, and only every now and then, when
the music stopped for a moment, a woman's voice could
be distinctly heard from the yeard:

"Blood-suckers, tyrants, a plague on you!"

In the evening there was dancing to the strains of the
band. The Khrimins Junior came, bringing their own
wine, and one of them went through the quadrille with a
bottle in each hand and a glass between his teeth, to the
intense amusement of the company. Some varied the step
of the quadrille by squatting down and shooting out their
legs in the Russian manner; the green-clad Aksinya
flashed by, raising a wind with her train. One of the
dancers stepped on the flounce at the bottom of her dress,
ripping it off, and Spike shouted:

"You've broken the plinth! Children, children!"

Aksinya had innocent grey eyes and an unblinking gaze,
and an innocent smile played constantly over her features.

In those unblinking eyes, in the tiny head poised on the long neck, and in the litheness of her figure, there was something snake-like; the yellow front of her green dress, her constant smile, made her look like an adder, rearing its length out of the young rye in spring to peep at the passer-by. The Khrimins treated her with easy familiarity, and it was only too clear that there were long established intimate relations between her and the eldest of the brothers. But her deaf husband saw nothing, and did not even look at her; he sat with his knees crossed, eating nuts and cracking the shells with a noise of a pistol shot.

Then old Tsibukin stepped out into the middle of the floor waving his handkerchief to show that he wished to dance, too; and a murmur passed from room to room, and was caught up in the yard:

"*Himself* is going to dance! *Himself!*"

It was Varvara who danced, while the old man merely waved his handkerchief to the music and tapped his heels, but the eager crowd outside pressing against the windows and peeping through the panes was delighted, for the moment forgiving him all—his riches and his injustices.

"Go it, Grigory Petrovich!" they shouted from the yard. "Stick to it! There's life in the old dog yet! Ha-ha!"

It was after one when the rejoicings came to an end. Anisim staggered up to the musicians and singers, presenting each with a new half-ruble piece by way of a farewell gift. And the old man, not quite reeling, but lurching unsteadily, saw off the guests, telling each:

"The wedding cost two thousand rubles."

While the party was dispersing it was discovered that someone had left his old coat in the place of the good new one of the Shikalovo tavern-keeper, and Anisim, suddenly on the alert, shouted:

"Stop! I'll find it this instant! I know who took it! Stop, I say!"

He rushed out into the street, trying to overtake one of the guests; he was caught and led home, where they pushed him, drunk, crimson with rage, soaked in sweat, into the room, where the aunt had already undressed Lipa; then the door was locked on them.

IV

Five days passed. Anisim went upstairs to bid Varvara good-bye before leaving. The lamps in front of the icons were all lit, and there was a smell of incense; Varvara was sitting by the window, knitting a red woollen stocking.

"Well, you haven't stayed very long with us," she said. "Tired of us, I suppose? We have a good life, here, we live in plenty, and we gave you a decent wedding, everything was as it should be; the old man says it cost two thousand. In a word, we live like true merchants, but it's dreary here. We treat the people badly. It makes my heart ache, my friend, to see how we treat them, how we treat them, by God! Whether we barter a horse, buy something, or hire help, it's always deceit, nothing but deceit. Deception on every hand. The vegetable oil in our shop is bitter, rancid—tar would be sweeter! Now, tell me, don't you think we could afford to sell good oil?"

"To each his own, Mother."

"But when we come to die? Oh, couldn't you speak to your father, couldn't you now?"

"Why don't you speak to him yourself?"

"Ah! When I tell him my mind, he answers me, just like you, with those very words: 'to each his own'. But in the next world nobody will ask what belonged to you and what to others. The judgement of the Lord is just."

"Of course nobody will ask about that," said Anisim and sighed. "There is no God, Mother. So there'll be no one to ask."

Varvara looked at him in amazement, laughing, and throwing out her arms. Her frank astonishment, and the way she looked at him as if she thought he must be mad, made him uneasy.

"Well, perhaps there is a God, but no one believes any more," he said. "When I was being married, I felt funny. It was like when one takes an egg from under the hen, and suddenly hears the chicken cheep inside, and I heard my conscience cheep, and while the wedding was going on, I thought: 'There *is* a God!' But when I left the church, it all passed. And how should I know whether there is a God, or not? When we were children we were not taught such things, and while the baby is still at its mother's breast, it hears nothing but the words: 'to each his own'. Father doesn't believe in God, either. Do you remember you told me once about some sheep being stolen from the Guntorevs? Well, I found out all about it: a Shikalovo peasant stole them; yes, it was he who stole them, but the hides found their way to Father's shop. . . . There's religion for you!"

Anisim winked and shook his head.

"The village elder doesn't believe in God, either," he went on, "nor do the clerk and the sexton. And if they do go to church and fast, it is only so that people won't talk and in case the Day of Judgement comes after all. Some people say the end of the world is at hand, for men have become weak, no longer honour their parents and all that. But that's nonsense. This is what I think, Mother: all our troubles come from people having no conscience any more. I see through people, Mother, I know them. When I see a stolen shirt, I know it is stolen. A man sits in a tavern, and you may think he's just drinking his tea, but I see not only that he's drinking tea, but that he has no conscience. You can go about all day long, and never meet a man who has a conscience. And all because nobody knows whether there is a God, or not. . . . Well, Mother, good-bye. Keep your health and spirits, and think kindly of me."

Anisim bowed to the ground before Varvara.

"We thank you for everything, Mother," he said. "You are very good for our family. You are a decent woman, and I am greatly pleased with you."

Deeply moved, Anisim left the room, but turned back once more, and said:

"Samorodov has got me mixed up in a certain affair: it will either make me rich, or ruin me. In case anything happens, Mother, I hope you will console my parent."

"Don't say that! God is merciful. But, Anisim, I wish you would be a little kinder to your wife, you look at one another like wild beasts; never a smile, never!"

"She's such a strange girl," said Anisim with a sigh. "She understands nothing, and never says a word. She's very young, she must grow up."

A tall well-fed white stallion harnessed to a gig was waiting for him at the porch.

Old Tsibukin sprang jauntily into the gig, and took the reins. Anisim kissed Varvara, Aksınya and his brother. Lipa was standing on the porch, too; she stood motionless, looking away, as if she had merely sauntered on to the porch and had not come to see her husband off. Anisim walked up to her and touched her cheek with his lips, ever so lightly.

"Good-bye," he said.

She did not look at him, but a strange smile crept over her face; her features twitched and everyone felt sorry for her, without quite knowing why. Anisim, too, sprang into the carriage and sat down, arms akimbo, like one confident of his good looks.

While the gig climbed the side of the gully, Anisim kept looking back at the village. It was a warm, sunny day. The cattle had been taken out to graze for the first time that year, and the women and girls accompanying them were dressed up as for a holiday. A red bull bellowed loud, rejoicing in its freedom, pawing the ground with its hoofs. Everywhere, down below, and up above, the larks were singing. Anisim looked back at the church, so graceful and white—it had just been whitewashed—and remembered how he had prayed in it five days ago; then he looked at the school with its green roof, at the stream in which he used to bathe and fish, and his heart leaped with joy, and he wished a wall would suddenly rise from the ground and prevent him from going any further, leaving him with nothing but the past.

When they got to the station they went up to the refreshment-room and had a glass of sherry each. The old man put his hand into his pocket to get out his purse, but Anisim said:

"My treat!"

The old man was moved, patted him on the shoulder and winked at the barman, as if to say: "See what a son I have!"

"I wish you would stay at home, Anisim, and help me with my business," he said. "You would be invaluable to me! I would plaster you with gold, Son."

"No, no, Father, I can't."

The sherry was sour and smelt of sealing-wax, but they had another glass each.

When he returned from the station the old man hardly recognised his youngest daughter-in-law. The moment her husband left the house, Lipa was transformed into a cheerful young woman. Barefooted, in a worn skirt, her sleeves pulled high up her arms, she was washing the steps of the porch and singing in a high, silvery voice; and when she carried out the heavy tub of dirty water, and looked up at the sun with her childlike smile, she was like a lark herself.

An old workman, who happened to pass the porch just then, shook his head and cleared his throat.

"What daughters-in-law God has sent you, Grigory Petrovich!" he said. "Real treasures!"

V

On the eighth of July, which was a Friday, Lipa and Yelisarov, nicknamed Spike, were walking back from the village of Kazanskoye, where they had been to celebrate the day of the Kazan Madonna, the patron saint of the church there. Far behind them came Lipa's mother, Praskovya, for she was a sick woman, and short of breath. It was getting on towards evening.

"O-o-oh!" exclaimed Spike in astonishment as he listened to Lipa. "O-o-oh! Well?"

"I am very fond of jam, Ilya Makarich," Lipa was saying. "So I sit in the corner, drinking tea and eating jam. Or else I have my tea with Varvara Nikolayevna, and she tells me something sad and beautiful. They have ever so much jam—four jars! 'Eat up, Lipa, don't stint yourself!' they keep saying."

"Ha! Four jars!"

"Yes. They are rich. They eat white bread with their tea, and as much meat as you like. They are rich, but I am afraid all the time, Ilya Makarich. Oh, I'm so afraid!"

"What are you afraid of, child?" asked Spike, looking back to see if Praskovya was very far away.

"At first, after the wedding, I was afraid of Anisim Grigorich. He was all right, he never did me any harm, but whenever he came near me, it made my skin creep, right to my bones. And I lay awake every night, trembling and praying. And now it's Aksinya I'm afraid of, Ilya Makarich. She's all right, really, she smiles all the time, but sometimes she looks out of the window, and her eyes are fierce, with a green light in them, like sheep's eyes in a dark shed. The Khrimins Junior keep on at her: 'Your old man has a plot of land in Butekino, about forty dessiatines or so,' they say, 'the soil is mostly sand, and there is a stream there. Why shouldn't you build a brick-works of your own, Aksinya,' they say, 'and we would be your partners.' Brick costs twenty rubles a thousand now. They'd make a pile. Yesterday at dinner Aksinya said to the old man: 'I want to build a brick-works in Butekino, and start business on my own.' She said it smiling-like. But Grigory Petrovich's face went all dark; you could see he didn't like it. 'So long as I'm alive,' he said, 'there will be no separate trading. We must all stick together.' She gave him such a look, and gnashed her teeth. . . . And when the fritters were served, she wouldn't have any."

"Ha!" exclaimed Spike. "She wouldn't?"

"And I'd like to know when she sleeps," Lipa went on. "She lies down for half an hour, and then up she gets and starts walking about the place, walking, walking, looking into every nook and corner, to see if the peasants haven't burnt or stolen anything. She frightens me, Ilya Makarich! And the Khrimins Junior didn't go to bed after the wedding, they went straight to the law-courts in the town; and people say it's all Aksinya's fault. Two of the brothers promised to build a works for her, and the third is displeased, and so the mill didn't work for almost a month, and my uncle Prokhor was out of work and went from house to house begging crusts. 'Why don't you go and work in the fields,' I says to him, 'or saw wood, instead of disgracing yourself like that?' and he says, 'I've forgotten what it is to work like an honest peasant. I can't work in the fields any more, Lipa.'"

They halted at the young aspen grove to rest and let Praskovya catch up with them. Yelisarov had been working as contractor for a long time, but he had no horse, and walked all over the district on foot, carrying a little sack containing bread and onions, and striding along rapidly on his long legs, his arms swinging. It was quite hard to keep up with him.

On the edge of the copse was a milestone. Yelisarov touched it to see if it was as strong as it looked. Praskovya joined them, breathing heavily. Her wizened, permanently alarmed face was now radiantly happy: she had been to church like other people, afterwards walking about the fair drinking pear-*kvass*. This sort of thing did not happen often in her life, and it seemed to her that today was the only happy day she had ever had. After resting, all three walked on side by side. The sun was setting, its rays penetrating the copse, lighting up the trunks of the trees. From somewhere ahead came the hum of voices. The girls from Ukleyevo were a long way in front, lingering in the copse, probably looking for mushrooms.

"Hi, lasses!" shouted Yelisarov. "Hi, my beauties!"

His cry was greeted with laughter.

"Spike's coming! Spike! Old fogey!"

And the echo laughed, too. And now they had left the copse behind. The tops of the factory chimneys could be seen and the cross on the belfry flashed in the sun: it was the village, "the place where the sexton ate up all the caviare at the funeral". They would soon be home now; they only had to descend into the great gully. Lipa and Praskovya, who had been walking barefoot, sat down to put on their boots; the contractor sat in the grass beside them. Seen from above, Ukleyevo with its willows, its white church and its little river looked picturesque and peaceful, but the mill roofs, painted a sombre colour in the interests of economy, spoilt the effect. On the opposite slope of the gully could be seen rye—in sheaves, in stacks, as if flung down in the storm, or, where it had only just been mowed, in rows; the oats were ripe, too, and gleamed in the rays of the setting sun with a pearly lustre. Harvesting was in full swing. Today was a holiday, tomorrow they would gather in the rye and the hay, and the next day would be Sunday, a holiday again; every day the thunder rumbled somewhere far away, the air was sultry and as if it were soon going to rain, and as they gazed at the field, each thought: if only the grain is harvested in time, and there was joy and a happy tumult in each breast.

"Hay-makers are getting good money this year," said Praskovya. "A ruble forty kopeks a day!"

And all the while people kept streaming back from the fair at Kazanskoye; women, mill-workers in new caps, beggars, children. . . . A farm-cart went by, raising a cloud of dust, a horse which its owners had been unable to sell trotting behind, looking as if it were glad it had not been sold; now an obstreperous cow was led by the horns; another cart passed, loaded with drunken peasants, their legs dangling over the sides. An old woman led by the hand a little boy in a big cap and enormous high-boots; the boy, though exhausted by the heat and the heavy boots, which did not allow his knees to bend, blew incessantly with all his might into a toy trumpet; they had already descended the slope and turned into the street, but the trumpet could still be heard.

"Something's come over our mill-owners." said Yelisarov. "Mercy on us! Kostyukov is angry with me. 'You've used too many shingles on the cornices,' he says. 'Too many?' asks I. 'I used as many as were needed, Vassily Danilich,' I says. 'I don't eat shingles with my porridge, you know.' 'How dare you,' says he, 'speak to me like that? You fool,' he says, 'you this and that! You forget yourself! It was I who made a contractor of you!' 'Ha,' says I, 'and what of it? I got tea to drink every day before I was a contractor, didn't I?' 'You're a pack of swindlers, all of you. . .' says he. I held my peace. *We* are swindlers in this world, I thought to myself, but *you* will be swindlers in the other. Ho-ho! Next day he wasn't so rough. 'Don't be angry with me, Makarich,' says he, 'for what I said to you. If I did say something I shouldn't have, after all, I am a merchant of the first guild, and your superior, and you should bear with me.' 'It's true you are a merchant of the first guild, and I am only a carpenter,' says I. 'But St. Joseph was a carpenter, too. It's a worthy occupation, one that is pleasing to the Lord, and if you choose to consider yourself my superior, you're welcome, Vassily Danilich.' And then, after that talk of ours, I got to thinking: which of us is the superior? The merchant of the first guild, or the carpenter? The carpenter, children, the carpenter!"

Spike thought for a while, and then added:

"Yes, my children. He who labours and endures, he is the superior."

The sun had now set, and a dense mist, white as milk, was rising above the stream, the churchyard and the clearings round the mills. Now, with darkness coming on apace, and the lights shimmering below, while the mist seemed to be concealing a bottomless abyss, Lipa and her mother, born into utter poverty, and reconciled to live in poverty all their days, giving up to others everything but their meek, timid souls, may have felt, for one short moment, that they, too, in this vast mysterious universe, in the infinite chain of living creatures, meant something, were superior beings; they enjoyed sitting on the top of the slope, and smiled blissfully, forgetting for a moment that they would have to go down into the gully sooner or later.

At last they were home again. The hay-makers were sitting on the ground near the gate, and in front of the shop. The Ukleyevo peasants did not usually hire themselves out to Tsibukin, who had to get his hay-makers from other villages, and it seemed in the half-light as if all round sat men with long black beards. The shop was open, and the deaf man could be seen through the door playing draughts with a boy. The hay-makers were singing softly, almost inaudibly, every now and then breaking off to demand in loud voices their wages for the day before, but they were not paid for fear they might go away before morning. Beneath the boughs of a birch-tree growing in front of the porch, old Tsibukin sat in his shirt sleeves, drinking tea with Aksinya; a lighted lamp stood on the table.

"Ga-a-a-ffer!" one of the hay-makers on the other side of the gate sang out in a taunting voice. "Give us half— only half! Ga-a-a-ffer!"

And then there was laughter and more soft, almost inaudible singing.... Spike sat down at the table to have some tea.

"So we went to the fair," he began relating. "We had a good time, children, a very good time, thanks be to God.

But something very unpleasant happened. Sasha the smith bought some tobacco, and handed a half-ruble piece to the merchant. And the coin turned out to be a false one." Spike looked round him as he spoke; he meant to speak in a whisper, but everyone could hear what he said in his hoarse, half-smothered voice. "And it turned out to be a false one. 'Where did you get it?' they asked him. 'Anisim Tsibukin,' he says, 'gave it me, at the wedding....' So they called the policeman, and he took him away.... Look out, Petrovich, mind you don't have trouble, people talk, you know...."

"Ga-a-a-ffer!" came in the same taunting voice from the gate. "Ga-a-a-ffer!"

Then there was silence.

"Ah, children, children..." murmured Spike rapidly and he got up; he was overcome with drowsiness. "Thanks for the tea and sugar, my children. Time to go to bed. I'm a-mouldering, I am, and all my beams are rotting. Ho-ho!"

Before going away, he said:

"It means the time has come to die!" And he gave a sob.

Old Tsibukin did not finish his tea but sat on, thinking; he seemed to be still listening to the sound of Spike's steps, though he was already far away by now in the street.

"Sasha the smith must have been lying," said Aksinya, guessing at his thoughts.

He went into the house, returning in a few minutes with a small bundle in his hands. He unwrapped it and brand-new rubles gleamed on the table. Taking one up, he put it between his teeth, then flung it on the tray; then he picked up another, and flung it down, too....

"The coins *are* false..." he said, looking at Aksinya, in a kind of wonder. "They're the ones.... The ones Anisim brought, his present. Here, child, take it," he whispered, shoving the bundle into her hands, "take it and throw it into the well.... Who wants them? And see there is no talk. There may be trouble.... Take the samovar away, put out the lamp...."

Lipa and Praskovya sat in the shed, watching the lights go out, one by one; only in the top storey, in Varvara's window, shone the red and blue lamps in front of the icons, and they seemed to bring peace, content and innocence. Praskovya could never get used to the idea that her daughter had married a rich man, and when she came to see her, she crouched timidly in the entry, smiling ingratiatingly, and they would send her out some tea and sugar. Lipa could not get used to it either, and after her husband had gone away, did not sleep on her own bed, but laid herself down anywhere, in the kitchen, or the shed, and every day she scrubbed the floors and did the washing, and imagined she was still a hired worker. This time, too, after she and her mother returned from their pilgrimage, they had their tea with the cook and then went into the shed and lay down on the floor, between the wall and the sleigh. It was dark there, and smelt of harness. The lights went out round the house, then the deaf man could be heard locking up the shop, and the hay-makers settling down to sleep in the yard. Far away, at the Khrimins Junior, someone was playing on the expensive concertina. Praskovya and Lipa fell asleep.

And when they were waked up by someone's footsteps, it was light, for the moon had risen; Aksinya was standing in the entrance of the shed, holding her bed-clothes in her arms.

"It'll be cooler in here," she said, stepping in and lying down almost on the threshold, her whole figure lit in the moonlight.

She did not sleep and kept sighing heavily, tossing about in the heat, throwing off almost all her clothes; and in the magical light of the moon, what a beautiful, what a proud animal she looked! A short time elapsed, and footsteps were again heard; the old man, all in white, appeared in the doorway.

"Aksinya!" he called out. "Are you there?"

"Well, what is it?" she answered crossly.

"I told you to throw the money into the well—did you?"

"I'm not such a fool as to fling good stuff like that into the water! I gave it to the hay-makers. . . ."

"Oh, my God!" said the old man, consternation in his voice. "You stubborn wench. . . . Oh, God!"

He brought his hands together in a gesture of despair and walked away, muttering to himself. A little later Aksinya sat up, heaved a deep sigh of irritation, gathered up her bed-clothes and went out of the shed.

"Why did you marry me into this house, Mother!" said Lipa.

"Everyone must marry, child. It is ruled by others, not ourselves."

They were ready to give themselves up to feelings of inconsolable grief. But there was someone, they felt, high up in the sky, looking down upon them from the blue, where the stars were, seeing all that went on in Ukleyevo, watching over it. And great as the evil was, the night was still and lovely, and there was justice in God's universe, and there would be justice, as still and beautiful as the night, and everything on the earth was only waiting to be merged with justice, as the moonlight merges with the night.

And both, their peace restored, pressed close against one another and fell asleep.

VI

News had long arrived that Anisim was in prison for counterfeiting and circulating false coins. Months passed by, more than half a year, the long winter was over, and spring had begun, and everyone in the house and in the village had got used to the idea of Anisim being in prison. And whoever happened to pass the house or the shop in the night remembered that Anisim was in prison; and whenever they tolled the bell for the dead, people somehow remembered again that he was in prison, awaiting his trial.

A shadow lay over the entire household. The walls of the house seemed to have become darker, the roof was rusty, the heavy, green, iron-bound shop-door was warped; and old Tsibukin himself seemed to have grown darker. He had long stopped having his hair cut or his beard trimmed, and there was a shaggy growth all over his cheeks, and he no longer leaped into his gig with a jaunty air, or shouted to the beggars: "The Lord will provide!" His strength was declining, and this showed itself in everything about him. People no longer feared him so much, and the policeman drew up a statement in his shop, although he got the same solid bribe as before; the old man had been summoned three times to the town, to be tried for trading in spirits without a license, and the trial had been put off three times owing to non-appearance of witnesses, and the old man was worn out.

He often went to see his son in prison, hired a lawyer for his defence, sent applications somewhere, offered candles for him in church. He presented the warden of the prison in which Anisim was confined with a silver glassholder bearing an enamelled inscription: "The soul knoweth its measure", and a long silver spoon.

"There is no one for us to turn to, no one," Varvara went about saying. "We ought to ask one of the gentry to write to the chief authorities.... If only they would let him out before the trial.... Why should the lad languish there?"

She, too, was grieved, but she had become stouter and sleeker, and she lit the icon-lamps as usual, and saw that everything in the house was in order, and treated visitors to jam and apple jelly. Aksinya and her deaf husband worked as usual in the shop. A new enterprise was afoot— the building of a brick-works at Butekino—and Aksinya went there almost every day in the gig; she drove herself, and when she met anyone she knew, she reared her head like a snake in the young rye, and smiled her naive, mysterious smile. And Lipa played all the time with her baby, born just before Lent. It was a tiny baby, thin and sickly, and it seemed strange that it could cry and look about and that people regarded it as a human being, and called it Nikifor. It would lie in its cradle, and Lipa would walk away to the door, and say, with a bow:

"Good day to you, Nikifor Anisimich!"

And she would rush back to it, and kiss it, then walk back to the door again, bow and say:

"Good day to you, Nikifor Anisimich!"

And the baby would kick out with its little red legs, laughing and crying at the same time, just like Yelisarov the carpenter.

At last a day was appointed for the trial. The old man set out for the town five days before the time. Then it was said that peasants from the village had been sent for as witnesses; Tsibukin's old workman went, too, having also received a summons.

The trial was to be held on Thursday, but Sunday passed, and the old man had not returned, and there was no news. Towards evening on Tuesday, Varvara sat at the open window, listening for the old man to come back. Lipa was playing with the baby in the next room. She dandled it, gleefully crooning:

"You'll grow up big, big! You'll grow to be a man and we'll go and hire ourselves out to work together! Together, together!"

"Oh!" said Varvara, shocked. "What's this about going out for hire, you silly? He'll grow up to be a merchant!"

Lipa began singing softly, but very soon forgot herself, and started all over again:

"You'll grow big, big! And we'll go out to work together!"

"There you are—at it again!"

Lipa stopped in the doorway with Nikifor in her arms, and asked:

"Why do I love him so, Mother? Why is he so dear to me?" and her voice broke, and her eyes glistened with tears. "Who is he? What is he? Light as a feather, such a teeny-weeny thing, and I love him as if he were a real human being. Look, he can't say anything, not a thing, and I understand everything he wants, just by looking at his eyes."

Varvara listened again: the sound of the evening train coming into the station reached her ears. The old man might be in it. She neither heard nor understood what Lipa was saying, and did not notice the minutes go by, but sat trembling, not so much from fear, as from violent curiosity. She heard a cart clatter noisily past, loaded with peasants. It was the witnesses returning from the station. The old workman jumped out of the cart as it drove past the shop, and walked into the yard. She could hear people greeting him in the yard, questioning him. . . .

"Debarred from all rights and property," he answered loudly. "Siberia, hard labour, six years."

Aksinya could be seen coming out of the shop by the back entrance; she had been selling kerosene, and had the bottle in one hand, and the funnel in another, while between her teeth she held some silver coins.

"And where's Dad?" she lisped.

"At the station," answered the workman. "He'll come home when it gets darker, he says."

When it was known in the house that Anisim was sentenced to hard labour, the cook began wailing in the kitchen at the top of her voice, as if for the dead, for she considered that decency required this of her.

"Why do you leave us, Anisim Grigorich, my bright eagle?"

The dogs were roused and began barking. Varvara ran up to the window, and stood there rocking herself from side to side in her grief; she shouted to the cook, straining her voice:

"Sto-op it, Stepanida, sto-o-op it! Don't torture us, for Christ's sake!"

No one remembered to heat the samovar, they all seemed to have lost their heads. Lipa was the only one who had no idea what had happened, and she went on fondling the baby.

When the old man returned from the station, nobody asked him anything. He said a word of greeting and then walked through the rooms in silence; he refused supper.

"There's no one for us to turn to," said Varvara when they were alone. "I told you you should have asked some of the gentry, you wouldn't listen to me then.... You should have sent in a petition...."

"I did what I could!" said the old man, with a wave of his hand. "After the sentence was read, I went up to the gentleman who defended Anisim. 'You can't do anything now,' he said, 'it's too late.' And Anisim said those very words: 'Too late.' But still, as I was leaving the court, I spoke to a lawyer; I gave him some money on account.... I'll wait a week, and then go up again. We are in God's hands."

Once more the old man went through the rooms in silence, and when he got back to Varvara, he said:

"I must be ill. My head is misty-like. I don't seem to be able to think clearly."

Then he closed the door so that Lipa should not hear him, and said:

"I'm worried about my money. Remember Anisim brought me those new ruble and half-ruble pieces just before the wedding, the week after Easter? I put away one bundle, but the rest I mixed with my own money. . . . When my uncle Dmitri Filatich (God rest his soul!) was alive, he used to go buying goods, sometimes to the Crimea, sometimes to Moscow. And he had a wife, and that wife, while he was away, buying goods, like I said, used to go about with other men. And they had six children. And when my uncle had taken a drop too much, he used to laugh and say: 'I can't make out which of them are mine and which aren't.' He was an easy-going man, you see. And I can't make out, which of my money is good, and which is false. It all seems false to me, now."

"Don't say that, for God's sake!"

"Yes, I go to buy myself a ticket at the station, take out three rubles to pay for it, and keep wondering if they aren't false ones. It makes me afraid. I must be ill."

"We are all in God's hands, say what you will," said Varvara with a shake of her head. "We must think about it, Petrovich. . . . Anything might happen, you're not a young man any more. If you were to die, your grandson might be badly treated. I keep worrying about Nikifor. The father's as good as gone, the mother's young and foolish. . . . You might at least leave him that plot of land, Butekino, really you might, Petrovich! Think it over!" continued Varvara persuasively. "He's a pretty little thing, it would be a shame! Go tomorrow and write out a paper. What's the use of waiting?"

"Yes, I forgot about the boy..." said Tsibukin. "I haven't seen him today. He's a nice boy, is he? Well, well, let him grow up, God bless him!"

He opened the door and beckoned to Lipa with his forefinger. She came up with the baby in her arms.

"If there's anything you want, Lipa dear, you just

ask for it," he said. "And eat whatever you like, we don't grudge you anything, all we want is that you should be well. . . ." He made the sign of the cross over the baby. "And look after my grandson. I have lost my son, but I still have a grandson."

Tears poured down his cheeks, he gave a sob and walked away. Soon after he went to bed and, after seven sleepless nights, fell into a sound sleep.

VII

The old man was away in the town for several days. Somebody told Aksinya that he had gone to see a notary about his will, and had willed Butekino, where she was baking her bricks, to his grandson Nikifor. She was told this in the morning, while the old man and Varvara were sitting in front of the porch, beneath the birch-tree, drinking tea. She locked both the street door and the yard door of the shop, gathered up all the keys in her possession, and flung them on the ground at the old man's feet.

"I will not work for you any more!" she cried in a loud voice and all of a sudden burst into tears. "It appears I'm not your daughter-in-law, but a mere servant! As it is everyone laughs: 'See what a fine servant the Tsibukins have found!' I never hired myself out to you! I'm not a beggar, not some jumped-up creature—I have a mother and a father."

Without wiping away her tears, she fixed her swimming eyes, blazing and squinting with resentment, on the old man's face, shouting at the top of her voice, her face and neck crimson with the strain:

"I will serve you no more! I'm worn out! When it comes to working, sitting in the shop day after day, going for vodka in the night, it's me, but when it comes to giving away land, it's her, the convict's wife with her little devil! She's the mistress here, the lady, and I am her servant! Go on, leave everything to her, the gaolbird, and may it choke her, but I shall go home! Find yourselves another fool, accursed tyrants!"

Never in his life had the old man abused or punished his children and he could not even imagine that anyone belonging to his household could speak rudely to him, or treat him disrespectfully, and now he was terrified and ran into the house, where he hid behind a cupboard. But Varvara was so dumbfounded she could not even get up and could only sit waving her arms as if warding off a bee.

"What's this, what's this?" she kept muttering in a horrified voice. "Must she shout so loud? People will hear her! If only she would be a little quieter.... Just a little!"

"You've given away Butekino to the convict's wife," Aksinya went on shouting, "go on—give her everything, then, I don't want anything from you! To hell with you all! You're a gang of thieves! I've seen enough, and I'm sick of it! You've robbed passers-by, travellers, you scoundrels, you've robbed the old and the young! Who sold vodka without a license? And the false money? Your chests are crammed with false coins—and now you don't need me any more!"

A crowd had by now gathered before the wide-open gate and stood peering into the yard.

"Let people see!" cried Aksinya. "I'll shame you before them! I'll make you burn with shame! You shall grovel at my feet! Hi, Stepan!" she called to the deaf man. "Come home with me this minute! Come home to my father and mother! I will not live with convicts! Pack up everything!"

There was some washing hanging on a line across the yard; she tore from it her petticoats and bodices, all wet as they were, and thrust them into the deaf man's arms. Then, in a frenzy, she dashed up and down, tearing everything off the line, throwing on the ground everything which was not hers, and stamping on it.

"Oh-oh, stop her!" moaned Varvara. "What's the matter with her? Give her Butekino, for Christ's sake!"

"What a wench!" they were saying at the gate. "There's a wench for you! Did you ever see such a passion?"

Aksinya rushed into the kitchen, where the clothes were being laundered. Lipa was alone, washing, the cook having gone to the river to rinse the linen. Steam was rising from the wash-tub and from a vat in front of the stove, and the kitchen was dim and stuffy. There was a heap of unwashed linen on the floor, and on a bench beside the heap, so that if he fell he would not hurt himself, lay Nikifor, kicking out with his red, skinny legs. Just as Aksinya entered the kitchen, Lipa tugged one of the chemises from the heap and dumped it into the tub, reaching out for a great scoop full of boiling water which was standing on the table. . . .

"Give it here!" said Aksinya, looking at her with hatred and snatching her chemise out of the tub. "It's not for the likes of you to touch my linen. You're a convict's wife, and ought to know your place, and what you are!"

Lipa gazed at her, too stunned to understand anything, but suddenly, catching the glance Aksinya cast at the baby, she understood, and went stiff with horror.

"This is what you get for stealing my land!"

With these words, Aksinya grasped the scoop full of boiling water and poured it over Nikifor.

A scream was heard, such a scream as had never before been heard in Ukleyevo, and it was hard to believe that so puny and frail a creature as Lipa could have screamed like that. Then a great stillness came over the yard. Aksinya went into the house in silence, smiling her curious innocent smile. . . . The deaf man, who had been pacing up and down the yard with the washing in his arms, now began hanging it up on the line again, silently, unhurriedly. And until the cook returned from the river, no one dared to go into the kitchen and see what was going on there.

VIII

Nikifor was taken to the Zemstvo hospital, where he died towards evening. Without waiting for anyone to send for her, Lipa wrapped up the dead body of her child in a blanket and carried it home.

The hospital, a new one with large windows, stood on the top of the hill; it was all aglow with the rays of the setting sun and looked as if it was on fire. The village spread out beneath it. Lipa went down by the road, and seated herself by a small pond just outside the village. A woman had brought a horse to the water, but the horse would not drink.

"Why don't you drink?" the woman said softly, as if astonished. "What's the matter?"

A little boy in a red shirt was squatting right at the water's edge, washing his father's boots. And there was not another soul to be seen, either in the village, or on the hillside.

"It won't drink. . ." said Lipa, watching the horse.

And then the woman and the boy with the boots went away, and there was nobody in sight. The sun had gone to bed in a broad sheet of gold and crimson, and long clouds, red and purple, stretched across the sky, watching over its sleep. Somewhere in the distance, goodness knows where, the bittern boomed, and it sounded like the hollow, melancholy bellowing of a cow locked in a shed. The cry of the mysterious bird was heard every spring, and no one knew what sort of a bird it was, or where it lived. On the top of the hill, beside the hospital, in the bushes round the pond, on the other side of the village and all over the fields, nightingales were pouring out their song. The cuckoo was trying to tell somebody's age, losing count every time, and beginning all over again. In the pond frogs were calling to one another, in harsh, angry voices, and you could even make out the words: "Ee ti takava, ee ti takava!"* What a noise everywhere! One would think that all these creatures were shouting and singing on purpose, so that no one should sleep on this spring night, so that everyone, even the bad-tempered frogs, should cherish and enjoy every moment of it: after all, we only live once!

A silver crescent moon shone in the sky, which was studded with stars. Lipa had no idea how long she remained sitting by the pond, but when she got up and began walking, she could see that everyone in the village was in bed, and the lights were out. It was probably about twelve versts to Ukleyevo, and she was very weak, and could not

---

* You're just as bad!—*Tr.*

give her mind to the task of finding the way. The moon shone, now in front of her, now on her left, now on her right, and the cuckoo, hoarse by now, went on shouting, as if laughing, and taunting her: "You've lost your way, you've lost your way!" Lipa walked fast and lost her head kerchief.... She gazed into the sky, wondering where her little boy's soul was—was he following her, or floating somewhere high up, near the stars, forgetful of his mother? How lonely it is in the fields of a night, amidst all this singing, when you cannot sing yourself, amidst incessant cries of joy, when you cannot rejoice yourself, when the moon looks down from the sky, as lonely as yourself, not caring whether it is spring or winter, whether people are alive or dead.... When there is grief in your heart it is hard to be alone. If only she could be with her mother, or with Spike or the cook, or with just anyone!

"Booh!" cried the bittern. "Boo-oo-h!"

And all of a sudden she distinctly heard a man's voice: "Come on, Vavila, harness the horse!"

A few paces ahead, by the very road-side, a bonfire was burning, the flames had died down, and only the embers glowed. There was a sound of horses munching. In the dusk could be made out two carts, one with a barrel on it, the other, much lower, loaded with sacks, and the figures of two men; one of the men was taking a horse up to the cart, the other stood motionless in front of the fire, his hands clasped behind his back. Somewhere near the carts a dog growled. The man leading the horse stopped and said:

"Someone must be coming down the road."

"Quiet, Sharik!" shouted the other one to the dog.

And from his voice you could tell he was an old man. Lipa stopped and said:

"The Lord be with you!"

The old man approached her, and at first said nothing. Then he said:

"Good evening!"

"Your dog won't bite me, will he, Gaffer?"

"No, no, you can pass. He won't touch you."

"I've been in the hospital," said Lipa, after a pause. "My little son died there. And I'm carrying him home."

Evidently what she said upset the old man, for he walked away from her and said hurriedly:

"Never mind, my dear. It was the will of God. Come on, lad!" he cried, addressing his companion. "Hurry up, can't you?"

"Your shaft-bow isn't here," answered the lad. "I can't find it."

"What's the good of you, Vavila!"

The old man picked up a coal and blew on it, so that his eyes and his nose were lit up, and then, after they had found the shaft-bow, he moved towards Lipa, still with the coal in his hand, and glanced at her; and his glance expressed compassion and tenderness.

"You're a mother," he said. "Every mother loves her child."

And he sighed and shook his head. Vavila threw something on the fire, and then stamped it out, and immediately all was intense darkness; the vision had disappeared, and once more there was nothing but the field, the star-studded sky, and the noisy birds, keeping each other awake. And the landrail was crying in the very place, so it seemed, where the fire had been.

But after a minute or two the carts, the old man and the lanky Vavila were visible again. The wheels creaked as the carts were dragged back into the road.

"Are you saints?" Lipa asked the old man.

"No. We live in Firsanovo."

"You looked at me, and my heart grew softer. And the lad with you is so quiet. So I thought to myself, they must be saints."

"Have you far to go?"

"To Ukleyevo."

"Get in, we'll take you as far as Kuzmenki. From there you can go straight on, we turn to the left."

Vavila got into the cart with the barrel, and the old man and Lipa into the other. They drove slowly, Vavila's cart leading the way.

"My boy suffered all day," said Lipa. "He looked so gently at me from his dear eyes, as if he wanted to say something, and couldn't. God in Heaven! Holy Mother of God! I kept falling to the ground from grief. I stood by his bed, and down I went. Tell me, Gaffer, why should a little baby have to suffer so much before dying? When grown-up people suffer, men or women, their sins are forgiven, but why should a little baby that has no sins suffer? Why?"

"Who can tell!" answered the old man.

They drove on in silence for half an hour.

"You can't know all, the why and the wherefore," said the old man. "A bird has two wings, and not four, because two are enough for it to fly with; and in the same way it is not given to man to know all there is to know, but only a half or a quarter. Man knows just what he needs to help him through life."

"I think I would feel better if I walked, Gaffer. The jolting shakes my heart."

"Never mind. Stay where you are."

The old man yawned, making the sign of the cross over his mouth.

"Never mind," he repeated. "Your grief is only half-grief. Life is long, there is yet good and evil to come. Oh, Great Mother Russia!" he exclaimed, looking from side to side of the road. "I have been all over Russia, and I have seen all there is to see in it, so you can believe me, my dear. There is good to come and there is evil. I went on foot all the way to Siberia, I've been on the river Amur and on the Altai Mountains, I settled in Siberia and tilled the land there, and then I felt homesick for Mother Russia and came back to my own village. We went back to Russia on foot; I remember once we crossed a river by the ferry, and I was so thin, so ragged, barefoot, freezing cold, sucking at a crust, and there was a gentleman on the ferry, God rest his soul if he's dead, and he looked at me with pity, and the tears rolled down his cheeks. 'Ah,' he said, 'black your bread, and black your life.' And when I came back I had neither house nor home, as they say; I had a wife, but I left her in Siberia, in the grave. And so I hired myself out by the day. And what do you think? After that there was evil in my life and there was good. And I don't want to die, my dear, I would like to live another twenty years, so you see there must have been more good than evil. Ah, but how great Mother Russia is!" he repeated again, glancing from right to left, and looking backwards.

"Gaffer!" said Lipa. "When a person dies, how many days does his soul walk about the earth?"

"Who can say? Wait, we'll ask Vavila, he has been to school. They teach them everything there, nowadays. Vavila!"

"Eh?"

"Vavila, when someone dies, how many days does his soul roam the earth?"

Vavila first brought his horse to a standstill before replying:

"Nine days. But when my Uncle Kirilla died, his soul lived in our hut for thirteen days."

"How d'you know?"

"For thirteen days there was a rumbling in the stove."

"Very well. Go on," said the old man, and it was clear he did not believe a word of it.

Near Kuzmenki the carts turned on to the highway, and Lipa went on on foot. It was getting light. As she was descending the slope into the gully, the church and huts of Ukleyevo were hidden by the mist. It was cold, and it seemed to her that the same cuckoo was still giving its call.

The cattle had not yet been driven out to pasture when Lipa got home; everyone was still asleep. She sat on the porch, waiting. The old man was the first to come out; the moment he glanced at her, he understood all, and for some time could not utter a word, and only stood there mumbling.

"Ah, Lipa," he said at last. "You couldn't look after my grandson. . . ."

Varvara was roused from her sleep. She threw up her hands and wept, and began to lay out the dead child for its coffin.

"And such a sweet little boy as he was. . ." she kept saying. "You only had one son, and you couldn't take care of him, you little silly."

There were funeral services in the morning and evening. The child was buried the next day, and after the funeral the guests and the clergy fell on the food so greedily

that one might have thought they had had nothing to eat
for days. Lipa served at table, and the priest, raising his
fork with a pickled mushroom on it, said to her:

"Do not grieve over the infant. For of such is the kingdom of heaven."

It was only after everyone had gone that Lipa really
understood there was no Nikifor any more, and never
would be—and, understanding, wept. She did not know
what room to go and weep in, for she felt there was no
place for her in the house since her boy had died, that
there was nothing for her to do here, that she was unwanted; and everyone else seemed to feel the same about her.

"Well, what are you bawling about there?" shouted
Aksinya, appearing suddenly in the doorway; in honour
of the funeral she was all dressed in new clothes, and her
face was powdered. "Stop it!"

Lipa tried to stop, but only cried louder still.

"Do you hear me?" shouted Aksinya, stamping her foot
in her rage. "Who d'you think I'm talking to? Get out of
here, and never dare to show yourself here again, felon!
Get out!"

"Come, come," said the old man, rousing himself. "Calm
yourself, Aksinya dear.... 'Tis natural she should
weep.... Her child is dead...."

"Natural, natural!" repeated Aksinya, mockingly. "She
can stay the night, but by tomorrow let her pack off!
Natural!" repeated Aksinya once more, and, laughing,
turned to go into the shop.

Early in the morning of the next day Lipa went back to
Torguyevo, to her mother.

IX

Now the roof and iron door of the shop have been
freshly painted and shine like new, gay geraniums blossom
in the windows as formerly, and what happened three
years ago in the Tsibukin household is almost forgotten.

Grigory Petrovich, the old man, is still considered the
master but in reality everything has passed into Aksinya's
hands; she it is who buys and sells, and nothing is done

without her consent. The brick-works is doing well; owing to the demand for bricks for the railway their price has reached twenty-four rubles a thousand; women and girls take the bricks to the station and load the trucks, receiving twenty-five kopeks a day for this.

Aksinya has gone shares with the Khrimins, and the mill is now called "Khrimins Junior and Co.". A tavern has been opened next to the station, and the expensive concertina is now heard in the tavern, and not in the factory; the postmaster, who has also set up in trade on his own, frequents the tavern, and so does the station-master. The Khrimins Junior have given the deaf man a gold watch which he is always taking out of his pocket and holding to his ear.

They say in the village that Aksinya has become very powerful; and this must be true, for when she drives to the works of a morning, with her innocent smile, good-looking, radiant with happiness, and orders people about all day long, you cannot help feeling her power. Everyone is afraid of her, at home, in the village and at the works. When she makes her appearance at the post-office, the postmaster leaps up, saying:

"Be seated, Ksenya Abramovna, do!"

A middle-aged landowner, a great dandy, in a coat of fine cloth and patent-leather top-boots, selling her a horse one day, was so entranced by her conversation that he let her have it at her own price. He held her hand long in his, and said, gazing into her mirthful, arch, innocent eyes:

"I would do anything in the world for a woman like you, Ksenya Abramovna! Only tell me when we could meet without anybody to disturb us."

"Why, whenever you like!"

Ever since, the middle-aged dandy drives up to the shop almost every day for a drink of beer. The beer is atrocious, bitter as wormwood. The landowner shakes his head but drinks it down.

Old Tsibukin does not interfere in business matters any more. He never has any money in his pockets, for he cannot distinguish between false coins and genuine ones, but he says nothing about it, not wishing anyone to know of this failing of his. He has become very absent-minded, and unless food is set before him, never thinks of asking for it; they have got used to sitting down to dinner without him, and Varvara often says:

"He's gone to bed without his supper again." And she says it calmly, for she has got used to it, too. Winter and summer alike he goes about in his fur-coat, staying at home only on very hot summer days. He usually walks about the village street, in his winter-coat with the collar turned up, taking the road leading to the station, or sits from morning to night on a bench outside the church gate. Sits there motionless. Passers-by salute him, but he never answers their greetings, for he retains his dislike for peasants. When addressed, his answers are quite polite and rational, but always very brief.

They say in the village that his daughter-in-law has turned him out of his own house and starves him, and that he lives on alms; some rejoice in this rumour, others are sorry for the old man.

Varvara has grown still stouter, her complexion still more brilliant, she still goes in for charity, and Aksinya does not prevent her. So much jam is made every summer now that there is no time to eat it up before next year's berries ripen; so it candies, almost driving Varvara to tears, for she does not know what to do with it.

People have begun to forget about Anisim. Once a letter came from him, in verse, on a large sheet of paper, in the form of a petition, written in the same exquisite hand, Evidently his friend Samorodov is serving a sentence at his side. Beneath the verses was written in an ugly, almost illegible scrawl: "I'm ill all the time here, very unhappy, help me for the sake of Christ."

One sunny autumn afternoon old Tsibukin was sitting by the church gate, with the collar of his winter-coat turned up so that only the tip of his nose and the peak of his cap could be seen. At the other end of the long bench sat the contractor Yelisarov, and next to him the school-watchman Yakov, a toothless old man of about seventy. Spike and the watchman were talking:

"Children ought to support the old people ... honour thy father and thy mother," said Yakov severely. "But

she, his daughter-in-law, has turned her father-in-law
out of his own house. The old man has nothing to eat or
drink, and there's nowhere for him to go. He's had no food
for three days."

"Three days!" exclaimed Spike.

"Yes. And there he sits, without a word. He's too weak
to speak. Why hush it up? He ought to have the law on
her. She'd get it, in the courts."

"Get what in the courts?" asked Spike, who did not
catch the watchman's words.

"What's that you said?"

"She's not a bad wench, she works hard. Women can't
get along without that ... without a little sin, I mean."

"Turning him out of his own house," continued Yakov
angrily. "Get a house of your own, I say, then turn people
out of it. Who does she think she is? The pest!"

Tsibukin listened to them without stirring.

"What does it matter whether it's your own house, or
someone else's, so long as it's warm and the women don't
quarrel..." said Spike and laughed. "When I was young,
I cherished my Nastasya. She was a quiet wench. And
she used to go on at me: 'Buy a house, Makarich, buy a
house! Buy a horse!' Even when she was dying, she kept
saying: 'Buy yourself a droshky, Makarich, so as not to
go about on foot.' But the only thing I ever bought her
was gingerbread, nothing more."

"Her husband is deaf and a natural," Yakov went on,
not heeding Spike. "A real natural, he has no more brains
than a goose. What does he understand? You can hit a
goose on the head, and still he won't understand."

Spike got up to go back to his home at the mill. Yakov
got up, too, and they walked away together, still talking.
When they were fifty paces or so away, old Tsibukin got
up, and shuffled after them with uncertain steps, as if he
were walking on ice.

The village was beginning to be plunged in twilight,
and the sun shone only on the top of the road, which
wound its way up the slope like a snake. Old women were
returning from the woods, with children running beside
them; they carried baskets filled with mushrooms. Women
and young girls were coming back from the station where

they had been loading bricks on trucks, and red brick-dust lay on their noses, and on their cheeks beneath the eyes. They were singing. In front of them went Lipa, singing in a piping voice, warbling away as she gazed up into the sky, as if she were delighted that the day, thank God, was over, and it was time to rest. Her mother, Praskovya, the day-labourer, walked with the crowd, carrying a bundle and as usual breathing heavily.

"Good evening, Makarich!" said Lipa, as she met Spike. "Good evening, dearie!"

"Good evening, Lipa dear!" answered Spike joyfully. "Wenches and lasses, be kind to the wealthy carpenter! Ho-ho! Oh, my children, my children!" Spike gave a sob. "Oh, my precious axes!"

Spike and Yakov went on, and everyone could hear them talking. Then the crowd encountered old Tsibukin, and there was a sudden lull. Lipa and her mother were at the back now, and as the old man approached them, Lipa bowed low before him and said:

"Good evening, Grigory Petrovich!"

Her mother bowed, too. The old man stopped, gazing at them in silence; his lips trembled and his eyes filled with tears. Lipa took a piece of buckwheat pie out of her mother's bundle, and offered it to the old man. He accepted it and began eating.

The sun had gone down; it no longer lit up even the top of the road. It was getting dark and cold. Lipa and Praskovya went on their way, crossing themselves continually.

1900

THE BRIDE

I

It was already nine o'clock in the evening, and the full moon was shining over the garden. In the Shumin house the evening service ordered by the grandmother Marfa Mikhailovna was only just over, and Nadya, who had slipped out into the garden for a minute, could see a cold supper being laid in the dining-room, her grandmother in her billowing silk dress hovering about the table, Father Andrei, the Cathedral priest, talking to Nadya's mother, Nina Ivanovna, who looked very young seen through the window, by artificial light. Beside her stood Andrei Andreich, Father Andrei's son, listening attentively.

It was cool and still in the garden, and dark shadows lay peacefully on the ground. From a long way off, probably outside town, came the distant croaking of frogs. There was a feeling of May, the delightful month of May, in the air. One could draw deep breaths, and imagine that somewhere, far beyond the town, beneath the sky, above the tree tops, in the fields and woods, the spring was beginning its own life, that mysterious, exquisite life, rich and sacred, from which sinful mortals are shut out. It almost made one want to cry.

Nadya was now twenty-three; ever since she was sixteen years old she had been dreaming ardently of marriage, and now at last she was betrothed to Andrei Andreich, the young man standing in the dining-room. She liked him, and the wedding was fixed for the seventh of July, but she felt no joy; she slept badly, her gaiety had deserted her. From the open windows of the basement kitchen came sounds of bustling and the clanging of knives, and the door, which closed by a pulley, banged

constantly. There was a smell of roasting turkey and
spiced cherries. And it seemed as if things would go on
like this, without changing, for ever and ever.

Someone came out of the house and stood in the porch.
It was Alexander Timofeich, or, as everyone called him,
Sasha, who had arrived from Moscow about ten days
before, on a visit. Long ago, Maria Petrovna, an impov-
erished widow gentlewoman, small, slight and delicate,
used to visit Nadya's grandmother, to whom she was
distantly related, asking for charity. She had a son called
Sasha. For some reason or other people said he was a
fine artist, and when his mother died, Granny, for her own
soul's salvation, sent him to the Komissarov school in
Moscow. A year or two later he got himself transferred
to an art school, where he remained something like fifteen
years, till at last he scrambled through his final examinations in the architectural department; he never worked as
an architect, but found occupation in a Moscow lithographical works. He came to stay almost every summer,
usually very ill, to rest and recuperate.

He was wearing a long coat buttoned up to his neck
and shabby canvas trousers with frayed hems. And his
shirt was unironed, and his whole appearance was dingy.
He was emaciated, with huge eyes and long, bony fingers,
bearded, dark-skinned, and, with it all, handsome. At
the Shumins' he felt as if he were among his own people,
and was quite at home in their house. And the room he occupied on his visits had long been known as Sasha's room.

He caught sight of Nadya from the porch, and went
out to her.

"It's nice here," he said.

"It's ever so nice. You ought to stay till the autumn."

"Yes, I know, I shall have to, I suppose. I shall probably stay with you till September."

He laughed for no apparent reason, and sat down beside
her.

"I've been standing here watching Mama," said Nadya.
"She looks so young from here. Of course I know my
Mama has her weaknesses," she continued after a pause,
"but just the same she's a marvellous woman."

"Yes, she's very nice," agreed Sasha. "In her way your

Mama is of course very good and kind, but ... how shall I put it? I went into the kitchen this morning early and saw four servants sleeping right on the floor, no beds, only rags to lie on, a stench, bugs, cockroaches.... Just the same as it used to be twenty years ago, not the slightest change. Granny's not to be blamed, of course, she's old—but your mother, with her French and her amateur theatricals.... You'd think *she*'d understand."

When Sasha spoke he had a habit of holding up two long, bony fingers in the direction of his hearer.

"Everything here strikes me as so strange," he continued. "I'm not used to it, I suppose. Good heavens, nobody ever does anything! Your mother does nothing but stroll about like a grandduchess, Granny does nothing at all, and nor do you. And Andrei Andreich, your fiancé, he does nothing, either."

Nadya had heard all this last year, and, she seemed to remember, the year before, and she knew it was the only way Sasha's mind could work; there was a time when it had amused her, but now for some reason it irritated her.

"That's old stuff, I'm sick of hearing it," she said, getting up. "Can't you think of anything new?"

He laughed and got up, too, and they both went back to the house. Good-looking, tall and slender, she seemed almost offensively well-dressed and healthy, as she walked by his side. She was conscious of it herself, and felt sorry for him, and almost apologetic.

"And you talk a lot of nonsense," she said. "Look what you just said about my Andrei—you don't know him a bit, really!"

"*My* Andrei.... Never mind your Andrei! It's your youth I grudge."

When they went into the dining-room everyone was just sitting down to supper. Nadya's grandmother, or, as everyone in the house called her, Granny, a corpulent, plain old woman, with heavy eyebrows and a moustache, was talking loudly, and her voice and manner of speaking showed that it was she who was the real head of the house. She owned a row of booths in the market-place, and the old house with its pillars and garden was hers, but every morning she prayed with tears for the Lord to preserve her from ruin. Her daughter-in-law and Nadya's mother, Nina Ivanovna, blonde, tightly corsetted, who wore pince-nez and had diamond rings on all her fingers, Father Andrei, a lean, toothless old man who always looked as if he were just going to say something very funny, and Andrei Andreich, his son and Nadya's fiancé, a stout, handsome young man with curly hair, rather like an actor or an artist, were all three talking about hypnotism.

"You'll fatten up in a week here," Granny told Sasha. "But you must eat more. Just look at yourself!" she sighed. "You look awful. A real prodigal son, that's what you are".

"He wasted his substance with riotous living," interpolated Father Andrei, bringing out the words slowly, his eyes twinkling, "and he was sent into the fields to feed swine."

"I love my old Dad," said Andrei Andreich, patting his father on the shoulder. "Dear old man. Good old man!"

Nobody said anything. Sasha suddenly burst out laughing, and pressed his napkin to his lips.

"So you believe in hypnotism?" Father Andrei asked Nina Ivanovna.

"I can't exactly say I believe in it," replied Nina Ivanovna, assuming a grave, almost severe expression. "But I have to acknowledge that there is much that is mysterious and incomprehensible in nature."

"I quite agree with you, though I am bound to add that faith narrows the sphere of the mysterious considerably for us."

An enormous juicy turkey was placed on the table. Father Andrei and Nina Ivanovna continued their conversation. The diamonds on Nina Ivanovna's fingers sparkled, and in her eyes sparkled tears, she was deeply moved.

"Of course I cannot venture to argue with you," she said. "But you will agree that there are many unsolved riddles in life."

"Not one, I assure you."

After supper Andrei Andreich played the violin, Nina Ivanovna accompanying him on the piano. He had graduated from the philological department of the university ten years before, but had no employment and no fixed occupation, merely playing at occasional charity concerts. In the town he was spoken of as a musician.

Andrei Andreich played and all listened in silence. The samovar steamed quietly on the table, and Sasha was the only one drinking tea. Just as twelve o'clock struck a fiddle-string snapped. Everyone laughed, and there was a bustle of leave-taking.

After saying good night to her fiancé, Nadya went upstairs to the rooms she shared with her mother (the ground floor was occupied by Granny). The lights were being extinguished downstairs, in the dining-room, but Sasha still sat on, drinking tea. He always sat long over his tea, in the Moscow way, drinking six or seven glasses one after another. Long after Nadya had undressed and got into bed she could hear the servants clearing the table, and Granny scolding. At last the house was quiet but for an occasional sonorous cough from downstairs, in Sasha's room.

II

It must have been about two o'clock when Nadya waked up, for dawn was beginning to break. The night watchman could be heard striking his board in the distance. Nadya could not sleep, her bed seemed too soft to lie down in comfortably. As she had done on all the previous nights this May Nadya sat up in bed and gave herself up to her thoughts. The thoughts were just the same as those of the night before, monotonous, futile, insistent—thoughts of how Andrei Andreich had courted her and proposed, how she had accepted him and gradually learned to appreciate this good and clever man. But somehow or other now that there was only a month left till the wedding, she began to experience fear, uneasiness, as if something vaguely sad lay in wait for her.

"Tap-tap, tap-tap," rapped out the night-watchman lazily. "Tap-tap. . . ."

Through the big old-fashioned window could be seen the garden, and beyond it lilac bushes, heavy with bloom, drowsy and languid in the cold air. And a dense white mist encroached silently upon the lilacs, as if intent on enveloping them. Sleepy rooks cawed from distant trees.

"Oh, God, what makes me so sad?"

Do all girls feel like this before their weddings? Who knows? Or could it be the influence of Sasha? But Sasha had been saying the same things over and over again, as if by rote, year after year, and what he said always sounded so naive and quaint. And why couldn't she get the thought of Sasha out of her head? Why?

The watchman had long stopped going his rounds. Birds began twittering beneath the window and in the tree tops, the mist in the garden cleared away, and now everything was gilded by the spring sunlight, everything seemed to be smiling. In a short time the whole garden, warmed by the caresses of the sun, had sprung to life, and drops of dew gleamed like diamonds on the leaves of the trees. And the old, neglected garden was young and gay for that one morning.

Granny was already awake. Sasha gave his harsh, deep cough. Downstairs the servants could be heard bringing in the samovar, moving chairs about.

The hours passed slowly. Nadya had been up and walking in the garden for a long time and the morning still dragged on.

And here came Nina Ivanovna, tearful, a glass of mineral water in her hand. She went in for spiritualism and homeopathy, read a great deal, and was fond of talking about her religious doubts, and Nadya supposed there must be some profound, mysterious significance in all this. She kissed her mother, and walked on at her side.

"What have you been crying about, Mama?" she asked.

"I read a book last night about an old man and his daughter. The old man worked at some office, and what d'you think, his chief fell in love with the old man's daughter! I haven't finished it, but I came to a place in it where I couldn't help crying," said Nina Ivanovna, and took a sip from her glass. "I remembered it this morning, and cried again."

"And I've been so depressed all these days," said Nadya after a pause. "Why can't I sleep?"

"I don't know, dearie. When I can't sleep I shut my eyes tight—like this—and imagine how Anna Karenina

looked and spoke, or I try to imagine something histori-
cal, something from olden times. . . ."

Nadya felt that her mother did not understand her, that
she was incapable of understanding her. She had never
had this feeling before, it frightened her; she wanted to
hide, and went back to her room.

At two o'clock everyone sat down to dinner. It was
Wednesday, a fast-day, and Granny was served meatless
borshch and bream with buckwheat porridge.

To tease Granny Sasha ate *borshch* as well as meat
soup. He joked all through the meal, but his jokes were
too elaborate and always intended to point a moral, and
it was not funny at all when, before coming out with a
witticism, he lifted his long, bony, dead-looking fingers;
and when the thought that he was very ill and probably
had not long to live crossed your mind, you felt so sorry
for him you could have cried.

After dinner Granny went to her room to rest. Nina
Ivanovna played the piano for a short time, and then she
went out of the room, too.

"Oh, Nadya dear," Sasha said, returning to his usual
after-dinner topic, "if only you would listen to me! If
only you would!"

She sat curled up in an old-fashioned arm-chair, closing
her eyes, while he paced quietly up and down the room.

"If only you would go away and study," he said.
"Enlightened, saintly people are the only interesting ones,
the only ones who are needed. And the more such people
there are, the sooner the kingdom of heaven will be on
earth. Then not one stone will be left on another, in this
town of yours everything will be turned topsy-turvy,
everything will change, as if by magic. And there will be
huge splendid buildings, beautiful parks, marvellous fountains, fine people. . . . But that's not the chief thing. The
chief thing is that then there will be no crowd any more,
as we now understand the word, that evil in its present
aspect will disappear, for each individual will have faith,
and know what he lives for, and nobody will seek support
from the crowd. Darling, little pet, go away! Show them
all that you have had enough of this stagnant, dull, corrupt
life! At least show yourself that you have."

"I can't, Sasha, I'm going to get married."

"Never mind that! What does it matter?"

They went out into the garden and strolled about.

"Anyhow, my dear, you've simply got to think, you've got to understand, how abhorrent, how immoral your idle life is," continued Sasha. "Can't you see that to enable you and your Mama and your Granny to live in idleness, others have to work for you, you are devouring the life of others, is that pure, now, isn't it filthy?"

Nadya wanted to say: "Yes, you are right", wanted to tell him she understood, but tears came into her eyes and she fell silent and seemed to shrink into herself; she went to her room.

In the evening Andrei Andreich came and played the violin a long time as usual. He was taciturn by nature, and perhaps he loved his violin because while playing he did not have to speak. Soon after ten, when he had his coat on to go home, he took Nadya in his arms and showered passionate kisses on her face, shoulders, and hands.

"My dearest, my darling, my beautiful," he murmured. "Oh, how happy I am! I think I shall go mad with joy!"

And this, too, she seemed to have heard long, long ago, to have read it in some novel, some old, tattered volume which no one ever read any more.

In the dining-room was Sasha, sitting at the table, drinking tea from a saucer balanced on the tips of his five long fingers. Granny was playing patience. Nina Ivanovna was reading. The flame sputtered in the icon lamp, and everything seemed still and secure. Nadya said good night and went up to her room falling asleep the moment she got into bed. But, just as the night before, she waked up at the first streak of dawn. She could not sleep, something heavy and restless lay on her heart. She sat up and put her head on her knees, thinking about her fiancé, her wedding. . . . For some reason she remembered that her mother had not loved her husband, and now had nothing of her own, and was completely dependent on Granny, her mother-in-law. And try as she would, Nadya could not understand how it was that she had regarded her mother as something special, remarkable, had not seen that she was just an ordinary, unhappy woman.

Downstairs, Sasha, too, was awake—she could hear him coughing. A strange, naive creature, thought Nadya, and there is something absurd in his dreams, in all those splendid parks and marvellous fountains. But there was so much that was beautiful in his naivety, in his very absurdity, that the moment she began to wonder if she ought to go away and study, her whole heart, her very being, was bathed in refreshing coolness, and she was plunged in ecstasy.

"Better not think," she whispered. "Better not think about it."

"Tap-tap," the distant night-watchman rapped out on the board. "Tap-tap . . . tap-tap. . . ."

III

Towards the middle of June Sasha was suddenly overcome by boredom and began to talk about going back to Moscow.

"I can't live in this town," he said morosely. "No running water, no drainage! I can hardly bear to eat my dinner—the kitchen is indescribably filthy. . . ."

"Wait a little longer, Prodigal Son," Granny whispered. "The wedding will be on the seventh."

"I simply can't!"

"You said you would stay with us till September."

"And now I don't want to. I've got to work."

The summer had turned out cold and rainy, the trees were always dripping, the garden looked sombre and unfriendly, and the desire to get away and work was quite natural. Unfamiliar feminine voices could be heard in all the rooms, upstairs and downstairs, a sewing-machine whirred in Granny's room. It was all part of the bustle over the trousseau. Of winter-coats alone Nadya was to have six, and the cheapest of them, boasted Granny, had cost three hundred rubles. All this fuss irritated Sasha. He sat and sulked in his room. But they managed to persuade him to stay, and he promised not to leave before the first of July.

The time passed quickly. On St. Peter's day Andrei Andreich took Nadya after dinner to Moscow Street to have yet another look at the house which had long been rented and prepared for the young couple. It was a two-storey house, but so far only the upper floor had been furnished. In the ball-room with its gleaming floor, painted to look like parquet, were bent-wood chairs, a grand piano, a music-stand for the violin. There was a smell of paint. On the wall was a large oil-painting in a gilt frame—a picture of a naked lady beside a purple vase with a broken handle.

"Beautiful picture," said Andrei Andreich with an awed sigh. "It's by Shishmachevsky."

Next came the drawing-room, in which were a round table, a sofa, and some arm-chairs upholstered in bright blue material. Over the sofa hung an enlarged photograph of Father Andrei with all his medals on, wearing a tall ceremonial hat. They passed into the dining-room with its side-board, and from there into the bedroom. Here, in the half-light, stood two beds side by side, and it looked as if those who had furnished the bedroom had taken it for granted that life would always be happy here, that it could not be otherwise. Andrei Andreich conducted Nadya through the rooms, never removing his arm from her waist. And she felt weak, guilty, hating all these rooms and beds and chairs, while the naked lady made her sick. She now saw quite clearly that she no longer loved Andrei Andreich, perhaps never had loved him. But she did not know how to say this, whom to say it to, and why to say it at all, and though she thought about it day and night she came no nearer to knowing. . . . He had his arm round her waist, spoke to her so kindly, so humbly, was so happy, walking about his home. And all she saw was vulgarity, stupid, naive, intolerable vulgarity, and his arm round her waist seemed to her cold and rigid, like an iron hoop. At any moment she was ready to run away, to burst into sobs, to jump out of the window. Andrei Andreich led her to the bathroom, touched a tap screwed into the wall, and the water gushed out.

"What do you think of that?" he said, and laughed. "I had them put up a cistern holding a hundred pails of water, so we shall have running water in our bathroom."

They walked about the yard for a while and then went out into the street, where they got into a droshky. The dust rose in thick clouds, and it looked as if it were just going to rain.

"Are you cold?" asked Andrei Andreich, narrowing his eyes against the dust.

She did not answer.

"Remember Sasha reproaching me for not doing anything, yesterday?" he said, after a short pause. "Well, he was right. Infinitely right. I do nothing, and there is nothing I know how to do. Why is it, my dear one? How is it that the very thought of one day wearing a cockade in my cap and going to an office makes me feel sick? How is it that I can't stand the sight of a lawyer, or a Latin teacher, or a town councillor? Oh, Mother Russia, Mother Russia! How many idlers and useless beings you still bear on your bosom! How many beings like myself, oh, long-suffering one!"

And he theorised about his own idleness seeing it as a sign of the times.

"When we are married," he continued, "we'll go to live in the country, my dear one, we'll work. We'll buy a little plot of land with a garden and a stream, and we'll toil, observe life. . . . Oh, how lovely it will be!"

He took his hat off and his hair waved in the breeze, and she listened to him, thinking all the time: "Oh, God, I want to go home! Oh, God!" They overtook Father Andrei just before they got back to Nadya's home.

"Look, there's my father!" said Andrei Andreich joyfully, and he waved his hat. "I love my old Dad, really I do," he said, paying off the cabby. "Dear old man! Good old man!"

Nadya went into the house feeling out-of-humour and unwell, unable to forget that all the evening there would be visitors, that she would have to entertain them, to smile, to listen to the violin, to hear all sorts of nonsense and talk about nothing but the wedding. Granny, stiff and pompous in her silk dress, was sitting beside the samovar, looking very haughty, as she always did when there were visitors. Father Andrei came into the room with his subtle smile.

"I have the pleasure and virtuous consolation of seeing you in good health," he said to Granny, and it was hard to say whether he was earnest or in jest.

IV

The wind knocked on the window-panes and on the roof. Whistling sounds could be heard, and the brownie in the chimney crooned his morose, plaintive song. It was one o'clock in the morning. Everyone in the house was in bed, but no one was asleep, and Nadya kept thinking she could hear the violin being played downstairs. There was a sharp report from outside, a shutter must have torn loose from its hinges. A minute later Nina Ivanovna came into the room in her chemise, holding a candle.

"What was that noise, Nadya?" she asked.

Nadya's mother, her hair in a single plait, smiling timidly, seemed on this stormy night older, plainer, and shorter than usual. Nadya remembered how, so very recently, she had considered her mother a remarkable woman and had felt pride in listening to the words she used. And now she could not for the life of her remember what those words had been—the only ones that came back to her were feeble and affected.

Bass voices seemed to be singing in the chimney, even the words "Oh, my God!" could be made out. Nadya sat up in bed, and tugged violently at her hair, sobbing.

"Mama, Mama!" she cried. "Oh, darling, if you only knew what I was going through! I beg you, I implore you —let me go away!"

"Where to?" asked Nina Ivanovna, in bewilderment, and she sat down on the side of the bed. "Where d'you want to go?"

Nadya cried and cried, unable to bring out another word.

"Let me go away from this town," she said at last. "The wedding must not, will not be, believe me. I don't love that man.... I can't bear to speak about him."

"No, my darling, no," said Nina Ivanovna quickly, frightened out of her wits. "Calm yourself. You're out of sorts. It'll pass. It often happens. You've probably had a quarrel with Andrei, but lovers' tiffs end in kisses."

"Go, Mama, go!" sobbed Nadya.

"Yes," said Nina Ivanovna, after a pause. "Only the other day you were a little girl, and now you're almost a

bride. Nature is in a constant state of metabolism. Before
you know where you are you'll be a mother yourself, and
then an old woman, with a troublesome daughter like mine."

"My darling, you're kind and clever, and you're
unhappy," said Nadya. "You're ever so unhappy—why do
you say such commonplace things? Why, for God's sake?"

Nina Ivanovna tried to speak, but could not utter a
word, only sobbed and went back to her room. Once more
the bass voices moaned in the chimney, and Nadya was
suddenly terrified. She jumped out of bed and ran into
her mother's room. Nina Ivanovna, her eyelids swollen
from crying, was lying in bed covered by a blue blanket,
a book in her hands.

"Mama, listen to me," said Nadya. "Think, try to
understand me, I implore you! Only think how shallow
and humiliating our life is! My eyes have been opened,
I see it all now. And what is your Andrei Andreich? Why,
he's not a bit clever, Mama. Oh, God, oh, God! Only
think, Mama, why, he's stupid!"

Nina Ivanovna sat up with a jerk.

"You and your grandmother keep torturing me," she
said, with a gasping sob. "I want to live! To live!" she
repeated, smiting her chest again and again. "Can't you
let me have my freedom? I'm still young, I want to live,
you've made an old woman of me!"

She cried bitterly and lay down, rolling herself up in
the blanket, and looking just a silly, pathetic little thing.
Nadya went back to her room and dressed, then she sat at
the window to wait for morning to come. All night she sat
there thinking, and someone seemed to be knocking at the
shutter outside and whistling.

The next morning Granny complained that the wind
had beaten down all the apples and split the trunk of an
old plum-tree. It was a grey, dim, joyless morning, one of
those days when you feel inclined to light the lamp from
the very morning. Everyone complained of the cold, and
the rain-drops tapped on the window-panes. After breakfast Nadya went to Sasha's room and, without a word, fell
on her knees before a chair in the corner, covering her
face with her hands.

"What's the matter?" asked Sasha.

"I can't go on like this, I can't!" she exclaimed. "I don't know how I could live here before, I simply can't understand it! I despise my fiancé, I despise myself, I despise this whole idle, empty life...."

"Come, come..." Sasha interrupted her, not yet realising what she was talking about. "Never mind ... it's all right...."

"This life is hateful to me," continued Nadya. "I won't be able to bear another day here! I shall go away tomorrow. Take me with you, for God's sake!"

Sasha gazed at her for a moment in amazement. At last the truth dawned upon him, and he rejoiced like a child, waving his arms and shuffling in his loose slippers, as if he were dancing with joy.

"Splendid!" he said, rubbing his hands. "God, how fine that is!"

She gazed at him unblinkingly, from wide-open eyes, full of love, as if fascinated, waiting for him to come out immediately with something significant, something of infinite importance. He had not told her anything yet, but she felt that something new and vast, something she had never known before, was already opening before her, and she looked at him full of expectation, ready for anything, for death itself.

"I'm leaving tomorrow," he said after a pause. "You can come to the station to see me off. I'll take your things in my trunk and buy a ticket for you. And when the third bell rings, you can get into the train, and off we go. Co with me as far as Moscow, and go to St. Petersburg by yourself. Have you a passport?"

"Yes."

"You will never regret it—never repent it, I'm sure!" said Sasha enthusiastically. "You will go away and study, and afterwards things will take their own course. As soon as you turn your life upside down, everything will change. The great thing is to turn your life upside down, nothing else matters. So we're off tomorrow?"

"Oh, yes! For God's sake!"

Nadya, who imagined that she was profoundly stirred and that her heart had never before been so heavy, was quite sure that now, on the eve of departure, she would suffer, be racked with anguished thoughts. But she had hardly gone upstairs to her room and lain down on the bed when she fell fast asleep, and slept soundly, with a tear-stained face and a smile on her lips, till the very evening.

V

The droshky had been sent for. Nadya, in her hat and coat, went upstairs to have one last look at her mother, at all that had been hers so long. She stood in her room beside the bed, which was still warm, and then went softly into her mother's room. Nina Ivanovna was asleep, and it was very quiet in her room. After kissing her mother and smoothing her hair, Nadya stood for a minute or two.... Then she went downstairs with unhurried steps.

The rain was coming down in torrents. A droshky, dripping wet, stood in front of the porch, its hood raised. "There's no room for you, Nadya," said Granny, when the servant began putting the luggage into the droshky. "I wonder you want to see him off in such weather! You'd better stay at home. Just look at the rain!"

Nadya tried to say something, but could not. Sasha helped her into the droshky, covering her knees with the rug. And now he was seated beside her.

"Good-bye! God bless you!" shouted Granny from the porch. "Mind you write when you get to Moscow, Sasha!"

"All right. Good-bye, Granny!"

"May the Queen of Heaven protect you!"

"What weather!" said Sasha.

It was only now that Nadya began to cry. It was only now that she realised she was really going away, a thing she had not quite believed, even when saying good-bye to Granny, or standing beside her mother. Good-bye, town! Everything came over her with a rush—Andrei, his father, the new house, the naked lady with the vase. But all this no longer frightened her or weighed upon her, it had become naive and trivial, it was retreating farther into the past. And when they got into the railway carriage and the train started, the whole of this past, so big and important, shrank to a little lump, and a vast future, scarcely perceptible till now, opened before her. The rain-drops tapped on the windows, there was nothing to be seen but the green fields, the telegraph-poles flashing by, the birds on the wires, and joy suddenly almost choked her. She remembered that she was going to be at liberty, to study, doing what used to be called in the old days: "Running away to the Cossacks." She laughed and cried and prayed.

"Come, come," said Sasha, smiling broadly. "Come, come!"

VI

Autumn passed, and after it winter. Nadya was now very homesick, and thought every day of her mother and Granny; she thought of Sasha, too. Letters from home were resigned and kindly, everything seemed to have been forgiven and forgotten. After passing her May examinations, she set off, well and happy, for home, breaking her journey at Moscow to see Sasha. He was just the same as he had been the year before—bearded, shaggy, still wearing the same long old-fashioned coat and canvas trousers, his eyes as large and beautiful as ever. But he looked ill and worried, he had got older and thinner, and coughed incessantly. And to Nadya he seemed dingy and provincial.

"Why, it's Nadya!" he cried, laughing joyfully. "My darling, my pet!"

They sat together in the lithographical workshop, amidst the fumes of tobacco smoke and a stifling smell of ink and paint; then they went to his room, which reeked of smoke, too, and was littered and filthy. On the table, beside the cold samovar, was a broken plate with a bit of dark paper on it, and both floor and table were strewn with dead flies. Everything here showed that Sasha took no thought for his private life, lived in a continual mess, with utter contempt for comfort. If anyone had spoken to him about his personal happiness and private life, had asked him if there was anyone who loved him, he would have been at a loss to know what was meant, and would only have laughed.

"Everything passed off all right," said Nadya hurriedly. "Mama came to St. Petersburg in the autumn, to see me, she says Granny isn't angry, but keeps going into my room and making the sign of the cross on the walls."

Sasha looked cheerful, but coughed and spoke in a cracked voice, and Nadya kept looking at him wondering if he was really seriously ill, or if it was her imagination.

"Sasha, dear Sasha," she said, "but you're ill!"

"I'm all right. A bit unwell—nothing serious. . . ."

"For goodness' sake," said Nadya, in agitated tones, "why don't you go to a doctor? Why don't you take care of your health? My dear one, Sasha dear," she murmured, and tears sprang into her eyes, and for some reason Andrei Andreich, and the naked lady with the vase, and the whole of her past, which now seemed as far off as her childhood, rose before her mind. And she cried because Sasha no longer seemed to her so original, clever and interesting as he had last year. "Sasha dear, you are very, very ill. I don't know what I wouldn't give for you not to be so pale and thin! I owe you so much. You can have no idea what a lot you have done for me, Sasha darling! You are now the closest, the dearest person in my life, you know."

They sat on, talking and talking. And now, after a winter in St. Petersburg, it seemed to her that something outmoded, old-fashioned, finished, something, perhaps, already half in the grave, could be felt in everything he said, in his smile, in the whole of him.

"I'm going for a trip down the Volga the day after tomorrow," said Sasha, "and then I'll go somewhere and take *koumiss*. I want to try *koumiss*. A friend of mine, and his wife, are going with me. The wife is a marvellous person. I keep trying to persuade her to go and study. I want her to turn her life topsy-turvy."

When they had talked themselves out, they went to the station. Sasha treated her to tea and bought her some apples, and when the train started, and he stood smiling and waving his handkerchief, she could see by just looking at his legs how ill he was, and that he was not likely to live long.

Nadya arrived at her native town at noon. As she drove home from the station the streets seemed to her disproportionately wide, the houses very small and squat. There was hardly anyone about, and the only person she met was the German piano-tuner in his rusty overcoat.

And the houses seemed to be covered with a film of dust. Granny, now really old, and as stout and plain as ever, put her arms round Nadya and cried for a long time, with her face pressed against Nadya's shoulder, as if she could not tear herself away. Nina Ivanovna, who had aged greatly, too, had become quite plain and seemed to have shrunk, but she was as tight-laced as ever and the diamonds still shone from her fingers.

"My darling," she said, shaking all over. "My own darling!"

Then they sat down and wept silently. It was easy to see that both Granny and Mama realised that the past was irrevocably lost. Gone were their social position, their former distinction, their right to invite guests to their house. They felt as people feel when, in the midst of an easy, carefree life, the police break in one night and search the house, and it is discovered that the master of the house has committed an embezzlement or a forgery— and then farewell for ever to the easy, carefree life!

Nadya went upstairs and saw the same bed, the same window with its demure white curtains, the same view of the garden from the window, flooded with sunshine, gay, noisy with life. She touched her table, sat down, fell into a reverie. She had a good dinner, drinking tea after it, with delicious thick cream, but something was missing, there was an emptiness in the rooms, and the ceilings struck her as very low. When she went to bed in the evening, covering herself with the bed-clothes, there was something ridiculous in lying in this warm, too soft bed.

Nina Ivanovna came in for a moment, and seated herself as the guilty do, timidly, with furtive glances.

"Well, Nadya, how is everything?" she asked. "Are you happy? Really happy?"

"Yes, Mama."

Nina Ivanovna got up and made the sign of the cross over Nadya and the window.

"As you see I have turned religious," she said. "I'm studying philosophy, you know, and I keep thinking, thinking.... And many things are as clear as daylight to me now. It seems to me that the most important thing is to see life through a prism."

"Mama, how is Granny really?"

"She seems all right. When you went away with Sasha and Granny read your telegram, she fell down on the spot. After that she lay three days in bed without stirring. And then she began praying and crying. But she's all right now."

She got up and began pacing up and down the room.

"Tap-tap," rapped the watchman, "tap-tap."

"The great thing is for life to be seen through a prism," she said. "In other words life must be divided up in our consciousness into its simplest elements, as if into the seven primary colours, and each element must be studied separately."

What more Nina Ivanovna said, and when she went away, Nadya did not know, for she soon fell asleep.

May passed, and June came. Nadya had got used to being at home again. Granny sat beside the samovar, pouring out tea and giving deep sighs. Nina Ivanovna talked about her philosophy in the evenings. She still lived like a dependent, and had to turn to Granny whenever she wanted a few kopeks. The house was full of flies and the ceilings seemed to be getting lower and lower. Granny and Nina Ivanovna never went out, for fear of meeting Father Andrei and Andrei Andreich. Nadya walked about the garden and the streets, looking at the houses and the drab fences, and it seemed to her that the town had been getting old for a long time, that it had outlived its day and was now waiting, either for its end, or for the beginning of something fresh and youthful. Oh, for this new, pure life to begin, when one could go straight forward, looking one's fate boldly in the eyes, confident that one was in the right, could be gay and free! This life was bound to come sooner or later. The time would come when there would be nothing left of Granny's house, in which the only way for four servants to live was in one room, in the basement, surrounded by filth—yes, the time would come when there would not be a trace left of such a house, when everyone would have forgotten it, when there would be no one left to remember it. Nadya's only distraction was the little boys in the next house who banged on the fence when she strolled about the garden and laughed at her, shouting, "There goes the bride!"

A letter came from Saratov, from Sasha. He wrote in his reckless, staggering handwriting that the trip down the Volga had been a complete success, but that he had been taken rather ill at Saratov, and had lost his voice, and been in hospital for the last fortnight. She understood what this meant, and a foreboding amounting almost to a conviction came over her. It vexed her that this foreboding and the thought of Sasha himself no longer moved her as formerly. She felt a longing to live, to be in St. Petersburg, and her friendship with Sasha seemed to belong to a past, which, while dear, was now very distant. She could not sleep all night, and in the morning sat at the window, as if listening for something. And there really did come the sound of voices from below—Granny was saying something in rapid, querulous tones. Then someone cried.... When Nadya went downstairs Granny was standing in the corner of the room praying, and her face was tear-stained. On the table lay a telegram.

Nadya paced up and down the room for a long time, listening to Granny's crying, before picking up the telegram and reading it. It said that yesterday morning, in Saratov, Alexander Timofeich, Sasha for short, had died of consumption.

Granny and Nina Ivanovna went to the church to order a service for the dead, and Nadya walked about the rooms for a long time, thinking. She realised clearly that her life had been turned topsy-turvy, as Sasha had wanted it to be, that she was lonely, alien, unwanted here, and that there was nothing she wanted here, the past had been torn away and vanished, as if burned by fire, and the ashes scattered to the winds. She went into Sasha's room and stood there.

"Good-bye, dear Sasha," she said. Life stretched before her, new, vast, spacious, and this life, though still vague and mysterious, beckoned to her, drawing her onward.

She went upstairs to pack, and the next morning said good-bye to her family, and left the town, gay and full of spirits—never to come back, she was sure.

1903

A.P.Chekhov.
27.10 — 9.11 1893.
Moscow.
Photo by D.Asikritov.

The Chekhov family.
1874. Taganrog.
Photo by S.S.Isakovich.

Anton Chekhov
on the day of his graduation
from the gymnasia.
15 June, 1879. Taganrog.
Photo by S.S.Isakovich.

A.P.Chekhov. January 1889.
St.Petersburg.
Photo by K.Shapiro.

The house in which A.P.Chekhov
was born. Taganrog.

M.P.Chekhov, A.P.Chekhov, M.Komeyeva,
L.S.Mizinova, M.P.Chekhova, Ye.Ya. Chekhova,
Alyosha Komeyev, A.I.Ivanenko, I.P.Chekhov,
P.Ye.Chekhov in the courtyard of the home
on Sadovo-Kudrinskaya St. in Moscow.
April 1890. Photo by Alexander Chekhov.

A.P.Chekhov in his home on Malaya Dmitrovka St. in Moscow. November 1891. Photo by Alexander Chekhov.

Maria, Anton, Ivan and Mikhail Chekhov in the study of the writer's Melikhovo house. 1892. Photo by A.A.Lesov

A.P.Chekhov.
1898. Yalta.
Photo by L.V.Sredin.

The building
of the Moscow
Art Theatre.
1902. Moscow.

The "Sreda" (Wednesday) literary group. L.Andreyev, F.Chaliapin,
I.Bunin, N.Teleshov, Ye.Chirikov, Skitalets, M.Gorky. 1902.

A.P.Chekhov (after his wedding O.L.Knipper). June 1901.
The Aksyonovo sanatorium (Ufa Gubernia).

A.P.Chekhov and M.Gorky. 1901

A.P.Chekhov. 1900. Yalta. Photo by L.V.Sredin.

A.Chekhov's home in Autka.

O.L.Knipper-Chekhova
and A.P.Chekhov.
1902. Yalta.

А. П. Чехов

ПОВЕСТИ И РАССКАЗЫ

На английском языке

Подробнее ознакомиться с содержанием
и оформлением наших книг можно по Интернету.
Наш адрес: **www.raduga.express.ru**

Оформление *Е. Кузнецовой*
Художественный редактор *Т. Иващенко*

Подписано в печать 09.10.2000.
Формат 84 × 100/32. Бумага офсетная.
Печать офсетная. Условн. печ. л. 10,92. Уч.-изд. л. 11,94.
Доп. тираж 3000 экз. Заказ № 1929. Изд. № 8883.

Налоговая льгота — общероссийский классификатор
продукции ОК-005-93, том 2;
953000 — книги, брошюры.

Лицензия ЛР № 020846 от 23 декабря 1998 г.
ОАО Издательство «Радуга»
121839, Москва, пер. Сивцев Вражек, 43.

Отпечатано
в ОАО «Можайский полиграфический комбинат»
143200, г. Можайск, ул. Мира, 93.